Praise for *DINGS*

This delightful book, written by a well-respected neurologist with decades of experience, explores the intricacies of neurologic disease while emphasizing the humanistic side of medicine. Written for lay consumption, the book gives a clear and authoritative description of the problems that the family of a child with subtle features of epilepsy may encounter in arriving at an appropriate diagnosis and treatment. This book rightfully belongs on the desk of anyone seeking an understanding of epilepsy in the child.

Michael E. Cohen, M.D., Professor of Neurology and Pediatrics, S.U.N.Y. at Buffalo; Past President: Child Neurology Society

As a veteran public-school psychologist, I see Dr. Fogan's novel as an insightful assist in identifying and diagnosing a child with epilepsy in the school setting. It belongs in the library of anyone who works with children.

Marlene Curwen, M.F.T., Retired School Psychologist.

I enjoyed this book. It provides a sensitive and accurate portrayal of a family's journey in understanding and coming to terms with a child's illness.

Joy Lottermoser, M.S., School Psychologist

Dr. Fogan's book takes a realistic look at the problem of recognizing children with complex partial seizures. Early diagnosis and treatment are critical for them to achieve their full potential. This novel will help educators and the public learn about this interesting problem and advocate for children.

Karen Nelson, R.N., M.S.N., District Nurse, Newhall, CA School District.

Dr. Fogan has written a captivating novel about a common condition surrounding which there is much public ignorance, misconception and fear: epilepsy. He writes of the parents and their child, the doctors whom they encounter and the stages along their joint clinical and emotional journey. *DINGS* is fascinating and educational reading for anyone touched directly or indirectly by epilepsy.

> **D. Alan Shewmon, M.D.,** Clinical Professor of Neurology and Pediatrics, Vice Chair of Neurology, David Geffen School of Medicine at UCLA.

DINGS portrays the process of psychologists helping families cope with the emotional struggles that can accompany a physical disorder. I recommend this book to family members striving to better relate to a child who has epilepsy.

> **Janet Miller Stier, Ph.D.,** Clinical Child Psychologist

DINGS will be especially helpful to educators. Physical illnesses must be identified and distinguished from emotional ones. It will alert teachers to the elusive symptoms of unrecognized epilepsy.

> **Karen Weiss**, Elementary School Teacher

DINGS

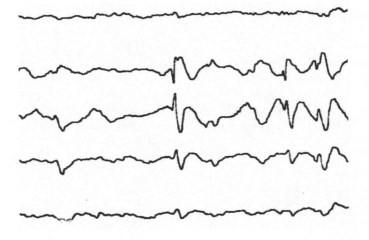

A Novel

LANCE FOGAN

AuthorReputationPress ®
Creativity & Branding

Author Reputation Press LLC
45 Dan Road Suite 5
Canton MA 02021
www.authorreputationpress.com
Hotline: 1(800) 220-7660
Fax: 1(855) 752-6001

Ordering Information:
Quantity sales. Special discounts are available on quantity purchases by corporations, associations, and others. For details, contact the publisher at the address above.

Printed in the United States of America.

ISBN-13:	Softcover	978-1-64961-276-2
	Hardcover	978-1-64961-278-6
	eBook	978-1-64961-277-9
	Audiobook	978-1-64961-325-7

Library of Congress Control Number: 2021905585

DEDICATION

There are currently three million people living with epilepsy in the United States of America and over sixty million others in the world.

This novel is dedicated to all the children who are affected by undiagnosed nonconvulsive epilepsy. These children require our immediate attention and care. Their families deserve our compassion, and the professionals who treat them merit recognition and support.

ABOUT THE AUTHOR

LANCE FOGAN, M.D., M.P.H., was born in Buffalo, N.Y. in 1939. He is Clinical Professor of Neurology at the David Geffen School of Medicine at UCLA in Los Angeles, California, and a Fellow of the American Academy of Neurology. He graduated from the State University of New York at Buffalo School of Medicine in 1965. His undergraduate studies in Anthropology and Linguistics promoted a two-and-one-half months' fellowship in tropical medicine working with an Australian general practitioner in Papua New Guinea during medical school. Lance promotes broad educations.

He earned a Master of Public Health degree from the University of Oklahoma while serving with the United States Public Health Service (1966-1968). Pursuit of neurology training at Case Western Reserve University Hospitals in Cleveland, Ohio (1968-1971) followed. In 1971, he joined the Kaiser Permanente Health Plan in Southern California where he practiced clinical neurology for twenty-six years until retiring.

Dr. Fogan has published original research on medical and neurological diseases. In 1988, the American Academy of Neurology awarded him the History of Neurology Prize for his paper, *The Neurology in Shakespeare.*

Since he retired in 1997, Dr. Fogan has continued to teach neurology.

He lives in Valencia, California. He and his late wife have two daughters. He is writing other projects including focusing on his grandsons' life experiences and the ways those have rekindled his own childhood memories.

FOREWORD

The characters and events in this book are fictitious. Any similarity to real persons, living or dead, is coincidental and not intended by the author.

The information included in this novel is not intended nor implied to be a substitute for professional medical advice. The reader should consult his or her healthcare provider to determine the appropriateness of the information for their own situation or if they have any questions regarding a medical condition or treatment plan. Reading the information herein does not create a physician-patient relationship.

ACKNOWLEDGEMENTS

I relied upon my clinical and life experiences in the preparation of this book. However, it was inspired and intellectually guided by my literary mentor, the international award-winning playwright, screenwriter, director and author Donald Freed.

I am also grateful to the skilled professionals who reviewed chapters pertinent to their expertise. Specific advice concerning medical, neurological and nursing scenes was offered by: Michael E. Cohen, M.D., Professor of Neurology and Pediatrics, University at Buffalo School of Medicine and Biosciences, Past President of the Child Neurology Society; Sandra Gault, R.N., B.S.N., District Nurse, Newhall School District, Newhall, CA.; Karen Nelson, R.N., M.S.N., District Nurse, Newhall School District, Newhall, CA.; Betty Shaby, A.N.P.C., M.S.D., Neurology Nurse Practitioner; D. Alan Shewmon, M.D., Chief, Department of Neurology, Olive View-UCLA Medical Center, Sylmar, CA., Clinical Professor of Neurology and Pediatrics, UCLA School of Medicine.

I appreciate the review and advice concerning the psychology aspects offered by: Lourdes Caseras, Ph.D., Clinical Psychologist and Psychoanalyst, University of Miami School of Medicine; Marlene Curwen, Retired School Psychologist, M.F.T.; Julian Kivowitz, M.D., Child Psychiatrist; Joy Lottermoser, M.S., School Psychologist; Janet Miller Stier, Ph.D., Clinical Child Psychologist; Wayne Tashjian, M.F.T., B.C.B.A., Director, Behavior Therapy Clinic.

Advice that added realism to the teacher and school interactions was offered by Ana Donovan, B.A., Third Grade Charter School Teacher and Karen Weiss, Elementary School Teacher.

Special appreciation goes to Paul Berkowitz. His valued friendship, wise counsel, encouragement and technical skills meant so much to me in completing this writing project.

My young grandsons guided the portrayal of Conner, the third grader around whom this story revolves. Thank you, Emmett and Perry.

I also want to acknowledge the too numerous to name friends and colleagues who made important suggestions that helped to enrich the narrative.

Finally, I would like to thank my family for their patience and encouragement as I pursued this project.

MARCH 5, 2007:
SOUTHERN CALIFORNIA

CHAPTER 1

"**A**rrrgghhrrr!" There it was again! Conner's temperature was 103.6 degrees. I was sitting on the side of our bed and had begun to dial the pediatrician when I heard it. The hairs on the back of my neck bristled. What was that? It was some loud, strange animal sound.

Sam's head shot off the pillow, his face cast with a bleary-eyed, quizzical expression.

I dropped the phone. "Conner's room!" We bolted down the hall. The dim moon through his bedroom window showed our little boy jerking and thrashing on his bed. I pushed past my husband. "What's he doing? Conner, what are you doing?"

Conner growled. It was a drawn-out, high-pitched cry that sounded like something from a horror movie.

"Turn on the light, Sam! Conner, what's wrong?"

Our eight-year-old was on his back, his body twisted in the covers. His head, arms and legs trembled and thrashed, emitting a long, drawn-out groan between clenched teeth. "Conner, honey. What are you doing? Wake up, Conner!"

"Oh, God! He's having an epileptic convulsion. I've seen 'em before, in Iraq. My brother had one as a kid, too." Sam bent over and grabbed at Conner's flailing arms.

3

"What do we do? What should we do?" Red streaks stained the pillow and bubbled out of my son's mouth.

"His lips are blue! He's bleeding! He's dying! Call Dr. Jackson. No! Call nine-one-one! Sam! Call nine-one-one! It's an emergency. Hurry! Hurry! We have to get him to the hospital!"

"Stay with him!" Sam turned and ran to the telephone in our room. A few seconds later he was back. "Let's get Conner in the car. We'll take him ourselves. It'll be faster. Let's go!"

"Yes! Okay! Come on!" Conner had stopped thrashing. He unclenched his jaws and released a long, hissing sigh through foamy pink bubbles frothing between his lips. I detected a faint odor—like urine.

"Conner? Conner, we're taking you to the hospital, honey." I stroked his damp forehead and pushed strands of light-brown hair away from his closed eyes. The only sound now was the rattle of his deep, noisy breathing and the roar of my pulse throbbing in my ears. I couldn't tear my eyes away from those bubbles.

"Ohhhh..." I knelt beside the bed and kissed his sweaty forehead over and over. His tiny hand felt cold and clammy in mine, yet only a few minutes ago he had been burning up with fever, coughing and sneezing.

Sam leaned over Conner. I had never seen my husband look so scared. "I'll change and get some pants and a shirt on. You'd better get dressed, too, Sandra. We might be at the hospital for hours or..." Our eyes locked.

"Yeah, as soon as you get back." I pressed my lips. "I'm not leaving him alone." I saw Grandma Audra's face—my closest relative that I could recall ever dying. I sat and cradled Connor's head in my lap as I rocked back and forth. Thank God he was breathing. I heard Sam's dresser drawer squeak and the closet door slam.

When he came back, I left Conner to get dressed but I can't remember doing it—only my shaking hands.

Sam hefted Conner into his arms. "He's so light, Sandra." Sam's eyes glistened. This was a man who had returned after a year of combat in Iraq less than two months ago. "Bring another blanket—a dry one.

We've got to wrap him. It's cold out." Sam adjusted our son's position in his arms a couple of times and headed out of the bedroom. Conner's bloody, red-lipped face flopped and hung down. I reached to steady his head.

"It'll be okay. Go get Madison, Sandra. I'll meet you in the car." His voice cracked. "Hurry!"

I ran to my daughter's bedroom and lifted the three-year-old out of bed. She opened her eyes wide. At first, she was too surprised to cry, but as I rushed around the room, grabbing clothes and blankets and her stuffed giraffe, her initial surprise erupted into wails of protest. Her mouth was an open cavern; I could see pinkness in the back of her throat.

"Shh, Maddie! Conner's very sick. We have to take him to the hospital. Be a good girl. We have to go." She was dry. I took her into the kids' bathroom and put her on the toilet. Then I put her in some Pull-Ups just in case. The house was quiet. I hurried down the stairs with her screaming and a blanket in my arms.

"No! I don't want to go! Thtop, Mommy!"

"Shush. It's all right."

Sam was sitting behind the wheel. Our SUV purred in the garage; its heater was already blowing warm air. Conner, very still now, lay stretched out across the back seat. Madison stopped crying. I strapped her into her car seat and covered Conner. The little girl whimpered again, looked down at her motionless brother and sucked on the Binky pacifier I stuck between her lips. I squeezed into the rear seat and held Conner's head on my lap.

My tight chest heaved with quick, shallow breaths. My mind flashed back to the night that Conner was born. Over eight years ago, again just after midnight, Sam drove me to the hospital like this. Except that night, we were going there so I could deliver our son. I bent over his face and tasted salt. I rubbed tears from my cheeks. "Oh, Conner. My baby!"

"How's he doing?" Sam looked back and then forward again. His head turned to the right and to the left as we rolled through a stop sign.

"He's asleep. Drive faster, Sam! Faster!"

5

This Southern California March night was chilly. Puffed clouds opened and closed as they drifted over an almost-full moon that washed light onto the distant, dark, purple mountains surrounding our valley.

A few minutes later, we pulled up to the emergency room entrance of the Valley View Medical Center. Madison looked at me and blinked into the bright hospital lights and the red glowing signs.

Sam put the car in 'Park' and pressed on the emergency brake. "Honey, I'll carry him in. He's heavy, Sandra."

"No! I'll meet you inside. You park and bring Madison!" I gathered Conner into my arms. "I can't pick him up, Sam! I can't pick him up!"

"There's a wheelchair—inside those doors. I'll carry him to it. You get him in there while I park." He got out, picked Conner up and carried him through the automatic doors, sat Conner down in the chair while I fixed the blanket over him. Conner's lips and chin were caked with dried, creased, red smears. He slumped over an armrest. I propped him back into a sitting position.

"Okay. I've got him."

As I pushed Conner through the open hospital doors I heard Madison's muffled scream for me behind her fogged-over window, "Mommy! Mommy!"

White clouds from the tailpipe puffed and floated and then melted into darkness as Sam got back in the SUV "We'll be with Mommy and Conner in a minute, sweetheart."

CHAPTER 2

An elderly woman with bottle-blonde hair was sitting at a desk in the reception booth. The skin around her dark eyes and throat was dry and wrinkled. She looked up from a magazine and opened the Plexiglas window. "Oh, my! I'll tell them inside that you're here. Just let me get some information." The hands on the large round clock behind her read twelve thirty-one.

"My son just had a convulsion. He's really sick. His temperature is over 103, almost 104." I turned my head and saw nurses in the emergency ward through glass doors. "He needs a doctor! Now!"

"Yes. Just let me get some information and then you'll be able to go right in. They're coming to get him."

A gray-haired, unkempt woman dozed in a maroon armchair along the wall on the other side of the room. She opened her eyes, sat up straighter, dropped her hand from her cheek and addressed an empty room: "Sure. Go ahead. Go riiiiiiight ahead. I've been waiting over an hour for somebody to see me, and they just walk right in. For Christ's sake, I'm sick, too, you know! For crying out loud!" Her voice was hoarse from years of smoking. A sagging lower lip pulled to one side and the woman's red, lower eyelids drooped. Ivory-colored stuffing protruded through a small tear in the Naugahyde where she braced her right elbow on the worn armrest. An unbuttoned cloth coat hung loosely on her thin torso to expose an old pink housedress with small blue roses printed all over it. Thick, flesh-colored stockings were rolled down to her ankles and her puffy feet were stuffed into a pair of pink, terry-cloth bedroom slippers.

Shut up! Shut up, won't you? I snarled to myself as I gritted my teeth and turned back to the receptionist.

The receptionist never looked up as she wrote down my information. "Now, Mrs. Franklin, you can see this little boy is really sick, with that bloody mouth and all. The doctor will see you soon. He just took care of you two nights ago."

I shifted from one foot to the other. Conner slumped toward one side of the large wheelchair again. I straightened him. "Can't we go in yet? He needs the doctor, right now! It's an emergency! Can't you see that?" What was she waiting for? What was she talking to that repulsive old hag for? What was she doing?

The receptionist's mouth twisted, and she was about to say something when doors whooshed open again. A tall blonde nurse wearing tan scrubs came toward us. "I've got your little boy, Mrs. Golden." She took charge of the chair and wheeled Conner back through the automatic doors. I took little skips alongside them to keep up. I used one hand to support Conner in the chair and tucked the blanket back around his body, with the other. We rushed past beds: old, pale-gray man upright in bed—clear plastic pronged-tubes plugged under his nose—rapid breaths—hissing—eyes closed—youngish brunette woman propped up on pillows reading magazine—dark red bag on a pole, dripping—needle in her arm at the end of red tubing.

"Dr. Choy, we need you." The nurse's voice was so much calmer than I expected. She wheeled Conner to a bed covered with a gray blanket that spread out all tight and neat over crisp white sheets. The pillow looked huge, full. Chrome side rails hung down. I stood back and watched as she and another nurse lifted Conner onto the bed. One took his feet and the other held him under his arms.

The tall blonde handed me the folded-up blanket I brought from home. "You'll lose this if you don't hang on to it. We'll take care of him now. You can wait there. We'll just take a minute. The doctor on duty is Dr. Choy. He's coming."

They left me standing alone as they pulled cream-colored cloth curtains around Conner's bed. I looked up when the curtains squeaked on metal rods in a track on the ceiling. The curtains closed. Bewildered and angry, I took a single step and stopped. I turned and surveyed the brightly lit ward. Disinfectant and other hospital smells wafted into my senses. Nearby, several nurses checked IV lines on poles, wrote in charts, or typed on computers at the central desk station. Only three of the other eight beds in the ward were occupied—all by adults. An elderly woman with blue-gray hair in an unbuttoned tan coat sat next to the old man getting the oxygen through the tube under his nose. I could make out black letters on the orange dust jacket of a closed book in her lap. I saw sensible low, thick-heeled black shoes. I started to turn away but then our eyes met. She smiled. I turned back and returned the smile: perfunctory, superficial.

Now Conner was in one of these beds, too, but I was out here. I turned back and heard muffled words behind the curtain. Before I could get what they were saying an Asian doctor was at my side chewing on something.

"I'm Dr. Choy. I'm on duty tonight. Mrs. Golden, right?"

"Yes, I am. Mrs. Golden. That's right. My son's in there." I jerked my head toward the curtain.

"Tell me what happened to Conner. That's his name, isn't it?"

How'd he get that information? I hadn't seen anyone talking to him. A light-blue stethoscope was draped around his shoulders. Dr. Choy was about my height, stocky and clean-shaven with short, straight dark hair. I saw no wedding band when he rubbed his nose. His right index and middle fingers had deep yellowish-tan stains. He wore dark green scrubs and tan, wooden clogs.

"Yes. My son started with a cold yesterday. He developed a real bad cough and was sneezing a lot. I took his temperature less than an hour ago, I think." I glanced at my wristwatch. "It was 103.6. When I went to phone Dr. Jackson—he's our pediatrician—we heard this horrendous sound, this God-awful scream. We ran to his bedroom and, my God, he was having a convulsion—at least that's what my husband thought it was. Conner was shaking and jerking all over. His mouth was all bloody, too. I don't know why. We drove here as fast as we could."

He nodded. "It sounds like he had a convulsion, but it seems to be over now. I'll examine him and then I think we'll be getting a head CT scan in addition to routine lab work. It will show if there's anything in his brain that could cause the seizure. Let's go into the conference room where we can sit down, Mrs. Golden." There was an odd movement when he spoke—his cheeks puffed in a funny, quick, disturbing way after every few words. It was peculiar, really odd. I'd never seen anyone do that.

"You think there could be something in his head then? Like a tumor, or something, Doctor?"

"We usually don't find a tumor, Mrs. Golden, and that's a fact." He shook his head. "But I have to make sure that there's nothing serious going on, especially with his fever. It's just a routine test we do when people have a seizure." He smiled wide and his eyes narrowed; their sides wrinkled up.

His comment made me feel a little more at ease. Maybe whatever was wrong with Conner wasn't that serious.

I spotted Sam and Madison crossing the large rectangular emergency ward. Sam had put Madison in the stroller that we kept folded in the SUV. I waved with a side-to-side, jerking motion. He walked toward us. Madison's head turned from side to side. She watched the nurses and sucked on her Binky. Sam took a deep breath. He looked pitiful as he peeked through the slight opening of the curtain—his moist eyes narrowed, and his jaw hung. Conner was on his side: a gray blanket partially exposed his pale back and bottom, and a nurse was taking his rectal temperature. An IV line had already been inserted near his left elbow and was secured by some white bandages. His arm was stretched out, taped to some kind of board.

"Sam, this is Dr. Choy. He said he's going to do a brain scan on Conner, and some other tests." My voice sounded higher pitched than usual. I trembled inside. "The doctor said that the scan will show if there's any serious problem inside Conner's head. But they usually don't find anything." I left out that word. The less I thought "tumor," the less chance there would be one. That's how I manage tough, confusing situations: don't think about it. Magical thinking helps.

Madison squirmed in the stroller and reached up to me. I lifted the toddler into my arms and held her close.

"There, there, honey. Mommy's got you." I kissed the top of her head and breathed in her scent. Mom used the same baby shampoo on me, and it always took me back to that time whenever I smelled it on her. Madison rested her head on my shoulder and sucked on the pacifier like nobody's business. She clutched her stuffed giraffe to her chest. Her head dropped to the crook of my neck. I smoothed her hair and kissed her ear. I shifted my weight from one foot to the other as I held her, a little dance that usually soothed her.

The men shook hands. "Yes, Mr. Golden. I'm Dr. Choy. How are you? Your wife just told me what happened. I'll be taking care of your son."

A tiny particle of white rice flew out of the doctor's mouth. I detected the pungent aroma of garlic and ginger in his breath.

Sam's eyes looked at the ID tag pinned to the doctor's scrub shirt: SAMUEL CHOY, M.D., Ph.D., Emergency Medicine. His gaze fixed on an open pack of cigarettes bulging from the pocket behind the tag and then up at the doctor's face. That desultory sneer had become too familiar in our home. How did Sam ever get along in Iraq? So many soldiers smoked.

The doctor didn't miss my husband's expression, either. Dr. Choy stared for a second. Then he looked down, cleared his throat and turned his attention back to me as a nurse opened the curtain around Conner's bed. Conner was on his back now. The gray blanket covered him up to his chest. He seemed to be in a deep sleep, breathing softly. The blood was gone from around his mouth, thank God.

"He's ready for you now, Doctor," she said. "I'll get his vitals into the computer. They're normal, except his rectal temp is 101.6. The five-percent IV D and W is going in at a slow drip."

"Thank you," I whispered. The nurse smiled and touched my hand as she and her colleague walked back to the nurses' station.

Sam looked pale. He gripped the back of a chair, his jaw clenched. Dr. Choy said, "Mr. Golden, a little while ago your wife described what happened to Conner at home. It sounded to me like he had a grand mal seizure." I clasped Sam's hand. The doctor turned his head and looked at an open door of a nearby room. "Here, why don't we sit down? We can go into the conference room." He stepped forward. "Has Conner ever had one before?"

Sam and I looked at each other. Before he could answer, I interjected, "No, Doctor. I—we—want to be where we can see Conner. Can't we stay here? No. He's never had a seizure. Of course not!"

The doctor's eyebrows lifted, and his eyes opened wider. I realized I had shouted. "I'm sorry, Doctor. I'm a bit upset and topsy-turvy now. No, Conner's never had anything like this before."

The doctor's face relaxed. He directed a slight smile at me, accompanied by several little nods. "Okay. We wouldn't be far away, but I understand that you want to stay close to your son. We've done vitals on him and drawn some blood for tests. We're also collecting urine and I've started him on a medication that should prevent any more seizures."

Medicine! What medicine?

"The CT scan will be done in a little while. The scanner is in the radiology department down the hall. They'll come for him shortly. It'll only take a few minutes. It could tell us why he had this seizure."

Why he had this seizure? We would know that…right now…good.

"Your son has a moderate fever. His temperature has come down a bit from what you said it was. Now, please tell me everything that happened before you brought your little boy in."

"Well, Doctor, as I said, Conner was sneezing last night. He was coughing a lot, too, and…" I told him everything. I knew I sounded rushed, and I kept looking at Conner as we all stood next to his bed. The IV dripped a clear liquid into his arm while pale-yellow urine ran from a clear tube under the sheet and into a clouded plastic bag hanging from another pole on the opposite side of the bed. "Is that tube stuck inside my son's bladder? That'll hurt, Doctor. Why'd you have to do that?"

"No, Mrs. Golden. Don't worry. The tube is not inside his bladder. It's a condom catheter stuck onto the end of his penis. Urine will just come out naturally. No, nothing's inside him."

Sam blinked hard a couple of times and wrapped his arm around my waist.

Dr. Choy leaned over and coughed into his fist. "Sorry." He glanced at Sam and then looked at me and smiled. "We're going to take good care of your son. He's going to be all right. Seizures are quite common and they're not always serious. Conner can be perfectly fine afterward." There were those funny little blowing cheek puffs again between his words.

The doctor coughed again and covered his mouth with yellow-stained fingers. He cleared his throat and stepped away from Conner's bed. "Why don't we all sit down in our conference room while the scan is being done? I need to ask you more questions about your son's medical history."

Sam and I nodded. Conner seemed comfortable now. Dr. Choy escorted us to the conference room and extended his right arm to usher us inside. It was just steps from my son's bed. I carried Madison and Sam pushed the empty stroller into the room.

"Would your little girl like some milk or juice?"

"No thank you, Doctor. She just needs to sleep. I would like to take her to the bathroom. She's potty-trained, but I don't want to over-test her. Where is it?"

I draped the blanket that had been over the stroller handlebars and carried Madison to the bathroom. The soles of my Keds squeaked on the linoleum floor. I set her on the toilet and waited for her to pee. The mirror reflected my drawn and worried expression. My brown eyes, pink from crying, were in stark contrast to my clear, pale complexion. I was slightly horrified that my hair, which usually lay neat and tidy in a pageboy cut, looked greasy and tangled. I wondered if that old rash would break out again with all this stress. The taste of pasta salad from supper came up in the back of my throat. I tucked my blouse back into my slacks and pulled down my sweatshirt. I frowned at my reflection.

Would I ever be able to lose those extra fifteen pounds I'd packed on when I was pregnant with our daughter?

"I'm done, Mommy!"

"That's a good girl, Madison, honey." I pushed the flush handle. We washed our hands.

We passed Conner's bed on the way back to the conference room. It looked like he hadn't moved. The IV dripped and it seemed like his urine bag was filling up. I sat Madison back in the stroller, eased the back down and covered her with the blanket. She closed her eyes and rhythmically sucked on her pacifier. She was fast asleep in less than a minute.

Sam and the doctor sat opposite each other at the rectangular wooden table. There were four dark, hard-back wooden chairs on each side and one chair at either end. I sat beside Sam across from the open door. I wanted to see Conner. Madison slept in her stroller behind me next to the wall.

Dr. Choy chuckled and slid several containers of Chinese-takeout to the other end of the table. Their top flaps winged upward and a pair of wooden chopsticks stuck out of one of the white boxes. The containers featured drawings of vicious-looking dragons with open mouths and Chinese writing in bright red. "I'm sorry. I was having my lunch when you arrived." He smiled. The pungent aromas of garlic and ginger filled the air.

Sam nodded. I set my mouth in a grim line. I could barely see the foot end of Conner's bed.

I looked down and noticed red blood splotches on the right shoulder of my sweatshirt where Conner's bloody mouth had touched it in the car.

"You can get that spot out pretty easily, Mrs. Golden. Just dab milk on it. That's a trick I learned from nurses early in my training. It works every time. The milk enzymes break down the blood cells." He had a broad smile with great looking teeth, sparkling almost.

"That sounds like a neat trick. I'll try it."

Conner's nurse appeared in the doorway and surveyed our little group. "CT can take him now, Dr. Choy."

"Good. I'll finish the physical exam when he gets back. It looks like he won't need any sedation; he's still postictal."

Postictal? I raised my brow and looked at Sam.

Dr. Choy picked up on my quizzical expression. "That means that Conner is still in a stupor, Mrs. Golden. It's routine after a convulsion. He'll sleep, probably for a few hours. He won't remember most of this when he wakes up. The radiology department will finish with his scan in a few minutes. After they bring him back, I'll take a look at it." He alternated his gaze between Sam and me. I liked him. He explained things.

The nurse smiled, nodded and walked away. Dr. Choy held a clipboard and occasionally he looked down to write notes as we talked. "Has your son ever had fainting spells or blackouts before?"

"No. He's always been healthy." A terrible weight settled on my shoulders. *Why did this happen? He's had high fevers before. We all have. Would he really be okay? Maybe he would be paralyzed. Could he die? Could Conner die tonight?* I gnawed my lip and shuddered. I looked down at my balled-up fists in my lap. I uncurled the fingers and looked up. Was this really happening? Maybe I would wake up and all this would just be a dream. God, was I going nuts?

Dr. Choy directed his queries to me and only occasionally glanced at Sam. I thought he did this because I had done most of the talking. I was the one who had answered most of his questions so far. What was wrong with my husband? He was always the one to take charge of a situation, to be in control. But, lately... I felt a rising frustration about my husband's silence. *He could be in this with me a bit more!* I stared at Sam sitting next to me. His head was down and his eyes focused on his lap.

"Has Conner ever complained of headaches?"

"Sometimes. But he doesn't seem to be too bothered by them; not for long. He usually stops complaining that his head hurts after a little while. If he says his head really hurts, I give him a Tylenol. The pediatrician warned me not to give aspirin because it could poison his liver and cause real problems at his young age. So, I use Tylenol for both my kids, but not much; a couple times a year, maybe. Headaches never seemed like they interfered with anything he really wanted to do unless he wanted to get out of school." I had begun to ramble again.

"Was there any vomiting with those headaches, or nausea, Mrs. Golden? Did he want to get into a dark room when he had those headaches?"

"You mean, like migraine? No. My mom used to get those, but she hasn't had one in years." I glanced at Sam. He sat perfectly still beside me, but now he leaned back with his hands folded across his abdomen. His eyes looked a little droopy. I smiled at him and reached for his hand. He nodded and squeezed mine.

Dr. Choy shot a quick glance at Sam but then turned his attention back to me. "Has Conner complained of any dizziness?"

"Well, only after spinning around in those games that kids play. You know. That's all."

"And you said that he's had no passing out or fainting spells, right?"

"That's right." I pressed the tip of my tongue against my upper lip. If anything like tonight happened before, I...I couldn't...

"Has he had any vision troubles?"

"No. Dr. Jackson checks his eyes with that eye chart every year. He says Conner's vision is fine. He seems to see all right to me, too."

"Any hearing problems or pain in his ears?"

"He gets ear infections occasionally, like when he catches cold. Dr. Jackson treats it with ampicillin. That's all. All the kids seem to get them much more than Conner does." I became aware that my foot had begun to bounce the way it does when I get tense and I cross my legs. I stopped it.

"Has Conner ever told you that he feels numb or gets weak anywhere?"

"No. No, he hasn't. Only when he hits his funny bone in his elbow sometimes, and he said that made his hand tingle. That happens to me, too, if I hit it the right way, Doctor. I mean the wrong way, don't I?" I chuckled and cupped my right palm under my left elbow.

The doctor looked up from his scribbling and smiled. "And what about rashes? Have you noticed any lately?"

"No, I haven't."

"Has he had his vaccinations? All the ones his pediatrician recommended?"

"Oh, yes. Both children are up-to-date with our doctor's recommendations." My foot jerked up and down. I uncrossed my legs and put both feet on the floor.

"What childhood diseases has he had?"

"None, really." I leaned forward and rapped my knuckles on the table twice. "I mean, that's what the vaccinations are for, right? I mean, I had chickenpox myself, but that was it. My kids haven't had it. None of their friends have, either."

"Does he take any medicines, prescription medicines, every day?"

"No, but I give the children a multivitamin. That's it. I'm wondering about those, too. Are they really necessary if they're eating well? Probably not, from what I've read."

Dr. Choy's expression didn't change. He continued, "And has he ever been in the hospital overnight for any serious illness or any surgeries?"

I shook my head. "No."

Sam's eyes were closed now. Was he awake? I became aware of a rhythmical squeak; I turned around. Madison's cheeks moved in and out with her Binky between her lips.

"And what about the relatives? Any diseases that run in the family? Anyone have seizures or epilepsy?"

Sam sat up straight and cleared his throat. So, he *was* awake. He turned to me and then back to Dr. Choy. "You know, actually, my younger brother had a convulsion when he was very young. He had a fever. I remember it like it happened yesterday now that I'm reminded of it. It was scary. He was shaking like Conner. It seemed like it lasted forever, but it probably went on for only a minute. It never happened again, thank heaven. He's fine, now."

What the—? My stomach dropped. "You said that tonight at home, didn't you? You never told me that before." I turned to Dr. Choy. "Could that affect Conner? Did that have something to do with what happened to Conner tonight? Could he have inherited it?"

"I never *told* you, Sandra, because I never thought about it until now. Jimmy's fine. Anyway, he never had another one. No one else did.

It was a long time ago, Sandra." He furrowed his brow and returned my fixed stare. "Sandra, it just *never came up*," The edge of irritation was clear in is voice.

Dr. Choy broke in: "It sounds like your brother had a febrile seizure, Mr. Golden. They're common in young children and not serious. Maybe five percent of people have them when they are very young and sick with a fever. And no, Mrs. Golden, I don't think that it's related to Conner's seizure tonight."

How could he be so sure? Why not?

The doctor smiled, nodded and wrote something else. "Thank you. You were both very helpful."

A middle-aged woman with short, wiry gray hair appeared in the open doorway.

Dr. Choy turned his head. "Ah, here's Mrs. Beck from the Financial Services Office. How are you, Mrs. Beck?" He turned back to us and said, "Mrs. Beck needs to get some information from you about your medical insurance and that sort of thing. Here, sit down, Mrs. Beck. I'll leave you to it."

"Hello. How are you?" She smiled and sat down.

I pushed my chair back to get some distance from the woman's cloying perfume.

The doctor looked over at Madison, still sound asleep in her stroller. "I'm just going to check on my other patients now. When Conner returns, I'll look at the scan and do a more thorough examination. We should be getting the blood tests back shortly. I'm concerned that he still has a fever. Depending on what those tests show, I'll probably recommend a lumbar puncture. I want to rule out meningitis as a possible cause of his seizure. It's another routine test. We'll talk about that when I get back." The chair screeched as Dr. Choy pushed back from the table and hurried out the door.

I looked up at the doctor, my mouth agape. Sam shook his head.

"Lumbar puncture? Isn't that a needle in the back, one of those long needles? Sam, I'd rather he not do that to Conner." My skull felt like it was being squeezed. "Sam, maybe we should get another opinion."

He turned toward me and placed his hand over mine but his expression was vacant. It was as though I was dealing with this alone and he was just, like, watching everything. I slumped in the seat and pulled my hand away from his. I closed my eyes and began to count slow, deep breaths.

Mrs. Beck began to shuffle some papers, her long fingernails painted pink at the tips.

We heard a whoosh of automatic doors and then squeaky wheels echoed as they approached the conference room. There was Conner, covered with a blanket on the gurney. The side rails were up and he was secured by a broad, black strap buckled across his stomach. The plastic IV bag hung on a pole attached to the stretcher and the full urine bag was between his feet.

Conner turned his head sleepily on the pillow as he was wheeled past the conference room. He saw us. "Mommy!"

The orderly looked in through the doorway and said, "He was a very good boy! He did fine, and we got him back in no time." The man's soft, Punjabi accent sounded musical.

I gave the financial officer a frosty glance and pushed my chair away from the table. She turned around in her seat and saw Conner on the gurney. "I'll come back in a little while." Mrs. Beck smiled, gathered her papers and left.

Sam was already out the door and reached Conner first. He clasped the hand without the IV. I leaned down and kissed his forehead. "Conner, sweetheart! How are you feeling?" I nodded my head toward the conference room. "Sam, keep an eye on Madison! No, wheel her out here."

Conner's eyes were wide and pleading. "Mommy, what happened? Where are we?" His breath was sour and his lips were wrinkled and dry.

"You're in the hospital, honey. You got sick, but you, you'll be all right, my darling boy," My voice trembled.

Sam returned with Madison in the stroller. She was still asleep, thank God. He squeezed Conner's little hand between both of his and forced a huge grin to hide the worry I saw in his unsmiling eyes.

Conner lifted his head and contorted his neck to look at the IV tube protruding from under a bandage at his elbow. "Why do I have that thing in my arm, Mommy? Take it out! Take it out! I want to go home!"

I brushed a lock of hair off his forehead. "Soon, honey, soon. When the doctor says so."

"I want to go home! *Now*!" Tears streamed down my son's cheeks. He slid his jaw from side to side and twisted his mouth. "Mommy, my mouth hurts. It hurts real bad."

Even though the blood was gone from his face, I noticed some red streaks remained on an upper front tooth.

The tall, blonde nurse moved from behind the nurse's station and approached the gurney. "Let's get Conner back into bed now, Mom," she said. Out of the corner of my eye I caught Sam's eyes move over her. *Seriously?*

I forced a smile and nodded. I followed the gurney back to his curtained cubicle. Sam was behind me pushing the stroller.

"Okay sweetie, we're going to lift you onto that nice bed. You just pretend you're on a magic carpet." The nurse said. She and the orderly lifted him smoothly onto the bed again. Sam and I sat on chairs on either side of him. Madison slept in her stroller next to me. The nurse adjusted the blanket and touched some control on the IV. "Dr. Choy will be right with you." She smiled at Sam and then at me. The curtains squeaked on their ceiling tracks as she pulled them closed around us.

Sam and I each held one of Conner's hands between the guardrails. He had become quiet. His eyes were closed again. I was momentarily alarmed that he had fallen back asleep so quickly. I watched his chest move up and down in slow, deep, regular breaths, pulling me back to a better time—a much better time before this night. I looked off, unseeing, until I heard Sam.

"He looks so peaceful now, honey."

CHAPTER 3

The automatic doors opened. I saw Dr. Choy stride toward us through a crack between the curtains. He pulled it open and slipped into our cubicle. Sam's jaw muscles began to work right away. I, too, detected the stale smell of tobacco.

I held my breath and looked up.

Dr. Choy looked down at Conner and cleared his throat. "Your son is still postictal; that's why he's sleeping again." He turned his gaze toward me. "I expect he'll sleep for a few more hours."

"Yes, we remember," Sam said and looked at me. I pursed my lips and nodded.

Dr. Choy said to me, "The CT scan shows that his brain appears normal." Then, he turned to look at Sam.

"Thank God!" I grinned at Sam and pumped my fist.

"Oh, that's great, Doctor. Thank you." He blinked quickly and looked down.

Dr. Choy nodded at each of us and continued, "That's very reassuring. We'll have to wait for the official results when the radiologist reads the scan in the morning, but it looks good to me."

He cleared his throat and said in a halting voice, "So, you know, uh, the question that we have to answer is, uh, why did Conner have this seizure?"

"The doctors said that my brother Jimmy's seizure was because of a high fever. Isn't that why Conner had it, too? His fever was high."

Dr. Choy tightened his grip on the guardrail and leaned over. He seemed to be studying our sleeping boy. "How old did you say your brother was when he had his seizure, Mr. Golden?"

"I think he was one, maybe two years old. He was really little."

"Hm." Dr. Choy straightened up. He rubbed his chin and turned to look down at Sam seated in the chair next to him. "You see, very young children can have seizures when they get febrile. That is, when they have a high fever, such as from a cold or the flu. Typically, we find no serious cause for those. But Conner is eight. That's a bit old to have a benign febrile seizure. We need to be sure that nothing serious has caused it."

Then he looked over at me. "I checked his blood-panel studies, and they're all normal. That's very good news. But the fever could be associated with meningitis or encephalitis. Those are serious infections in the nervous system that would need to be treated right away. We wouldn't want to miss that."

Oh, God. "Meningitis!" My stomach cramped. I searched Sam's face. He looked at Conner and said nothing.

Dr. Choy lowered the guardrails on the sides of the bed, first on his side and then he walked over and lowered the rail on mine. I slid my chair over to give him room. He walked back to Sam's side again, pulled down the cover and began moving Conner's head up and down off the pillow. "Any stiffness in the neck would suggest that your boy has one of those serious infections. It's not stiff."

The doctor turned Conner over and pulled open the hospital gown. He examined Conner's thin back and legs and then rolled him onto his back again to examine his chest and belly. "Just searching for spots and rashes on his skin that could be a sign of disease. They're subtle things that can tell us a lot," Dr. Choy explained. I looked at the tone of Conner's apricot-complexioned skin with new interest.

It seemed that he paid particular attention to Conner's hands. He prodded and pushed his fingers into Conner's belly. Then he moved his hands smoothly along both sides of our boy's neck, under his armpits, his groin and his inner elbows.

He inserted his stethoscope's earpieces and listened to Conner's chest, moving the end to different areas. Occasionally, the doctor held his breath; other times he looked up at the ceiling and closed his eyes as he listened.

He turned and grabbed an instrument with a dark-green cone attachment off the wall. I recognized it as one like something the kids' pediatrician uses. He pushed a button and used the illuminated end to peek into Conner's ears. "No redness in the canals. That's good."

Next, he propped open Conner's eyelids with his fingers and shined a flashlight into each of pupil. I stood. The light underscored greenish flecks in Conner's brown iris. I saw the pupil get smaller in the beam of light. I had all kinds of questions about what he was looking for but I didn't want to interrupt the doctor doing his work. I glanced over at Sam. He watched the doctor, too. Finally, Dr. Choy propped open Conner's eyelids again and touched each of Conner's eyeballs with a small wisp of cotton that he took from a jar at the bedside. That could not feel good. I imagined the sharp, irritated feeling when wind blew something in my eye. Conner blinked, even though he was asleep.

Dr. Choy must have seen me shudder because he looked at me and said, "This doesn't hurt, Mrs. Golden. That's normal; a normal response tells me his brainstem—the back of his brain—is working well."

"Oh," I said, without comprehending what he meant.

Now Sam was on his feet. "What did you do, Doctor?"

"I just touched his cornea with this wisp of cotton to test the corneal reflex."

"Uh-huh," Sam said.

Throughout the examination Dr. Choy murmured, "Fine, good." When he said that, I nodded and looked at Sam. I started to feel a little hope and tried to smile. *Maybe everything really was fine and we could go home.* I had forgotten all about that mention of a spinal tap.

The doctor propped open Conner's mouth with a tongue depressor and directed his flashlight inside. "Look! He bit his tongue. Right there! Do you see that? That's where all the blood came from."

He leaned back for us to have a look, too. I could see that the whole left side of Conner's tongue was swollen and dark blue. There was a red jagged cut along the edge.

My hands flew to my mouth. "Oh, my God. That's awful!" I groaned and lowered my hands. "People can bite off their tongue during a convulsion, Doctor. I heard that. They can even swallow it, can't they?"

"No, no, Mrs. Golden. It's pretty common to bite the tongue during a grand mal seizure. Don't worry. This is not a serious injury; it will heal in a few days. I promise you; no one has ever bitten off his tongue during a seizure. Nor is it possible to swallow the tongue. Those are old wives' tales. You said that he wet himself at home. That also happens routinely during a seizure. Loss of bowel control can also occur."

Dr. Choy pulled out a small rubber hammer the color of red clay from a lower pocket on his scrub shirt. He tapped the triangular tip on Conner's elbows and knees.

"What does that tell you, Doctor Choy? Why do you do it?" I watched his face and felt a wave of self-consciousness rush over me. *Why do I keep talking so much? Asking so many questions?* "I hope you don't mind these questions..."

"No. I encourage questions. Many people don't ask enough of them. The reflexes can tell us if there's a neurological problem, Mrs. Golden. It can tell us if the problem is in the central nervous system—that's the brain and the spinal cord—like with a stroke. If it is, then the reflexes are really brisk and jumpy, and the hand or foot jumps real hard when we hit the tendon."

I glanced at my elbow.

"If the problem is in the peripheral nerves—like the nerves that go out into our arms and legs—then they won't jump when we hit the tendon, or hardly at all." He scraped the pointed metal tip of the hammer's handle across the bottoms of Conner's feet. My feet tingled and my toes curled as if in sympathy with the sensation I imagined Conner was feeling at that moment.

"He has good reflexes. Everything seems normal. He still has a fever, though. I want to make sure that we are not missing a treatable infection

in his nervous system. So, I would like to perform a lumbar puncture—
that's a spinal tap—to examine the fluid in his spinal column. It would
tell us if there's an infection."

"Oh, no, Doctor! Do you have to do that? I don't want Conner to
have that. He's so little. I think it would be too dangerous." I looked
at Sam. I wanted him to agree with me—he *had* to agree with me. I
draped my body over Conner's. I glared up at my husband. Why didn't
he say anything?

Sam grimaced but maintained his stony silence. I straightened up;
my fists clenched at my sides. I could feel my lips press closed in a tight
line and push my tongue hard against the back of my front teeth.

"I understand that you're worried, Mrs. Golden. Look, this is a
routine test. It takes just five to ten minutes." He paused. A little puff
of his cheeks squelched an inaudible burp that I saw rise up his torso.
"We do it as an outpatient procedure in the office, and when it's over
most patients are surprised at how easy it was. More times than not, they
say, 'You mean, that's all there is to it, Doc?' Mrs. Golden, I promise
this test is very safe."

"You had a 'spinal' when you had the kids, didn't you, Sandra?"
Sam had a croak in his voice now that he finally spoke. He cleared his
throat. "I remember that," he said.

This was what Sam said? *This* was my *support?* "Yes, but that's
different from what he wants to do to Conner!" My voice cracked with
irritation.

"It's basically the same thing, Mrs. Golden, except you had an
anesthetic injected into your spinal canal to numb you. For this test, I
don't put anything in. I take out a small amount of spinal fluid to study
in the lab for infection and other problems. Don't worry; Conner's body
will replace the fluid within a half-hour."

I heard Sam ask, "Will you analyze the results yourself?" My
shoulders drooped.

"I send the spinal fluid to the lab for a technician to examine. But,
yes, I get the results to interpret and make a diagnosis."

"Gee, Doctor, um, the needles, you know, they're, ah, they're real long." Sam stammered. "I've seen pictures of them someplace, in some book or other. It must, uh, really hurt a lot, doesn't it?"

I jerked my head with quick nods. A surge sprang into my chest as I looked at my husband. At last, Sam was showing a little support for me. I turned to Dr. Choy.

His eyes locked with Sam's. "They're long needles only because the tip has to reach deeper, Mr. Golden. That needle doesn't hurt any more than shorter ones. It just has to go deeper, that's all. And it usually doesn't hurt at all, or not much, anyway. I numb up the area with a local anesthetic. You need to know the possible side effects of a spinal tap, though. I clean off the skin with a sterilizing solution first, but there is a very remote possibility that the spinal tap can cause an infection. I have never seen it, but you must know that it can happen. Local soreness occasionally occurs. And, on average, one out of three patients gets what's called a 'post-spinal headache.' We really can't predict who will get that headache."

"If you do this test, uh, I remember they told me that I had to lay flat for a long time after my spinals when I delivered my children. What about that, Doctor?"

"It doesn't make any difference if you lie down for twenty-four hours or for five minutes following a spinal tap. One out of every three people still gets that headache no matter how long they lay flat, and it can last a few days. We do spinal taps here just about every day. It's very routine, Mrs. Golden.

"Having said all that, I recommend Conner have this procedure because he has a fever, and he had a convulsion. Meningitis and encephalitis can cause his seizure, and it's critical to know if that is the case, here."

"But, you said the CT scan was normal. Doesn't that mean he doesn't have an infection? Why do it then?"

"Meningitis usually doesn't show on the scan. The best way to rule it out is to examine spinal fluid. If the spinal fluid does not show any sign of infection, you can take him home. I am also going to refer Conner to a specialist—a neurologist—to find out why he had the convulsion in the first place. Meanwhile, as I've said, I started a medication to prevent him from having any more seizures."

"Wait. Does that mean you expect he could still have *another* one?"

"It's possible, Mrs. Golden."

I sensed he was trying hard to hide his annoyance. Although we were the same height, the way he tilted his head made me feel like he was looking down his nose at me. His cheeks puffed in and out like a bellows, fast and more pronounced than before. His lips tightened into a slight grimace.

Sam pinched the bridge of his nose with his thumb and index finger. "I really think that Dr. Choy should do the test, Sandra. We want to be sure that Conner doesn't have meningitis. We wouldn't want that…" His voice trailed off.

I felt this compulsion—this duty—to protect Conner. I still wasn't convinced about what the doctor wanted to do. "You make it sound so safe and simple. But I've heard bad things about spinal taps, Doctor. I remember my uncle told me once that one paralyzed a friend of his. It was a long time ago, but I remember it."

Dr. Choy smiled and shook his head. "No, I don't think so, Mrs. Golden. This procedure is often done *after* people are *already* paralyzed. That's probably what your uncle was referring to. Now, I really think the spinal tap should be done. My nurse will give you the release form that you need to sign. It covers what we've talked about. Why don't you go back to the conference room now to wait while I do it? By the way, is Conner allergic to Lidocaine? You know, the numbing medicines that dentists use?"

He was talking so rationally. Doctors' facts: they didn't mean he was right; doctors were not always right. I just didn't want Conner hurt anymore.

The men's voices interrupted my turmoil. "No. I don't think so, not that we know of, anyway. He's never needed it before. Isn't that right Sandra?" Sam turned questioning eyes toward me and shrugged.

"Wha—what?" I turned to Dr. Choy. "No. That's right. And Doctor, we'll be with Conner when you do this."

"No, Mrs. Golden. It would be best if you both waited in the conference room."

His firm expression and the way he shook his head surprised me. "But—I'm his *mother*! I should be there *with* him." I paused to let it sink in. "Okay?"

"I will have my nurse assist me. That is all that I will need. As I said, the procedure takes just about ten minutes. You'll be able to be with him as soon as I finish. Please, go with your husband. We'll come and get you as soon as I finish."

He was emphatic. His hard stare made me uneasy. I knew that I couldn't argue him out of it. I looked at Sam and bit back my protest. I murmured, "Is that okay with you, Sam?"

Sam got behind the stroller, "Yes. We'll wait there."

When we walked into the conference room Mrs. Beck was at the table waiting for us with her paperwork spread out and stickers indicating where we were supposed to sign. I completed the financial and insurance forms in just a few minutes. I thanked her when she wished us and our son well as she left the room.

I walked over to check Madison. Sam had pushed the stroller near the wall behind him. She was fast asleep under the blanket. The pacifier had dropped from her mouth and was under her shoulder. I watched the blanket that covered her chest rise and fall for a moment. I put the pacifier in my pocket and sat down.

Sam sat across the conference table. We stared silently at each other. Funny, I hadn't even heard the wall clock before, but its ticking pierced me now. I glanced over at it and then looked back into his eyes. He shrugged.

I dug a tissue out of my pocket and blew my nose.

"Hey," Sam said softly. He reached across the table. I reached out, too. He placed both hands on top of mine and squeezed. "Sweetheart, the doctor *did* say we'll be able to take him home soon. Sandra?"

"Oh, Sam!" I whispered. I lowered my head onto my outstretched arms and closed my eyes.

CHAPTER 4

*S*everal minutes later, Dr. Choy and a nurse were behind the curtain with Conner. The boy was sound asleep, still under the combined postictal stuporous effects of his convulsion and the sedative effect of the intravenously administered anti-seizure medication.

The nurse unwrapped a sterile spinal-puncture kit and placed it on a metal stand next to Dr. Choy. The doctor positioned the boy on his side. He pulled Conner's knees up to his abdomen to round out the spine and open the spaces between the bony vertebrae. Conner moaned softly in his stupor and tried to straighten his body, but Dr. Choy held the boy's flexed torso and legs still with his hands for several seconds until the boy relaxed.

The doctor washed and dried hands and inserted them into sterile gloves with a loud snap. He donned the sterile gown from the kit and sat on a stool to swab rusty-brown antiseptic solution over Conner's lower back. Then his fingers felt the spaces between the boy's vertebrae under the skin. Dr. Choy decided which space in the lower vertebral column had the best opening to insert the long spinal needle. As he'd done a hundred times before, he covered his patient's naked back with the sterile paper drape from the kit, the center of which had been cut open to gain access to the spine.

He injected the local anesthetic. "We're lucky he's still postictal; otherwise, we'd have a real fight on our hands," Dr. Choy said as he looked up at the nurse standing opposite him over Conner. "This local anesthetic burns. It's usually the most uncomfortable part of the whole procedure, you know."

He placed the anesthetic syringe on the tray and picked up the spinal needle. That needle could look a foot long to a patient, but it measured less than four inches. He pushed the sharp tip into the numbed skin, confirmed that his aim was correct and pressed the needle deeper. It slid smoothly into Conner's back.

Dr. Choy exhaled. No movement, no cries, no moans from his patient. *At least I haven't hit bone yet,* he thought. The doctor pushed the needle deeper until he felt the reassuring "pop" as it penetrated the thick, fibrous ligamentum flavum membrane that enclosed the spinal canal. He pulled out the hollow needle's stylet. Colorless, clear cerebrospinal fluid immediately dripped out the end of the now-empty, hollow-bored spinal needle. The tension in the doctor's shoulders dissolved as these welcome first drops fell onto a towel he had placed on the floor for this purpose.

He attached a long, thin measure-marked plastic manometer tube to the end of the needle and watched the colorless fluid climb slowly up the tube. The surface of the fluid undulated up and down slightly with each of Conner's breaths. It finally stopped rising at the 140-millimeter mark: the pressure in the cranial cavity and spine was normal.

Samuel Choy mused at the similarities between spinal fluid and seawater as he watched the fluid: both liquids shared the same chemistry. This fact had fascinated him ever since medical school.

And he recalled his grandmother's sea stories. Grandma Liu grew up along the Pearl River in southern China. Her pet cormorant was trained to dive for fish for the family to eat and to sell. With her funny laugh and with a gesture of fingers around her throat, she had described how a tight ring around the bird's throat prevented it from making the fish its own meal. He loved her stories from China.

The nurse broke his reverie from the opposite side of the bed. "If I ever need a spinal tap, Dr. Choy, I want you to do it." *His weak smile masked the pleasure he felt at the compliment.*

He removed the manometer and placed a collection tube under the end of the needle. A few drops splashed onto his clogs. "The fluid looks clear.

Good. It's unlikely Conner has an infection," he said to her. He collected three tubes of spinal fluid for testing. Then he pulled the long spinal needle out of the boy's back.

"I'll take the vials down to the laboratory. You won't need me now, will you?"

"No. I have everything under control here. The orders are written. Go ahead." He nodded at her, and she left.

Dr. Choy turned Conner onto his belly. He wiped away a red drop oozing from the puncture site and washed the antiseptic solution from the boy's back with a warm, damp towel. Then he dried the skin and placed a Band-Aid over the puncture, retied Conner's hospital gown and rolled the boy onto his back.

"We're all done, Conner."

Conner stared up with uncomprehending eyes.

Dr. Choy covered him with the blanket and snapped the bed's guardrails back into place.

OCTOBER 2006:
SOUTHERN CALIFORNIA

CHAPTER 5

I carried my coffee into the den to answer the phone. There was the photograph of Sam, smiling in uniform, next to it. He was nearing the end of his year-long deployment to Iraq with the California Army National Guard. My heart pounded and the muscles in my jaw tightened whenever the phone rang. I drew a deep breath and let it ring a few more times, deciding. I exhaled and tried to empty my mind of those secret, awful fears. I put the coffee down and reached for the receiver.

"Hello."

"Mrs. Golden?"

A woman's voice. "Yes, speaking."

"This is Janet Dorsey. Conner's teacher, Mrs. Golden."

The tightness in my chest eased. "Oh. Hi, Mrs. Dorsey."

"How are you, Mrs. Golden?"

"I'm good. How are you? What's going on?" If she was calling about some volunteer project she wanted me to do she was out of luck.

"Well, I have some concerns about Conner that I'd like to discuss with you. Do you have a minute?"

"Ye-es. What's wrong? We just got home. He never told me anything—anything about school." I suddenly felt queasy. I sucked in a breath and gripped the phone tighter in my slick palm. I sank onto the couch, reached for the coffee cup, hesitated and pulled my hand back.

"His schoolwork is not—well, he's not progressing as I would like, Mrs. Golden. Could we get together and talk? We could meet here at school. If you're pressed for time, though, we can discuss it now."

I sat forward on the edge of the couch and my knees started to bounce together. "Please tell me about it now. It wouldn't be very easy for me to come to the school these next few days." A delivery truck squealed to a stop across the street. I watched the driver—a black guy in a brown uniform with matching baseball-type cap—move around in the cab. The teacher's voice droned on. I forced my legs to stop moving and focus on what she was about to say.

"I understand. Well, frankly, I am a bit perplexed, Mrs. Golden. Usually—actually, most of the time—Conner completes his work very well. Sometimes he stands out in his comprehension and cooperation. But then…for instance, let me tell you about yesterday. Maybe he told you?"

"No, he didn't tell me anything." My voice was louder than I had intended. "Tell me. What?" I opened my mouth wide and the tension in my jaw started to relax.

"Well, he left more than half of his spelling words out. That has happened before, and he often doesn't complete his homework. Is he getting enough sleep at night? I am aware that his father's in Iraq. That has to be hard on the whole family. How is Mr. Golden?"

"Uh, he's doing fine, thank you." Her interrogatory tone annoyed me. I bit my lower lip and shook my head. "But, back to Conner, he really doesn't tell me much about what's going on at school. I ask him who he ate lunch with and what he did at recess and what lessons he had that day. I try to get him to open up, but he won't. I guess that's like most kids."

Conner didn't talk about Sam even with me—not that much anyway. I was sure he must be worried about his dad, like I was. He had to. That must be what the teacher meant. Sam's absence must be affecting him more than I thought. He had wet his bed a couple of times the past few months, too. And why didn't he ever talk about his father? He was shutting that side down. He and Sam used to do so much together before Sam was called up last January. Play catch, ride bikes—I just couldn't do those things with Conner like Sam did. At least, not in the same way.

I grasped the phone with both hands. My armpits felt damp. I stared out the window for a few seconds; the truck driver was now at the front door of the house across the street.

Mrs. Dorsey's voice brought me back. "Yes, I agree. Well, that's so much like children his age, you know."

"I had no idea that he's having trouble with his schoolwork though, Mrs. Dorsey." I blinked rapidly and twisted a lock of hair with my fingers. "What's the matter? Conner does his homework. I check that he has his assignments and his papers in his backpack every morning. I ask him about it."

I stood and went to the window. The driver was back in his truck. Seconds later, he gunned the engine and moved off, leaving gold and red leaves whirling in the street. It brought up a memory: a taste of apples. I could still hear the crunch and taste the sweetness of the crisp apples I used to enjoy when I was at college back east a couple of decades ago. "What do you think is going on with Conner at school, Mrs. Dorsey?"

"Well, Mrs. Golden, his homework is often incomplete. When I ask him why he didn't finish, Conner can't really explain why. I sent a note home with him about it a few days ago. Did you—"

"I didn't get any note. He didn't *bring* me a note." A note? Did he drop it? Did he lose it? "Look, Conner is very responsible. I mean, sometimes he ignores me and he doesn't answer me. But he's a kid. Kids are always in their own little world."

"I've mentioned my concerns about Conner to our principal, and she—Dr. Signet—observed him in the classroom for a few minutes this morning. In fact, we have been observing him for a while. I can't explain why your son isn't doing better work. I know that he's capable of it, Mrs. Golden."

How could this be? There had been no inkling. Unless…Sam…too distracted? I rubbed one wet palm against my slacks and then the other as I transferred the phone from hand to hand.

"Dr. Signet and I would like to arrange a Student Study Team conference to discuss what's going on with Conner. SST is a multidisciplinary team; I would like to invite you to meet with us. I'll be there, along with Dr. Signet and Millie Shaw, Conner's teacher from last year. You know Millie. She remembers Conner very fondly, too. Our school psychologist, Maryanne…uh…Offermantel…she'll be there, too, and a few other staff members. We'll share our observations with you, and you'll have a chance to tell us your ideas about what's going on and how we can help your son."

"School psychologist? Why a psychologist?" My voice rose again. "My family, uh…" *Dad…After Vietnam he was real hard to live with…* Mom nearly left him…so many counseling sessions…not much good. He calmed down…nightmares…took an awful long time. Mom said he was still not right. "Do you think there's something wrong with Conner in that way? Do you think it's that serious? Is that what you're saying?"

"It's routine for the school psychologist to take part in these meetings, Mrs. Golden. She is trained to identify specific learning and behavioral problems that could affect a child's work. School psychologists use tests, psychological tests, to appraise a child's learning abilities and identify interfering conflicts. That sort of thing. It's a standard method used to evaluate children. Conner seems to have—well, how should I put it? —a lack of engagement. We think that a psychologist's input would really help."

I looked up. I felt several vertebrae pop in my neck. My Psych 101 course—Jesus that was boring—I hated it. Jeanie had been going to a therapist for years. It hadn't gotten my friend very far. She was still as neurotic as ever. "Then, certainly I could attend the meeting. It sounds like it would be important for Conner. When would it be? I'd have to arrange to have someone watch my children."

"We actually had an SST meeting scheduled for tomorrow afternoon, but that student's family had something come up and they've asked for a postponement. I was thinking that you could take their appointment. It so happens that most of the same staff members would be attending. Is there any way that meeting would work for you?"

What would they say? What would I have to do? *Why wasn't Sam here? For Christ's sake, I need him here, not in Iraq.* I realized that I was clenching my jaw and my teeth ground from side-to-side.

"Mrs. Golden, I believe we can resolve whatever is going on with Conner. We just want to make sure that everything he needs is being provided for him."

"I understand. I know you're trying to help, Mrs. Dorsey. It's too bad my husband can't be there, too."

"This will work out, Mrs. Golden. When is your husband expected home?"

I closed my eyes, arched my back and rolled my neck in a couple of circles. Then, when I extended it, I felt another satisfying pop. I thought about the article I had to finish. And the other pieces I had promised to write for two more periodicals. The paperwork—I had to balance books that Tom, the partner in our construction company, expected me to do while Sam was away. I flashed on a memory and closed my eyes: I was twelve again, in the sixth grade, trying on makeup with my best friends, Judy and Marsha. We were at Judy's house. I could still see the pink- and blue-flowered wallpaper; her canopied bed matched the wallpaper. We laughed and screamed and slammed the bedroom door against Judy's younger twin brothers. Life was much simpler, so much easier back then. I shook my head, sighed and blinked. The wan smile that creased my face reflected in the glass covering the face of our grandfather clock, just feet away.

"Mrs. Golden?"

I turned from the reflection. "Uh, Sorry. Sam will be home in less than three months—in January." *My salvation.* I blurted, "Do you think that this could wait until he's home so that he could attend, too?" I immediately realized how foolish that question was. "No, I guess that wouldn't be practical. We should address this as soon as we can, shouldn't we, Mrs. Dorsey? Okay, we'll meet tomorrow after school. I'll arrange for Conner and Madison to have a playdate. How long will this meeting take?"

"Not more than an hour. I know it's short notice, but this is really important for Conner, and for you, too. We're lucky there was a cancellation. We'll see you in the principal's conference room next to her office at 3:30 tomorrow. I'll let you know if there's any scheduling problem with our team. Okay?"

I mumbled my assent, and we said our goodbyes. I replaced the receiver onto its cradle. I had pressed it against my head so hard that my ear stung. My heart pounded. There was a sour taste in the back of my throat. I stood there, confused and annoyed. Why did she call now? What had I missed? I grabbed the coffee cup and walked into the kitchen. How could I have missed this? What was she talking about? Conner seemed fine. He was not any different from his friends. He always did his schoolwork—I think. What did I miss? I leaned against the cream-tiled counter next to the sink, poured my coffee down the drain and concentrated on my breathing. *Slow it down. Settle down, Sandra.*

I had always presented an image of strength to the outside world; at least I thought I did. But ever since Sam's deployment, I had been discouraged by a growing constellation of worries and responsibilities. This was when I needed to rely on my life experiences. I knew myself. I had always just gone with the flow before. I had always done that, and things always seemed to have worked out.

The late-afternoon sun cast long shadows on our back lawn. Gold and rust reflections from the windows over on the next street sparked memories. I recalled my college days with sharp and sudden longing: my turn-of-the-century Victorian dormitory, the same colorful late-afternoon sun reflecting off of campus windows…my roommates, our dreams, planning careers, weddings, husbands, children and reunions… all of that quick-moving time.

As I stared, unbidden images wove between shadows on the lawn. I squeezed my eyes shut; in that blackness those images wove into a word-painting:

> *Wolves snarling, circling—*
> *Terror-filled eyes now watching—*
> *Falling, caught in nets.*

These phantasmagorias assaulted and captured a part of my mind— my soul, even. They developed deep in my unconscious emotional and perceptional world. Fortunately, Professor Mayer recognized this ability in me. He nourished it and encouraged me. They were that practiced "haiku-part" of my mind that birthed during my college years. Haiku were just three lines, three streams of thought that spoke of contrasting concepts in a way that combined and completed them into a meaningful closure. They required interpretation—some thought. Haiku were beautifully provocative.

The sound of the children playing upstairs shattered my reverie. Conner squealed with laughter and I heard Madison's adorable, lisped yell, "Mommy, Mommy! We want ithe cream!"

As we sat down for dinner, I wondered what to say to Conner—how to ask him why he wasn't finishing his school assignments. Madison scooped some gravy-covered rice and peas and dropped half of the spoonful onto her plate. A few grains of rice stuck in her hair. Conner sat across from me. He pushed pieces of roast beef around his plate and mixed them into his rice and peas while he made low, growling motor sounds.

After a moment, "Conner, honey, Mrs. Dorsey called me today. She said that you haven't been finishing your schoolwork. Why is that?"

His head shot up. "I do, too, Mom! I do, too!" he yelled. Suddenly tense, his face reddened. He left his chair and stood next to the table. Madison dropped her spoon and stared at him. Her bib was completely in her rice now.

"Well, she says that you don't finish your work. Why would she think that?" His expression hardened. "Sit down, Conner."

He remained standing, one bent knee balanced on the seat of his chair. "I don't know! I do everything. I do everything just like the other kids, Mom." His voice trembled. He sat down again and pushed his plate away. His water glass almost tipped over. My hand shot out to steady it. Conner's eyes narrowed and filled with tears. Madison watched her brother.

"Don't worry, honey. Mrs. Dorsey just set up a meeting for me to talk about how you're doing in school. You and Madison will have a play-date tomorrow afternoon while I'm at the meeting."

I looked at them. Madison started to play with her rice and peas again. She mimed feeding the spoon to her stuffed giraffe, which was stuck beside her in the booster seat. I reached across and put my hand over one of Conner's. He snatched it away and wiped his eyes with his sleeve. He looked down at his plate, his expression defensive. I tried to smile.

I hated that everything was in my lap. I did not sign up for this. Sam would be home in January—not soon enough. Why didn't I appreciate how serious he was about the National Guard when I married him? It was peacetime, for Christ's sake. I should never have allowed him to continue to sign those Army reserve contracts. I was such a fool.

"Okay. Are we ready for some of that pie?"

That evening Conner sat at his desk. He was in his pajamas marking a paper with crayons. I leaned against the jamb of his open bedroom door and stared at the dark world outside his window. *Would he wet his bed again tonight?* I made a mental note to monitor how much he drank during and after dinner. Buried in thought, I tapped my fingers lightly on my lips.

He looked up and noticed me standing there. His "Hi, Mom," registered vaguely. He turned back to his drawing. After a moment he looked back. "Mom? Mommy?"

I turned away from the window. "Huh? Oh, it's time for bed now, honey. Did you brush and floss and go to the bathroom?"

"Yeah, Mom."

"Is all your homework done? Let me see it."

"There is none. I didn't have any to do tonight."

"Oh, okay. I want you to show me your homework every night, Conner." I glanced at his drawing: a stick figure with a large, round, pink head, black dots for the eyes and nose, and a straight line to indicate the mouth. Several jagged yellow and red lines emanated from the sides of the head like lightning bolts.

"That's good, honey. What is it?"

"Oh, it's just what I think about sometimes."

I looked out again into the night. "Uh-huh." After a moment, I said, "Okay, hop into bed now. I'll tuck you in."

Conner put his crayons back into their box. I caught the briefest whiff of crayon-wax as crumpled paper flew into the wastebasket. Those yellow and green crayon boxes haven't changed since my own grammar school days: fresh, new-tipped rows of crayons with all of those colors in those flip-tops at the beginning of the school year.

He climbed into bed. I bent down and kissed the top of his head. His soft, sweet smell conjured images of his infancy: pinkness, chubby cheeks and limbs, giggles and diapers. I smiled and switched off the overhead light. "I love you, honey. Sleep tight in your cozy, warm bed."

"I love you, too, Mom. And I love Daddy and Madison, too."

CHAPTER 6

It was gray and misty when I drove to school the next afternoon. Autumn clouds dominated the sky. The windshield wipers' slow, steady syncopation reminded me of that old tune I loved but could never remember its name. I gripped the steering wheel hard. Conner—our Conner seemed to be in trouble. What was going on? Sam wasn't renewing his Guard contract, but—now! I needed him here, now! He should be home with us.

I didn't remember parking. I didn't even remember most of the drive here. I sensed that I was slouching, shuffling toward the school door. I took in a deep breath, sucked in my stomach and straightened up. Get a grip on yourself, Sandra. Conner would get up to speed. This committee would fix things. *We would fix it.* Mrs. Dorsey said Conner could do better. Well, I *knew* he could.

The scent of fresh rain permeated the air. I had always loved rain, especially walking in the rain back in New England…majestic, old college buildings…umbrellas.

I was totally aware now. I felt brighter, lighter. The cloud around me lifted. I tried to imagine what this meeting would be like, what I might have to face. "Not progressing…" Mrs. Dorsey had said. What was that? I would hear the SST Committee out. *Then, I would show them what Conner was capable of.*

The members of the SST were already in Principal Signet's conference room when I arrived. They stood chatting around a long oak table. One woman was on her cell phone, others were holding white Styrofoam coffee cups. There was Conner's teacher. Her back was to me. Mrs. Dorsey was in her mid-thirties, tall with long, dark hair. She stood next to the only man in the room. Both were laughing.

Everyone turned toward me as I entered the room. I looked down and patted the sides of my tan slacks. I sucked in my stomach; I hoped that it looked flatter. My heart pounded. Coffee aromas mixed with a sweet, spicy scent of cologne.

Someone offered coffee. "No, thank you." I flashed a smile. I recognized the principal from other school events and nodded at her on the other side of the table as she caught my eye.

Dr. Signet walked toward me. "Ah, here's Mrs. Golden. Thank you for coming." Dr. Grace Signet had been principal of Conner's school, Valley Ranch Elementary, for the past six years. The school had already won several academic awards during her tenure. She was a slim brunette of medium height, in her mid-forties, attractively dressed and softly perfumed. Her light-pink lipstick framed her very white, perfect teeth when she smiled. She seemed friendly enough, but there was no mistaking the take-charge, business-like demeanor beneath her friendly façade.

She introduced herself and we shook hands. Her direct gaze made me drop my eyes. I touched the back of a chair with my other hand. Mrs. Dorsey smiled and silently mouthed "hi" to me from across the room.

The principal sat down at the head of the conference table; then the others did, too. The man and Mrs. Shaw, Conner's second-grade teacher, sat on either side of me; everyone else sat opposite us. Once the screeching of moving chairs stopped, Dr. Signet looked around and perfunctorily thanked everyone for making the time to come to the meeting. I noticed the slightest hint of a Southern drawl in her voice.

I was impressed. She was so smooth. As if they would not have come when she told them to be here. Anyone could see that she was top hen: how they all looked at her, how they all immediately stopped talking.

The principal nodded at Mrs. Dorsey sitting to her right, then turned back to me and explained that Conner's teacher had concerns about his progress in third grade.

Dr. Signet said that the issues we would address today had also been observed last year, when Conner was in the second grade. She nodded at Mrs. Shaw sitting next to me. "Mrs. Golden, all of us here today take great pride in our school's educational program. We care about each of our student's achievements, and that is why we are meeting. We want to explore these concerns and discuss what approaches should be taken that would benefit your son."

I nodded. I began to thank her but it came out as a croak. I cleared my throat and smiled at the group. My stomach had started to growl, though. I made another throat-clearing noise to hide the sound.

Dr. Signet introduced her staff. Miss Maryanne Offermantel, the school psychologist, sat across from me. The psychologist smiled and conceded that she was new to the school district. "Call me Miss O. Everyone does. My name is awfully long, I know," she said in an incongruously husky voice. Her right index and middle fingers were yellow-stained.

I already knew Mrs. Dorsey and Mrs. Shaw. Mrs. Dorsey's face brightened with a wide smile and warm, green eyes. I nodded at Mrs. Shaw. We had met several times last year on Parent-Teacher nights. She looked at me and smiled in a way that made me believe she really did remember me.

"This is Stanley Anton, Mrs. Golden. He's our special-education teacher." Mr. Anton lowered his head politely and smiled. I thought he could be a double for, what's-his-name, that actor? But the principal continued her introductions before I could think of it.

"Deepi Shipra is our school nurse, Mrs. Golden. She has some information about your son that she will offer regarding his health reports."

The woman bowed her head. A bright, round, orange-red spot that Indian women paint, struck me—at least it looked like it was painted. Or was it stuck on her forehead right between her dark full eyebrows? She was middle-aged, slight and dark-skinned. Her jet-black hair was pulled straight back into a bun. A broad, white collar was open at the top of her soft, blue-skirted nurse's uniform. The woman's gold pierced earrings dangled from thick earlobes, and I counted at least ten thin, gold bracelets on each wrist. That was a lot of gold. My gaze moved back up to her face. She beamed a warm smile that revealed—more gold! One upper-front tooth was gold. I smiled to myself at the spectacle; some sort of *memsahib* stuff I guessed, or whatever. The woman oozed friendliness. I liked her immediately, and she hadn't even said a word. I nodded and returned an effusive smile.

Throughout these introductions, I cast repeated glances at the psychologist. She was probably in her late twenties, but her chubby, baby-faced features made her appear even younger. Her black skirt and white blouse were tailored to her stocky figure. She wore dark-pink lipstick that matched her painted fingernails. A green jadestone dangled from a long silver chain around her thick neck, and an unflattering blonde bob partly concealed a pair of matching earrings. When I first entered the conference room I had noticed a small, blue-and-red butterfly tattoo on Miss O's right ankle. It just peeked out above her black pumps. Within minutes I disliked this young, "party girl" school psychologist.

Dr. Signet commenced the session. The school nurse read from her report. Her Indian accent was precise and sharply articulated. She rolled her *r*'s: "Conne*r* Golden doesn't appea*r* to have any health *p*roblems, and his vaccinations a*r*e up-to-date. His weight, vision and hea*r*ing tests are all normal. He's a healthy boy!" Nurse Shipra looked up from her records; she and that gold tooth grinned at me. "I *r*emember how keen he was in his vision and hea*r*ing tests. You have a ve*r*y nice boy, Mrs. Golden."

I nodded and smiled back. "Thank you," I said softly. Even this lovely woman's eyes smiled; the dark wrinkles beside them deepened.

"Mrs. Dorsey, Janet, you've had Conner in your classroom for a couple of months now. You have concerns about his work. Would you tell us about them?"

"Thank you, Grace," she said, and then she turned her attention toward me. "Conner is well-behaved, he is respectful and he's popular with his classmates. And, yes, Conner is intelligent—I'm convinced of that, Mrs. Golden. Nevertheless, he occasionally skips, or he doesn't complete his work assignments. He leaves out answers; he just leaves them blank. I have asked him about it several times, but my questions only upset him. I don't understand why he does that—leave out whole answers, I mean. Like in spelling tests, it is as if he doesn't even seem to hear what I've told the class to do. It is that, or he chooses to ignore me. I'm just not sure what's going on. I've worked with many children who have Attention Deficit Disorder—ADD. But, that doesn't seem to be his problem, in my opinion."

The school nurse broke in, "His hearing test last spring was normal."

Mrs. Dorsey continued, "He is capable of doing the work, Mrs. Golden. His reading scores are excellent, but overall, he needs to apply himself more. He has told me about his dad being in the Army in Iraq, so I assume that he worries about him. That would only be natural, and it probably contributes to some of these concerns. Another factor could be that he is not getting enough rest. Is Conner getting enough sleep at night, Mrs. Golden?"

"Yes, he is! I see to that." I shifted around in my seat and quickly surveyed the group watching me.

"I'm sorry that I have to say this, Mrs. Golden, but his academic performance is just not up to third-grade expectations." She glanced at the pencil she had begun to roll under her palm. Then she looked up at the principal and then at me. "I'm considering if we should put Conner back in second grade. I mean, at least for a trial period. It might be less stressful for him." She looked at her principal again.

I gnawed on my lower lip. My brow tightened. Flabbergasted, I felt an eyelid start to twitch. I looked at the principal and then back at Mrs. Dorsey. How could this be? It couldn't be that serious. I would have known. They never really said.

I saw Dr. Signet move her tongue behind her closed lips as she watched me. After what seemed like an eternity, she said, "Uh, huh. Thank you, Janet. Those are significant observations. What do you think, Millie? Conner was in your second-grade class last year."

I turned to look at her. She seemed like a very pleasant and sweet person on the few occasions we had met last year.

Mrs. Shaw looked down at the table as she began to speak. "Yes, well, I have to agree with what Janet has said. I was favorably impressed by your son at the start of last school year, Mrs. Golden, but it became apparent to me that, on occasion, he just wasn't attentive." She turned to me. "Certainly, it wasn't the majority of the class period, but it was noticeable. I wondered what the problem could be, too. Like Mrs. Dorsey, I was aware that his father had gone off to war while Conner was in my class. I thought that that had a lot to do with it, as she did." She nodded at Mrs. Dorsey. She turned back to me and added with a rueful smile, "We had exchanged views about the effect of his absence on Conner only recently."

I sat in numbed silence. Conner should have been held back? Is that what Mrs. Dorsey said? My eyes darted around the table. Everyone looked at me; it was as if they were searching my face. I hadn't seen this frequent lack of attentiveness that Mrs. Dorsey and Mrs. Shaw described. Well, maybe…sometimes, when I called to Conner, it would take a while for him to answer, if he answered at all. But didn't all kids get kind of rebellious like that?

I disagreed with their observations. My armpits were wet now; my hands were cold. "Now, wait! Conner is a responsible child. He is very good with his little sister. He does his homework. He's very cooperative around the house." I added that Conner liked reading Lego books before bed and enjoyed playing videogames with friends. "He's a whiz with those digital games. Sometimes, he has helped me to get my computer to work properly. But—" What was I saying? That stuff wasn't relevant here. Not to them, anyway. And not now.

I noticed the principal's brows draw together as her eyes narrowed. Her gaze darted between Mrs. Dorsey and me a couple of times. I stopped talking. I bit my lip. Paroxysms of dark emotions started to smother me. I breathed deeply and then bent forward a little as everyone's attention was on me. My stomach gurgled. My face flushed and tingled. I stared at the tabletop and pressed my toes down inside my shoes. Then I raised my eyes. I spoke softly, "I never suspected that Conner was having such problems at school. I remember that Mrs. Shaw mentioned to me last year that he could be doing better, but—that was second grade! She never said anything about needing to do something. It didn't seem that serious!"

My voice started to rise. "Why didn't anyone suggest we do something last year?" I looked at the principal. Her mouth barely opened as her jaw shifted ever so slightly off to one side. She looked expectantly at Mrs. Shaw.

"I had considered discussing my concerns with Dr. Signet, but then, with his father at war…that could be so stressful. I decided just to continue to watch and see how he progressed. And his performance *did* improve last spring. So, I advanced him to the third grade." Mrs. Shaw kept her gaze on me this whole time.

I returned her stare. "Conner reads, and he seems like all of his friends. I would have seen what you are talking about if it is as serious as you say! But, I haven't seen anything like that." All those accusations… Conner's face floated before me. His image intensified my resistance to what they were saying. I was determined not to let him be moved back a grade. That was not where he should be. I straightened in my seat and clasped my hands in front of me. I regarded each of them with a challenging gaze.

Dr. Signet exchanged a glance with Miss O. Did I really just see that psychology woman shake her head a little? It was…but still…it was the tiniest of movements.

The principal looked at me and spoke in a direct, even tone. "Mrs. Golden, the staff has summarized the situation. Conner is not doing the quality of work of which we think he is capable. Based on our discussion this afternoon, I believe that your son would benefit from a psycho-educational evaluation. I am recommending this testing for him. It should uncover any cognitive or emotional problems that are contributing to his difficulties. Miss Offermantel would administer the tests here at school."

"What kind of tests?" I leaned forward and pressed my hands onto the tabletop. My fingers spread like claws. I tried to imagine what those others saw sitting before them—a lioness protecting her cub? That was what I was now. They were silent. I looked at the principal and then at the psychologist. Mrs. Dorsey and even Mrs. Shaw had spent hours

50

with him in class. What did they see that I had missed? Sure, his grades could be better, but...

"What are these tests? Can they tell you what to do for Conner?" I asked again, a bit louder than I had intended,

I could feel all the tension in the room. Some looked down at their hands or just at the table in unreadable silence. The psychologist glanced at the principal. Dr. Signet parted her lips slightly as if she were about to speak but said nothing.

Miss O. looked at me; rather, her gaze was at my chin. She spoke slowly at first, then her voice became stronger and louder. "Mrs. Golden, the standard practice is to use a multidimensional test battery because learning problems and attention and emotional difficulties can overlap. Each test is designed to appraise a child's psychological make-up. For example, 'Draw-A-Person' will be used to help establish my rapport with your son. The way he depicts body parts and clothing can also partially aid in assessing his cognitive level."

The psychologist described the rest of the tests. "They provide information about Conner's attitudes, beliefs, motivations and other mental abilities." She moved her tongue across her lips and made a sucking sound. She nodded at Mrs. Dorsey. "Depending on Conner's level of cooperation, I will administer the tests over two to three weeks for an hour every few days. This would be done during class time. I'll also examine some of his classwork, which Mrs. Dorsey will provide."

Mrs. Dorsey nodded at Miss O. and then looked at me. I sensed that Mrs. Dorsey understood my resistance, my turmoil.

Miss O. waved her hand in Mr. Anton's direction. "Our special-education teacher may also do some academic testing." He flashed a smile at Miss O. that instantly disappeared when he looked back at me. "Will you give us permission to perform this testing, Mrs. Golden?"

Before I could reply, she pulled a form from her briefcase and held it in her hand. "Do you have the legal power to act for his father while he is deployed?"

I blinked rapidly. Maybe it was illogical, but I was totally irritated, furious with this woman. "Yes, of course I do," I snapped. Mrs. Dorsey dropped her head.

Miss O. slid the form across to me with that yellowed finger and passed a ballpoint pen to me with her other hand.

"Well, if you really think that these tests are necessary, okay, I'll sign this. I'm sure that Sam will agree, too. I'll tell him about the tests when we talk on the computer in a couple of days."

I ran my eyes quickly up and down the form a couple of times as I felt everyone watch me. I could only concentrate on a sentence here and there. After a moment, I scrawled my name and the date at the bottom of the page and slid it back to Miss O.

Her chubby face broke into a toothy smile. "Please tell Conner about the testing, Mrs. Golden. Reassure him that the tests are easy. Some children find that they are like a game. They can even be fun, like drawing houses and trees. Explain that these tests will help us find out why he's having these problems and how we may help him."

I wondered how I would explain to Conner why he had to take these tests when I had only just found out he was having problems in the first place. I only said, "I hope they will."

"Okay, then. I think we made definite progress this afternoon." The principal's gaze traveled down each side of the conference table. "Thank you, everyone. We all thank you for joining us, Mrs. Golden."

She collected the papers spread out in front of her and shuffled them into a neat pile. Then she put them into a manila folder. Chairs screeched on the wooden floor as everyone stood up. The SST members came over to shake my hand as they filed out.

Dr. Signet said, "We'll let you know when the testing will be done, Mrs. Golden. I will keep you informed on your son's progress." She offered her hand in a firm handshake and smiled; her eyes pierced mine. I watched her disappear around the corner. That woman was made of granite. She had everything under control. I just hoped this would solve something, everything.

I turned around. Mrs. Dorsey was last to leave the room. She grasped my icy-cold hand with her warm fingers. I pulled my hand away and slid it into the pocket of my slacks.

"I'm sure that those tests will be very helpful, Mrs. Golden. They have really turned things around for many of my students. It's best not to let a situation like this continue without getting a handle on what's happening. I'm sure the evaluation will help Conner, too. You'll see."

"I just…I don't know. I hope so." I broke into a nervous laugh. "It's obvious to me, though, that from now on I will have to actually make sure that he's done his homework."

"That's the ticket," she grinned. "I expect he'll make great improvement. You'll see."

Later that evening Conner sat behind me while I sliced tomatoes next to the sink. He was humming one of the theme songs from his favorite digital game as he colored in his *World Art for Children* book.

His high-pitched voice was so adorable when he hummed and sang softly to himself, oblivious to the world. His crayons were scattered on the kitchen table. I considered how to tell him about the upcoming tests without worrying him. Finally, I wiped my hands on a dish towel and turned around.

"Conner, honey, you know I met with Mrs. Dorsey and some other teachers at school today. I told you yesterday. They want you to take some special tests. Writing tests. They'll ask you some questions, and you just have to write down the answers."

"Will the other kids take the tests, too?" He continued drawing.

"No, honey. Only you this time."

He snapped around and glared; his eyes narrowed. I had messed up.

"Why? Why do I have to? What did I do, Mom? What did I do wrong? No! Don't make me!"

"You didn't do anything wrong, Conner. It's just that your teacher said that you could do better work at school than you are doing. She wants to find out why you're not, and these tests should be able to explain what the problem is. There will be a lady giving you the tests. I met her today. She told me that the questions are pretty easy to answer—"

"What lady?"

"Her name is Miss Offermantel. She is the school psychologist. She's someone who talks with children and asks them some questions to see what they think about certain things."

He muttered, "A school sy...gist...gist...sygist. Oh, Mom. I don't want to do it! I don't, Mom!"

I sounded out the word and added, "She said that there's lots of drawing, too, and you'll like that. You're good at drawing." I walked over to him and cupped his chin in my palm. Our eyes met. "I want to know, too. What's going on, buddy? Can you tell me? Is it Daddy? Are you worried about Daddy? Is that it?"

Conner pressed his lips into a thin line. His jaw tightened. He sniffed back tears and shouted, "I'm doing just as good as Michael and Jimmy and Braden, Mom! I am! I am!" He bunched up the bottom of his sweatshirt and wiped his nose.

I pulled him close. He clasped his arms around me, tight. "It's okay, honey. It'll be okay. Oh, my little man. Don't worry, Conner. You'll do fine." I drew back to look down into his face. I brushed my hand over his hair and gave him a wink. "They said that lots of kids take these tests. You aren't the only one."

He asked through choked sobs, "Will you be there, Mom?"

"They said that they just wanted to be with you. No, honey. I won't be there. It'll be during your regular school day. You'll probably like doing it. The school psychologist will show you what to do." I looked at him for a moment, bent down and kissed his cheek and then the top of his head. I returned to my slicing at the cutting board. He would be prepared. He would do fine.

I could feel Conner stare at me. Then I heard him turn back to his coloring. He was silent now.

CHAPTER 7

I t was a couple of weeks after the SST meeting when the school psychologist phoned. Miss O. described what transpired between Conner and her that morning. That morning? They were supposed to let me know! For the first few seconds, though, all I focused on was that image I had of her.

"Mrs. Golden, I'm sorry, but Conner gave me *no* cooperation in my attempts to initiate the psycho-educational testing today. None at all. I really can't explain what his problem was. He was extremely tense, very anxious. Didn't you tell him about these tests as I suggested at the Student Study Team conference? A little preparation beforehand usually takes the sting out of the testing."

"The testing was today? No one told me. The principal had said that I would be notified when the testing would take place. No one told me a thing."

"I'm sorry about that, Mrs. Golden. Something came up on our scheduling. This morning became available. As I said, Mrs. Golden, I got nothing accomplished today. Conner was so resistant. He wouldn't attempt *anything* that I asked him to do. He was crying. He kept asking to go back to his classroom. No matter how I approached it and encouraged him, he refused to cooperate. I finally had to take him back without achieving anything. Did you let him know about the testing?"

"Yes, I told him, just as you had advised, In fact, I told him about it later that same night after the SST meeting. He's a cooperative boy,

Miss O. He is very polite. Was he rude? What happened? I really don't understand."

"Well, he wouldn't attempt anything that I suggested. He would have nothing to do with any of it."

"Conner became defensive when I told him about the tests, Miss O. He wanted to know what he had done wrong and why he would be the only one who had to take them. I tried to reassure him. I told him that a lot of kids take them and that they were fun to do. That's what you said. He seemed to settle down after our talk—well, a little bit. What you're telling me is very surprising, very out of character for my son." My voice rose. "*You're* the psychologist, Miss O. What do *you* think? What is *your* explanation? What happened?"

"I had never met your son before, Mrs. Golden. I tried to befriend him with small talk, but he was very suspicious right from the start. Janet Dorsey told me that you had mentioned to her how much Conner and his father used to do together before Mr. Golden went to Iraq."

I was silent for a few seconds. "Yes. Yes, I did."

"It occurred to me, Mrs. Golden, that all of the significant people in his life right now are female—people in his home and his teachers in school. Perhaps he would be more comfortable if we arranged for a male school psychologist to administer the tests. I know of one at another school. We could give that a try."

"Gee, Miss O. I don't see why. But, you might be right about that. Yes. Yes, I agree. I mean...um, I'm sorry, Miss O. You are the professional here. But, yes, Conner might be more comfortable talking to a man. He really could use another man in his life right now."

"Mrs. Golden, if I had tried to get him to work on the tests without his full cooperation, the results would not be accurate. I cannot over-emphasize the importance of these tests. Conner was just so distrustful and uncooperative today."

Here was another problem for me. They couldn't even get the testing done that they insisted on. I closed my eyes. I wanted to just melt into my chair and disappear. "Since it's as important as you say, what do you suggest we—*I*—do, Miss O.?" My voice was flat. "The committee was so sure that this would give us something to work with."

"Well, the district could arrange for another try at testing with that male school psychologist, as I said. There are two other possibilities, Mrs. Golden. Your husband is on active military duty right now, and the military has their own healthcare plan: Tricare—"

"Yes, I know about Tricare."

"Well, Tricare provides child- and youth-counseling services for family members. I know they will provide support for school issues. Alternatively, if your health insurance covers outpatient psychotherapy, you could get the testing done privately. Ongoing supportive therapy with a male therapist might be very helpful for Conner."

I brightened. Here was a new possibility. "Sam's construction business provides excellent health insurance for all of our employees and their families. Our policy could take care of Conner."

"I should advise you that there might be a co-pay charge even with the insurance."

I stood up and moved the phone to my other ear. Here was something—a new plan! "I'll call our insurance office and find out what I have to do. I know a friend's child who is getting counseling. She is very pleased how her son is doing with that psychologist. I'll call her and find out the name of the therapist. Thank you."

"Okay, then. I will keep the school's records open until Conner completes the tests with another school psychologist or a private clinical psychologist. Just let us know if we can help here on our end."

"Thank you, Miss O. Goodbye." I put the receiver down.

As they so often did, my thoughts took the tangible form of a haiku. They had become like prayers—secret prayers—for me. I didn't tell anyone when I had them. They just popped into my imagination and twisted my thoughts into another kind of reality. Haiku were just so natural for me. I didn't even know how I formed them—I just did. Haiku coalesced and interpreted parts of my life at that moment. I easily understood this one:

> *Eagle alighting—*
> *Its wings spread, then enfolding—*
> *Chick fearful, but safe.*

That image was clear to me.

CHAPTER 8

We walked hand-in-hand into the psychologist's office on a late-October afternoon. Conner wore his favorite shirt: a long sleeved pull-on with blue horizontal stripes and a blue crew collar.

After a brief introduction and handshakes, Dr. Frank Thomas smiled and said to Conner, "You can call me Frank, okay Conner? I think it would be best for your mother to sit out in the waiting room while you and I talk and get to know one another. We'll see her in a little while."

Conner's damp hand squeezed mine. His eyebrows drew together, and his face drained of color. I looked at Dr. Thomas, flashed a quick smile down at my son and patted Conner's head. I fought my desire to enfold Conner in my arms. "That's fine, Conner. I'll wait outside, honey, in the waiting room. I will be right out there. You're going to like Dr. Thomas. Don't worry." I dropped his hand.

Conner stretched his neck to maintain visual contact with me until the very last second. I wiggled my fingers at him, turned and closed the door.

⌘

Dr. Thomas had met with me in his office about a week before. He sat in a worn, dark, stuffed leather chair that creaked with old-school comfort. Its patina molded to his form. I sat opposite on a leather sofa.

Between us was a low table, empty save for a box of tissues. It barely hid his shiny burgundy loafers with copper pennies in the cross-straps. I hadn't seen shoes like those in years. They must have been some holdover from his college days of thirty or forty years ago. They seemed appropriate for his persona, though, with his thick, gray hair parted straight down the middle.

"One reason that I chose to see you about his school problems, Dr. Thomas, is that I thought a male therapist might be better for Conner. The school psychologist actually suggested it. Conner's father is deployed in Iraq. He has been gone for almost a year. My two men," I chuckled, "miss each other so much, you see."

Dr. Thomas nodded, flashed a smile and crossed his legs.

"Most people in his life now are female. The school psychologist wondered if that contributed to his lack of cooperation during her testing."

"I see. Mrs. Golden, this perception that your son may relate to a male therapist where he didn't with the female psychologist at his school could make a difference in what I can accomplish." He raised his eyebrows in a quizzical fashion and asked, "There is no other male relative or adult around?" He shifted in his roomy chair and switched his crossed leg.

I shook my head. "None. When his father was home, Conner and he were together a lot. They played baseball, handball, went biking and they swam at the community pool. I really do not do those things with him. Conner even went to work with his dad occasionally at our construction business. He does like to help me in the kitchen when I cook, though. My parents moved out of town when they retired so there isn't even a grandfather around. Sam's father died when Sam was young."

"Okay. First, let me tell you that I admire you for what you are doing. I really give credit to mothers who are single caregivers. I realize that your husband is at war, but you, too, are a hero." His wide grin revealed sparkling white teeth beneath his thin mustache.

I appreciated what he said but I dutifully protested, "Oh, no, Doctor." I lowered my eyes and spoke to his knee, "Sam isn't doing something *much* more important. I mean Sam *is* doing something much more important." I shook my head and looked up again with a sheepish grin. My face felt warm. "He's in *real* danger over there." I twisted my wedding ring around and around with the fingers of my right hand. I looked at the charcoal skirt that I had paired with my white blouse under my dark-red cardigan.

"All right, then. Why don't you tell me what's going on with your son. What have you noticed about his behavior that concerns you?"

"Apparently, Conner is not completing his classwork. His teacher said he has a 'lack of engagement'—whatever that means—and he isn't working up to his potential. Also, the school psychologist couldn't get him to cooperate with her to do the psycho-educational evaluation. Conner is a very obedient child. He always does as he's told. I just don't understand what's going on with him."

"What do you think this behavior is about?"

"I can only think that it has something to do with his father not being here. It has been almost a whole year this time. Sam will be home in a little over two months—in January—for good. He is not re-upping. Conner was five and a half when his father left us for Iraq for a year the first time. That was in January, two thousand four. Our daughter Madison was only four months old. Then Sam came home, uh, that was in January, two thousand five?—yes, two thousand five—for a year before he was called up and he left *again*—for *another* year. That was in January, two thousand six. Absence of a father at that young age—? That's all that I can imagine. Wouldn't you agree?"

"Yes, that can be a stressful dynamic. I will work with Conner to explore what forces are operating and how they're affecting him. Tell me about Conner's birth and medical history."

"I had an uncomplicated pregnancy and delivery with Conner. Everything was normal with both of my children. He has always been a healthy, normal child."

"Is he on any regular medications?"

"No, he isn't. I give him an occasional Tylenol for bad fevers; otherwise, he takes only a daily vitamin." I crossed my legs and sank deeper into that soft, tan leather sofa.

"Do you have siblings?"

"No. I'm an only child, Dr. Thomas."

"What about your husband? Does he have any siblings?"

"Sam has a younger brother. He's well."

Dr. Thomas scribbled some notes in the pad on his lap. "Does anyone in the family have a psychiatric disease? I need to know the history of distant relatives, too."

"Um, no. I mean, I don't know for sure about distant relatives. Both of our parents lost touch with their few cousins." I saw him look at my crossed-over leg bouncing up and down. I put both feet on the floor.

His gaze moved back to my face. I suddenly felt out of control: a man directing questions at me—challenging me, the "little woman." I still hadn't completely shaken that paternalistic paradigm after all of my thirty-six years. It was cultural, all around us. Mom accepted it with Dad, and with her father. She just got along. That was not the Sandra I showed to the outside world. At least, I hope I didn't.

"Do you work outside the home, Mrs. Golden?"

"No. I'm a stay-at-home mom, but I freelance for different publications. I majored in literature and creative writing at college, you see. I write human-interest stories and I interview personalities, that kind of thing. Usually, they're five hundred up to two-thousand-word articles. The pay is pretty good, and I enjoy it. It keeps me as busy as I want to be. With young kids, it's just right. I worked for my dad's plumbing business until Sam and I got married in nineteen ninety-seven. We met on a blind date."

Dr. Thomas grinned.

"Yeah, it was one of those things. I was twenty-seven. I helped Sam out in his construction business until Conner was born the following year. While Sam's away I've been helping with the paperwork and bookkeeping in my husband's and his partner's construction firm. It keeps me in the real world, so to speak. It's good, I think."

"What about Sam? What's his background? How old is he?"

"He's thirty-eight, two years older than me. He has a younger brother. Sam enlisted in the Army Reserves when he was eighteen in order to help pay for college. He studied engineering. He was called up to fight in the Gulf War in nineteen ninety-one. He was twenty-two then, I think. He and his partner started their own construction company a few years before we married. I help with bookkeeping in their office, like I just said. Tom—that's our partner—basically is running the whole thing until Sam comes home. The company is pretty successful the way they set it up. Well, Tom says business might be slowing a bit, lately. Then, Sam was called up again in two thousand three—just a few months after our daughter, Madison, was born. He was there for a year. He's an officer: a captain in a California Army-National Guard Engineering Battalion."

"How do you feel about his deployment?"

"I don't know. He has a family, but he thinks serving is the right thing to do. Sam is very patriotic. Military service is a family tradition for him; it goes way back. But—two tours—at his age and with a family…" I shook my head. "But he's due to come home for good in a little more than two months, knock on wood." I used the arm of the sofa to pull myself forward and knocked on the table with my knuckles. Dr. Thomas shifted his gaze from my hand back to my face. We smiled.

"The children will have to get to know him all over again, especially Madison. He was gone during most of her first year. They only started to get to know each other when she was two. Now he's been gone again for another year."

As the psychologist wrote notes, I scanned his office. The walls had several diplomas and certificates. I could see a rich green golf fairway through the window just across the street.

He looked up from his pad. His pencil dropped out of his hand and down into the crack between the chair's rust-colored cushion and the armrest. I watched him maneuver his hand and rub and roll the pencil back into his grasp. "How is the family getting along while he's away, Mrs. Golden?"

"To be candid with you, Doctor, I have been having a rough time. I've been so worried about Sam in Iraq. It's crazy over there. All those bombs, ambushes and…I keep the news off when the kids are around, but we video-chat with Sam every week. I think that helps the children stay closer to their dad. Then again, sometimes I think we all miss each other even more because of the chats.

"And now I've had to deal with the school complaining about Conner's classwork." I forced a smile. "But Sam will be home soon." I leaned over and knocked on the wooden table again. "He has been a very responsible husband and father. Well, maybe it doesn't sound like it with him being halfway around the world."

I pursed my lips as a surge of anger tightened my throat. "I do resent that, Dr. Thomas. Yes I do. I resent it a lot. He has to be so loyal to the Army when we need him here at home—home with us. He says somebody has to do it, to protect all of us. For crying out loud; it's so complicated. And he could get killed over there. Where would that leave us?" I gnawed my lip and looked away. "Ahhhh!"

"You seem agitated, Mrs. Golden. Would you like to plan some sessions to talk? We could arrange that."

He looked at my foot again. I uncrossed my legs.

"No. Sam will be home soon, and that should help everything. I just had to let it out." I smiled sheepishly. "No, let's work with Conner. Let's help him first. I'm fine."

"Well, I want you to know that I'm available for you."

"Thank you. I appreciate that."

The psychologist cleared his throat. "How does Conner get along with his peers and his sister?"

I beamed and leaned forward again. "Conner is a terrific kid. I have to tell you that. He's obedient and responsible. Well, most of the time. He has lots of friends. They come to our house; he goes to theirs. I think that he's very popular at school. He's great with his three-year-old sister."

"Has he had any change in his appetite?"

"No. He has his likes and dislikes, of course, but I'm pretty satisfied with his eating habits. His weight is good, too."

"Is there any persisting bedwetting at his age?"

"He's had some accidents in bed, but not for quite a few months now. No, I wouldn't say *persisting*. I try to get him to go to the bathroom before bedtime. That seems to work. Other moms have mentioned the same kinds of things with their kids, too, so it seems to be not that unusual at his age. It's pretty rare with him now. However, when I did the laundry a few weeks ago I noticed dried urine stains in his underpants. He must not have been able to get to the toilet in time. I didn't mention it to Conner. I didn't want to embarrass him...there's no need to bring it up unless it becomes a pattern."

"Uh-huh. I think that's good judgment on your part. I would agree with your approach. And what about sleep? Does he get eight hours every night?"

"Yes. Sometimes he stays up late to play a video game on weekends; that's okay with me, but he still gets his eight hours then, too."

"Have you become aware of any new fears of things or situations that had not been a problem for Conner before?"

"No. I haven't seen anything like that."

"Have you noted any self-destructive behaviors, Mrs. Golden? Like head-banging or injuring himself on purpose?"

"No, nothing like that, thank God. That would indicate some kind of depression or suicidal behavior. Isn't that right?"

"That's right. Has Conner ever mentioned suicide or talked much about death in any way that disturbs you?"

"No! Conner is usually quite cheerful. Those kinds of thoughts don't bother him—at least, not that I've heard from him."

"So, the problem, as you see it, is that Conner is not performing well in school. So, what about his concentration? How's that?"

"Well, I—I don't know why he's not doing well. His teacher can't find a reason either. Yet, she still said that they were considering moving him back a grade. Then there was that attempt to do the psychological testing at school, and he wouldn't cooperate with the school psychologist. That is simply not like my son. It's beyond me why he—he's always completed school assignments. He is really a good boy. That's what I don't understand."

"Mm hm. Okay, I think I've got all the information I need at this point." The psychologist put his pencil and notepad aside and leaned forward. "I won't make any assumptions concerning Conner's difficulties until I've worked with him awhile. However, the psycho-educational testing is an important tool that we use to help identify the root of learning problems. I will arrange to get a different school psychologist to administer the tests. I will also ask Mrs. Dorsey and Miss Offermantel to send me samples of your son's schoolwork to look at. With your permission, I'd also like to consult with your son's pediatrician."

"Of course."

"Would you like me to inform Mr. Golden about your son's progress with me? I could communicate with him in Iraq via audiovisual websites."

"No, but thank you. I will tell Sam about Conner's appointments. As I've already said, the children and I talk to him on the computer each week, and we send each other e-mail all the time."

"Yes, you did say that. I think that's great. Isn't cyberspace amazing? I don't understand how it works. Does anyone?" He shook his head and smiled. "Do you have any questions that you'd like to ask me, Mrs. Golden?"

This psychologist fostered my confidence. I believed that he would be able to figure out what was going on with Conner and be able to help him. We covered a lot of ground that day.

I drew a deep breath. "Well, what about—I mean, I have insurance through my husband's construction company. You accept insurance, don't you?"

"Yes, of course." He asked some questions about the policy. "I will expect direct payment should there be any problem with your insurance provider. But, I don't anticipate anything like that."

"No. There shouldn't be. I've already looked into it." I added a soft, quick laugh.

"Good," he returned my smile. "Okay, now for some ground rules. I will meet with Conner alone unless there is a particular reason at times to include you. The discussions I have with Conner are totally confidential." He at the ceiling for a couple of seconds and then locked his eyes onto mine. "They have to be so that I can build trust with your son and he *wants* to confide in me. However, if Conner tells me anything that I believe could result in him hurting himself or, ah, anyone else, I must report that to the authorities. Of course, I would also share that information with you."

I nodded and immediately dismissed that concern.

After Conner's fifty-minute session, Dr. Thomas opened his door and invited me back into the office. Conner stood up and turned to face me as I walked in.

I was relieved to see that he had a wide smile across his face. "Did you have a good session, honey?"

"Yeah, Mom. I like him *loads* better than that lady at school. Much, *much* better. She made me feel like, like bad. Frank is nice, Mom." Conner's eyes darted between me and the psychologist.

"I knew you'd like him, honey." I took Conner's hand as he smiled broadly at the psychologist.

"I have hopes that we'll be great friends." Dr. Thomas smiled down at Conner.

Dr. Thomas escorted us back to the empty waiting room. "I'll arrange to get Conner's psycho-educational testing started at the school. Of course, there will be a different school psychologist to administer the tests this time, Conner." The psychologist looked at me and said, "The communication I've already had with his teacher a couple of days ago suggests to me that he doesn't have any attention-deficit problems. I'll consult with his pediatrician, too. All right, then. We'll see each other next week, okay, Conner?"

CHAPTER 9

The children were up in their rooms a few days later while I was clearing the supper table. Something banged overhead. "Conner, honey, what was that? Would you please bring down the book that I have been reading? It's on the nightstand next to my bed."

No answer. "Honey? Conner! Will you please bring down my book?"

I went to the bottom of the stairs and again called to him. "Conner? *Conner*, do you hear me?" I waited. What could he be doing? I trudged up the stairs. "Conner!"

"Wh—what, M-Mom?"

His voice sounded different: flat, disconnected. I reached the second floor, "What do you mean *what*? I have been calling you, Conner. What are you doing?" Madison was playing with her dollhouse. She didn't look at me as I passed her door. It crossed my mind that Conner had wet his bed this morning. He had wet his pants a couple of days ago, too. I discovered that when I did laundry. What was going on with him? I'll have to ask Dr. Thomas what he thought about it.

"Um, I'm...I'm playing with my...my videogame," Conner stammered.

I walked into his bedroom. Conner stood over the small, plastic case of his handheld videogame that was on the floor. His hands were cupped in front of him. Why didn't he pick it up rather than just stand there? "What happened? Why didn't you answer me? What's it doing on the floor?"

"I don't know." He mumbled with defiance. He stared at the floor and didn't look at me.

I didn't like his attitude. I started an angry-burn. "Well, did you drop it? It cost a lot of money, you know!"

"No! I don't know! I don't know! I don't know!" Conner's voice cracked and his eyes filled with tears as he bent down to pick it up.

"You have to be more careful, Conner!" What was going on with him? How did he get so cranky all of a sudden, just since dinner? "No more videogames, young man! It's bedtime. You are over-tired. Go brush your teeth. Don't forget to floss this time. Put on your pajamas. I'll be back to tuck you in after I check on your sister." I shook my head. "God, I wish your father was here!" My voice broke.

Conner put his arms around my waist. "Mommy, don't cry! I'm sorry for everything! I don't want to make you sad. I don't mean to. I don't know what happened. Maybe I shouldn't have been born. Maybe I should just go away or jump off a cliff!"

Dr. Thomas' warnings a few days ago flashed in my mind. "What? What are you saying, Conner?" Where did that come from? What brought that on? His words seemed to slice everything out of me. I suddenly felt so hollow. Tears welled in my eyes. I gripped his shoulders as I crumpled onto my knees. Now at his eye-level, I practically shouted, "What are you talking about? Do not say that, Conner! Don't *ever* say that!" I softened my voice. "You know we love you." I wrapped my arms around him and held him tight.

He rested his head on my shoulder and gulped back a sob. "I just wish I'd never been born."

"Conner! Honey, why did you say that? Don't you ever say that again. *Promise me!* We all love you so much. We're going to help you. I *promise*. School will get better. Did something happen at school today? Or at Dr. Thomas' office a few days ago? Something you talked about when you were there? Is that it?"

I pulled back. His teary eyes stared at me. "Was it something like that, Conner?"

He choked back tears. "No, Mom. I like him." He wiped his runny nose with a sleeve.

"Dr. Thomas will help you. We'll all help you, Conner. Everything will be fine. You'll see, and Daddy will be home soon." I bent my head and kissed his forehead.

He shrugged and turned his head to look at a framed photo on his bedside table. It was a picture of Conner and his father. They were shaking hands across a chessboard, looking into the camera with huge smiles. Conner sniffed and used his sleeve to wipe his cheeks.

"I'll go brush." He wriggled out of my embrace. He hung his head. "I'm sorry, Mom." Still on my knees, I watched him shuffle toward the bathroom. I squeezed my eyelids shut and more tears streamed down my cheeks. My tight throat ached. I pressed my fists against my chest.

Madison appeared in the doorway. "Whath wrong, Mommy?" She threw herself on top of me and wrapped her arms around my waist. She pressed her cheek against my collarbone. "Why are you crying, Mommy? Why ith Conner crying? *Thtop* it, Mommy!"

My toddler began to wail as she thrust her little hand into one of mine. I pushed myself off the floor and pulled a tissue from the pocket of my slacks. I wiped away Madison's tears and then my own. "Oh, honey. It's all right. Everything's going to be all right." I smiled at her and sniffled back my last sobbing gasps. "Let's get ready for bed. Daddy will be calling in a few hours."

"Can I get into bed with you for a little while? Pleath, Mommy, can I?" She asked through hiccupped sobs. The tip of her pink tongue protruded between her front teeth.

I smiled and brushed a stray lock of hair out of my daughter's eyes. "Sure sweetie. Sure you can."

She ran to her bedroom to get her bed toy. Then I saw her run past to snuggle under my bed covers. Her tears had already disappeared.

Later, alone in the darkness, I stared at the smooth white ceiling. I counted the rise and fall of my clasped hands on my chest. I listened for familiar nighttime house sounds: the soft ticking of the bedside alarm clock that I'd had since I was a girl; the sound of an occasional car driving down the street; the muffled rumbling of the dishwasher churning in the kitchen downstairs.

It took a long time for my thoughts to slow and for my mind to settle. Then a breeze made branches move and scratch against the house. The rattle of our windows sounded like someone breaking in. I felt so much pressure. I moaned softly and rolled onto my side. My chest and head felt so tight. I didn't know if I could help anyone, anymore. For a moment, I felt lost. I didn't know how to keep my family strong. In the morning, I would call Dr. Thomas to discuss Conner.

A beam of light from the street illuminated the framed black-and-white photograph of Mom and Dad that hung on the wall. They were so young twenty-five years ago. I could almost hear Mom's voice: "Sandra! Turn off that light *right now!*"

I shuddered. My eyes closed. I drifted into a restless sleep and a dream that I would not remember the next day.

I called the psychologist's office in the morning. My hands trembled as I held the phone. When Dr. Thomas returned my call I had settled down—kind of. I couldn't take Conner's threat that seriously. Not really! After all, kids said stupid things when they were upset. But, Dr. Thomas had told me that he would have to report any suicidal gestures and thoughts to the authorities. But, no, not for this—right?

"Oh, thank you for calling me back, Dr. Thomas. Last night was a rough one for all of us. Can I tell you about it?" There was silence and I continued, "Conner said, um, he told me that he wanted to run away. He said he wished he hadn't been *born*! And that he thought that he should jump off of a cliff. That's the kind of thing you said you—like if he wanted to hurt himself—you would need to report that, right?" I was beside myself again. I bit my lower lip.

"Tell me what happened. In what context was that statement made?"

I told him how I got angry at Conner for dropping his digital game console and his subsequent reaction. "It was just, like, he just seemed to shatter. It was as if he just gave up on everything. He looked so pitiful, Dr. Thomas. He said he wanted to go away and that he wished he had never been born and that he might jump off a cliff. I didn't know what to do for him. It hit me hard, really hard."

"I see. He was upset, you said. He was crying and you were, too."

I sensed that Dr. Thomas was trying to handle me ever so delicately. "That's right. It was terrible. I just held him tight. We both were crying. I remembered what you said—your rules. You said you'd have to report this to authorities to prevent any—any catastrophe."

His voice was calm and reassuring. "Of course, you should listen to a child's expressed intentions, but you don't always have to take them literally. We must also consider the context in which that exchange took place, Mrs. Golden. Remember, anxiety expresses itself in many ways. I'm working with Conner to help him deal with his fears and perceived loss of control."

"So, you *don't* think this is a serious turn for Conner?"

"No. I don't think it is. I really don't."

The psychologist continued to reassure me. I still had some doubts. How did he really know what Conner would do? Then again, I didn't take Conner's threat that seriously, either. I mean, he was so upset last night when he said it, there, in his bedroom. Today, he seemed fine, his usual self, as he prepared for school. I prayed that Dr. Thomas was right. So, I just let it go. I just let it happen, like the Taoists. I went with what Dr. Thomas said, and I felt this weight rise off me.

Dr. Thomas started to talk about Conner's fears. The way he said it hit me. "Fears? *His* fears? Who *doesn't* have fears, Doctor? I feel that I'm the one struggling to keep control—just keeping my family strong. Sometimes I could scream. I am just waiting for Sam to get home. I need his help, his support. His being here will make all the difference in the world for us. I'm sure of it. He has done enough for 'God and Country.' I'm just trying to keep us going, Dr. Thomas. That's what I have to do. Now, though—all of these problems, especially Conner's school problems. I don't want them to move him back a grade."

"Mrs. Golden, you *are* dealing with your family's problems. You are facing them. You are taking action. That is so healthy. You're doing a great job. You *are* in control, Mrs. Golden. It's very important that you remember that. And I don't believe we need to take Conner's comments any further right now."

"He was really upset, Doctor. We all were. And there was something else, Dr. Thomas. Conner wet his bed yesterday. He wet his pants a few days ago, too. That's unusual for him. It's been awhile since he's done that."

"Hm. You say this is sporadic? Anxiety is the usual culprit at his age. Let's just keep track of it."

"Okay. Yes. I'll do that."

"Okay. I will see you when you bring Conner in for his next appointment in a couple of days. Meanwhile, if you ever need to talk, call me. I'm always here for you. You know that, don't you?"

"Yes, Dr. Thomas. I know that. Thank you." I smiled. "You have been helpful. I feel a little better, now."

"Well, I'm glad."

I hung up the phone.

CHAPTER 10

S am had to postpone these chats for three weeks while he was on some military operation, but now there was my Sam's broad, gap-toothed smile. It was so good to see him. His face took up the whole screen, which at times froze or showed delayed movements or out-of-sync speech. But, oh, this wondrous technology! I saw other soldiers with guns moving around behind him. Conner sat in the swivel chair in front of the monitor and Madison stood next to him. I leaned in from behind the children.

These chats were the highlight of the week for all of us, but they never lasted long enough. Sam had less than two months left of his tour. Then, he would be home for good. At least he would never volunteer again. He had been our war hero long enough. Now, it was someone else's turn.

Sam's hair was clipped short and looked darker than usual. His fair complexion was darker, too. Was it the lighting of the monitor, or maybe all that sun over there?

"Daddy! Daddy! I thee you!"

Conner giggled at his little sister's excitement. Madison held her stuffed giraffe up to the screen. "Can you thee us, Daddy? Thay hello to Willie, Daddy!"

The kids were always so excited during these video chats. They were especially important for Madison, an opportunity for my daughter to get to know her daddy better. I doubted that she really knew him. Conner was already nearly five and a half when his father left on his first tour so they had a chance to create a bond before Sam deployed that time.

Sam's clean-shaven face—angular, with a powerful, square jaw—looked thinner than usual today. That great jawline attracted me to him when we met on our blind date in 1996. He looked so good in his desert fatigues with that engineer insignia and his captain's bars.

I let the kids chat with him for about five minutes. Then I said, "Okay, kids, go downstairs and finish your breakfast. I need to talk to Daddy for a little while. I'll be right down." The children blew kisses and Sam did, too. When they left, I sat on the swivel chair that Conner had just vacated and scooted in closer to the monitor.

Once they were out of earshot, I began. "I hate it when we can't get to chat with you every week. We missed seeing you, not to say how worried we were."

"I know. That shouldn't happen again, Sandra."

"Sam, you look thinner. Are you losing weight? Are you feeling okay?"

"I've lost a few pounds. Sometimes it gets to be over one-hundred-twenty degrees out here, Sandra. We're like pigs in a sauna with all our gear on. But I'm good. So, what's new?" He smiled across cyberspace. "How are you, honey?"

"I'm good, too. But what are you doing? Have you been going out on missions a lot? Building things, doing repairs?"

"Yeah, we've fixed a few bridges. Not much going on this week. It's been quiet." He smiled more broadly and added, "Really."

I wasn't sure I believed him. He was always trying to protect me. I heard the thumping of helicopter blades in the background. "You wouldn't tell me any different now anyway, would you? I know you, Sam Golden. Please, I want to know—I *have* to know that you are okay. You've been gone so long, darling."

"I'm fine. Really, honey. Really! So, tell me what's been happening at home. Did you get the garage door fixed?"

"It's all taken care of." I sighed and gnawed my lower lip.

"What's wrong, Sandra?"

"A lot has happened since we last spoke. I—I am worried about Conner, Sam. His teacher said that he's falling behind in his classwork. He is in third grade, and he is falling behind! His teacher, Mrs. Dorsey— you don't know her—she thinks he's not working up to his potential." I imitated the teacher's comments in a falsetto voice. "I know you don't need to hear this right now, you have enough to worry about, but—"

"What do you mean? What's going on?" His smile disappeared.

"The school asked me to come to a special meeting about Conner. His teacher, Mrs. Dorsey, and Mrs. Shaw, his teacher from last year, were there, too. You remember Mrs. Shaw?"

"Yeah, I remember. She's the one with—"

"Yeah, that's the one." I swallowed hard. In a choked voice, I said, "The principal was there, and that school psychologist. She was very young and a real piece of work, Sam. They said Conner doesn't finish lots of his assignments at school and he doesn't do some of his homework. But, Sam, Conner tells me that he *does* do his homework! I check it; maybe not every time. I guess I will have to now. Anyway, they wanted to do some special testing on him—psychological testing—but, for some reason, Conner just would not cooperate that day. He never took the tests. And they said that they're considering dropping him back to the second grade. That would be *terrible,* Sam!"

"Wow. That's not good. They can't do that." Sam scratched his head and slowly shook it side to side.

I caught myself before I told him that Conner had said he wanted to jump off a cliff. Sam didn't need to hear that. It wasn't like he could do anything for Conner, anyway. He was in Iraq, for God's sake.

"The school psychologist suggested that some psychotherapy could help. I took him to a private psychologist, Sam. Conner began treatment—those are his sessions—a few weeks ago. He started just after we last spoke. He's been going once a week. Dr. Thomas spent an hour alone with me first. I outlined Conner's problems at school. I told him all about us, too. You know, the family history and those kinds of things. Conner really likes him, honey. I do, too. Our insurance is paying for just about all of it."

"You think it's that bad? And this has been going on for a whole *year*?" I saw Sam shift in his seat. "I thought everything was going all right with everybody at home. Now, they want to fail him? Because he's not doing his homework? I certainly *forgot* to do my homework when I was a kid. Didn't you? Just keep after him. But, psychotherapy! Gee! Is it really that serious?"

"It's not only that he doesn't do all his homework that they want to drop him back to second grade, Sam. It's complicated. They said that he doesn't pay enough attention in class, too."

"What's going on with him? Is the psychiatrist helping?"

"He's a *psychologist*, Sam, not a psychiatrist."

"What's the difference? We've had some sessions with clergy and psychiatrists here about our families and stresses back home. I guess it helps. Listen to me: I'll be home in less than two months, just after the New Year. It's been hard for all of us. Sandra, I have to go now. I'm sorry; my company has a training assignment. I'll talk to you next week. I'll be home soon. I love you. I know you've got your hands full. Stay strong, honey."

Stay strong? "I love you so much, Sam. Please! Be safe! Come home safe. I need you! *We* need you! I'm sorry I had to dump all that bad news on you like that. It's so lonely without you."

Sam smiled, wiped the corner of his eye and sat up straighter. "I love you. Until next week…" He blew me a kiss and the screen went dark.

I sat there.

CHAPTER 11

I was just about to leave to pick up Conner from school a few days after my chat with Sam when the phone rang.

"Hello. Mrs. Golden?"

"Oh, Dr. Thomas, how are you?"

"Very well, thank you. I just got Conner's psycho-educational test results back. As they promised, a different school psychologist had administered them, and it's very good news. Conner's cognitive skills are above-average. The testing indicated that there is no reason why Conner should not be performing at least at his grade level. Additionally, there was no evidence to suggest that he had Attention Deficit Disorder. I really didn't suspect that was a problem."

"That is wonderful news. I don't want Conner to need Ritalin, or whatever medicines doctors give kids to control ADD. It seems that it's all that we hear about these days." My relief turned to frustration. "So, why isn't he doing better? What do you think is going on with him?"

"Well, the good news is he doesn't have any serious cognitive problems. That is so important. My work with Conner has uncovered some clues. He has a lot of anxiety—more than the typical child his age. I believe your husband's prolonged absence is affecting Conner's work at school. How could it not be? Who wouldn't be affected? Especially a child...there is so much internal turmoil. Conner worries about the entire family. He worries about you, too. Your apprehensions and your

77

attempts to maintain some semblance of a normal family life with his father absent are bound to bounce off you. Conner is quite perceptive, quite bright."

I ran my tongue across my lips. "I see."

"Mrs. Golden, could there be any other concerns? Are there any financial or other health problems in the family? You know, worries that could reflect onto him?"

"No. Nothing like what you are saying, thank God. Our construction business is doing well, although our partner has said that all of the frenzied home and apartment building in the country can't go on at this pace forever. He has started to see an occasional contract cancelled. But that's neither here nor there as far as Conner goes."

"Okay, then. Let's just continue our weekly therapy sessions for a while. Conner needs to feel safe in order to be able to confidently express himself. Keep monitoring his homework. Keep encouraging him as you have been doing."

"Yes. I will. Conner really likes his appointments with you, Doctor. I'm very thankful."

"That's good to hear. Thank you telling me. I look forward to seeing your young man at his next appointment."

CHAPTER **12**

I t was mid-November. I took the children for their flu shots. I hadn't bothered to call our pediatrician about Conner's school problems or his recent bed-wetting. I'd see what he had to say about them now.

When the nurse called our names, Madison started crying. I had to carry her screaming into the exam room. Another mother smiled at me; her little girl looked up from her toy with a quizzical expression. We were not the only ones upset in that office. Conner had a worried expression, too.

Dr. Bob Jackson was young and jovial. He never wore a doctor's white coat over his open-necked shirts, jeans and tan canvas shoes. He was tall and skinny and had a short beard. He always wore his shoulder-length, sandy-blond hair in a ponytail. I had heard that the doctor played saxophone in gigs with four friends on weekends. He was well-liked by his young patients and their mothers. I caught every flirtatious glance that the young nursing assistant cast his way.

Dr. Jackson knocked, opened the door and strode into the exam room. He smiled genially as we shook hands and exchanged greetings. He fist-bumped Conner. When he approached me, Madison, still in my arms, turned her head away and buried her face into my shoulder. She sobbed even harder.

"Aw, I'm sorry, Madison." The doctor peeked around my shoulder to give the toddler a broad grin. She snapped her head away from him again. Her chin quivered and tears streamed down her plump cheeks.

Dr. Jackson wrote in the charts as we visited. He finished the kids' physical examinations quickly, never skipping a beat in his age-appropriate interactions with them. He knew all the popular computer games that Conner liked to play. He even did a mini-examination on Madison's toy giraffe that she held in her lap. Diverted from her initial fear, she squealed with laughter when Dr. Jackson tickled Willie under his front legs.

"You have two very healthy children here," Dr. Jackson said. He perched on a high stool and scribbled another note. "How is the family doing, overall?" He tucked the ballpoint into his shirt pocket and looked up.

I thought about Conner's recent bed-wetting episode. I would tell him about it when we were alone. Conner would wilt in embarrassment. It was probably part of all the stress he was under, as the psychologist said, but I had better mention it. "Dr. Jackson, I'd like to talk with you when you're finished with the children. Conner has started seeing a psychotherapist: Dr. Frank Thomas."

"I know. He called me after I received your release that his office sent. I just had routine check-up information for him." He glanced over his shoulder to look at Conner. Conner was on the exam table, his attentive gaze focused on the doctor. "What's going on, Sandra?"

"Well, his schoolwork hasn't been what his teacher thinks it should be. Apparently, the school had similar concerns about him last year, too, but they never really told me about them. Conner took some psychological tests at school. It took two attempts. The first time, he was too nervous—"

"No, I wasn't Mom!" Conner gripped the edge of the exam table and leaned toward me. "I was not. I—"

"Don't interrupt me, Conner!" I heard the bite in my voice. My gaze swung between the doctor and my son.

Dr. Jackson looked at the boy. Conner looked at the floor as his eyes welled up. I felt my face flush. "I'm sorry, Conner, but please don't interrupt me, honey."

I described everything that had happened since the school psychologist tested Conner. "Dr. Thomas thinks that Sam's being away for so long is definitely having an effect on Conner. Like it is on all of us."

"Of course it is." The pediatrician nodded sympathetically and winked at Conner. "How is Conner responding to the therapy?"

"I think it's helping. His teacher has noticed improvement with his homework. I make certain he has finished his assignments before he hands them in. But she hasn't noticed that he's improved his classroom work that much."

"I have, too, Mom!"

"Conner, I'm still talking!"

The sounds of voices and of infants crying in the waiting area penetrated the closed door of the exam room. "Conner and Madison, you two kids wait here while I talk with your mom. We'll just be outside the door," Dr. Jackson said.

"Don't thut the door, Mommy. No!" Madison yelled. She clasped her stuffed toy to her chest and rose from her little chair.

"Okay, honey. Mommy will be just outside the door. I'll keep it open."

The children watched us go into the corridor. The door remained open a few inches and I made sure that Madison could see me.

Dr. Jackson said softly, "With Sam still in Iraq, I imagine that you *all* have a lot to be anxious about. I agree with the psychologist. Conner's worries about his dad being at war probably have a lot to do with his schoolwork. Kids may not talk about it much, but they get stressed just like adults do. That's what it sounds like to me. Don't you agree, Sandra?" The doctor's eyes widened as his shoulders hunched up. I saw his mouth smile, but his eyes were focused on the wall clock down the corridor.

"I know, but the school said that Conner started to have difficulties early *last* year, before Sam even left on this second tour. I don't know what to think. I didn't want to say this in front of Conner, but the psychologist thinks that even some depression, along with anxiety, is his problem."

"Again, Sandra, I think that psychotherapy is the right thing to do for Conner right now. Dr. Thomas didn't suggest that I consider any psychotropic medications when he called me. He hasn't mentioned meds to you, has he?"

"No. He hasn't. And I don't want him to take any drugs."

"Look. You're doing a great job, Sandra. I know how tough it's been for you acting as a single mom during your husband's deployment. Hang in there."

"Thank you, Dr. Jackson. I try. I do. Sam is scheduled to be rotated home in a month and a half, so we'll get him home, soon. Moreover, he is not going back. He's finished with the military."

"That's wonderful news."

I drew a deep breath. "But there's another problem, Doctor. Conner has started to wet the bed again. It doesn't happen often, but recently I have found urine stains in his underwear when I do laundry, too."

"Is he just wetting, or does he lose his bowels, too?"

"No. Just wetting. I've been restricting his fluids at supper and after, too."

He nodded. "You're right to restrict fluids at night. It's not that uncommon, even at eight, especially if he's under a lot of emotional strain. That probably explains it. I don't think there is anything to worry about if it only happens occasionally. Is he complaining of any pain or burning when he urinates? Any fevers?"

"No. He hasn't told me that it hurts. I haven't asked him, though. He's not wetting that often, either."

"I could get a urine specimen today just to make sure—to check if there's any infection or any problem that needs looking into. If his wetting is infrequent, like you said, then I think we can wait on that. The wetting should stop with time. Let me know if it doesn't."

I nodded. "Thank you. I appreciate your reassurance."

"Tell Sam 'hello' and be sure to say that I appreciate what he's doing." He shook my hand and we stepped back into the exam room.

"You kids must really be proud of your dad, and he'll be home soon, too. That's great! Okay, my nurse will come in to finish up. I'll see you all next year. Call whenever you need to, Sandra. 'Bye kids."

Dr. Jackson's ponytail swayed in rhythm with his quick steps back to his office.

CHAPTER **13**

The next day was Saturday. I slid a tray of brownies into the oven and went to answer the front door. I waved to Maggie Lee as she dropped off her son, Michael, for his playdate with Conner.

"Hi, Mrs. Golden! Mmmmm! Something sure smells good!" He hurried past me. "Is it your brownies? You make the very best brownies, besides my mom."

"Hi to you, too, Michael. Yes, you'll get some as soon as they're ready. Conner gave me the order." I liked this bright, well-behaved boy. He and Conner got along well together.

From the top of the stairs, Conner yelled, "Hey, Michael! Come on up!"

"Yeah!" He raced up. Less than a minute later both boys bounded down the stairs and charged into the den; each held a videogame from Conner's collection.

I had been reluctant to buy the videogame console. So much of the gaming software was rated "T" for teenagers. Some of those games were very violent. But, Sam disagreed. He said the games were appropriate for Conner's level of maturity. I thought that he usually over-gauged Conner's interests and abilities for his age. Sam accused me of being over-protective, and Conner protested that all of his friends had those games. What were their parents thinking? I ultimately relented and bought the unit, but I still wondered if I gave in too easily. I always came in to check what game he and his friends were playing.

"What are you guys going to play?"

"Race cars!" Conner shouted as they hooked up the unit. "Mom, my arm hurts from that shot." He turned to Michael: "I got a flu shot yesterday. Dr. Jackson's nurse said it wouldn't hurt, but it does." He looked at me. "Gee, Mom."

"I hate shots," Michael told him and pressed his own upper arm.

I leaned over and lifted Conner's sleeve.

He pulled his arm away. "Ooooh, don't *touch* it, Mom!"

"I won't. It looks a little red. I could put some ice on it."

"Nah. I guess it's not that bad, Mom. And Daddy says that I should put up with a little hurt once in a while." He grinned at Michael and said, "That's what soldiers do."

"It'll feel better soon, okay? And shh, don't shout." I pointed at the ceiling. "Madison is taking a nap." The little girl had thrown a tantrum when Conner told her that she couldn't play with him this afternoon. He usually let Madison watch him play on the console when they were alone, but when he had a friend over all bets were off.

"Sorry, Mom," he said in an exaggerated whisper.

"Just keep it down, boys. The brownies will be done in a little while." They booted up the system. Soon, their wide-eyed gazes careened from one side of the TV screen to the other along with their cars. I watched them for a moment, but by then I didn't even exist to them.

I headed upstairs to check on Madison. My little devil wasn't napping as she was supposed to; she was kneeling on the floor, playing with her dollhouse. Sam had lovingly designed, built and painted it to our daughter's specifications right before he left for Iraq this last time. It even had a delicate front porch that Sam painstakingly fabricated out of balsa and other woods. The toddler had been delighted with his construction; now, she had a whole family living inside.

"Mommy's going to check her e-mail and see if there's anything from Daddy, okay?"

Distracted, Madison nodded.

"Okay, I'll be right back to check on you, honey. The boys are playing downstairs. The brownies will be done soon." I quietly walked away for some downtime.

Later, the brownies had cooled and I had poured milk into the children's glasses. The kids were sitting around the kitchen table. Michael stuffed a thick piece of brownie in his mouth and mumbled, "Conner…mmm…already had brownies, Mrs. Golden. He was… mmm…chewing…mmm…and swallowing them…mmm…when we were playing. He was acting really weird."

"I was not!"

"Well, I *saw* you chewing *something*, Conner."

"No I wasn't."

"You were, too!"

"Was not!"

They argued back and forth. I had no idea what they were talking about. I studied their faces for a moment and searched for a clue. Conner could not have been eating brownies; I had only just pulled them out of the oven a few minutes ago.

"Conner, you know the rules about eating in the den! What were you eating in there?"

"I *wasn't* eating anything, Mom. I promise! I wasn't."

Michael stared coldly at him.

Conner pointed to huge chunks of brownie that Madison had dropped on the floor. "I'll eat those, Mom."

"No! Mine, Conner! Mine!" Madison yelled.

I bent down to clean the mess. The boys began laughing about something that happened at school. I poured more milk into their glasses.

I had no idea what Michael had been talking about, and their strange argument was soon forgotten.

JANUARY 2007:
SOUTHERN CALIFORNIA

CHAPTER 14

Conner played with his Lego bricks in his bedroom all morning. He had hundreds of them in various shapes, sizes and colors. As usual, they were scattered all over his pale, oak floor. Nearly every day I had to tell him to stop messing up his room and that he had to clean up his toys when he finished playing with them. But, I didn't mind today. Sam would be home this afternoon.

I stepped over Lego bricks and around Conner doing some "light-and-polite" dusting to get the house ready, eating up the time until we drove to the airport.

Conner went with us to a lot of galleries and museums. Sam and I were intent to give him—and now Madison—the feeling that learning was important and fun. Relatives knew to bring him mythological and historical souvenirs from their trips—his favorite *objets d'art*. They were aware of his interests in the military and in history because Grandpa Larry, my dad, liked those subjects. His Grandpa Larry had been a soldier during the Vietnam War. Now he was teaching Conner all about world history, especially military history. My dad and Conner had spent a lot of time together before my parents moved out of town to their retirement resort in Arizona.

The labeled shelves above Conner's desk contained his "museum." It was important to him that he had his own museum. He had influenced his friends, too. They wanted to get their own souvenir collections once they saw his museum. I liked that these moms told me how Conner had inspired their own children.

Mythology was Conner's favorite subject. He knew so many myths. He would tell me the significance of, in his words, "a bunch of gods that had lived a long time ago in Greece and in Egypt and in other places." He even played a mythology-themed computer game every day. I was so thankful for that game. It was very educational. Conner would wax on about it: "I can get Zeus and Kronos and Hercules and Prometheus and Osiris to fight and do loads of stuff, Mom." I could not keep up with all of the mythology that he loved to describe. Frankly, I just didn't find it that interesting. He felt special, too, because he could also teach his Grandpa Larry about mythology whenever they spoke on the phone. I loved to hover close and listen when they talked. Dad strung him along with all kinds of questions.

Conner looked up from where he was sprawled on the floor with his Lego bricks. "I wonder if Daddy will bring me anything. I hope he will, Mom."

"I would be surprised if he didn't bring you at least one souvenir, honey."

Conner could find Iraq on his globe. He had taped a small cut out soldier he made over that country.

"Mom, when I was little, you know—like Madison—I thought that Daddy knew everything. Now I know that he doesn't. I know the people in Iraq speak a language that even Daddy doesn't know. Mom, Madison still says that Daddy is the smartest man in the whole wide world. She says it like that, too. She's funny, Mom. Daddy is real smart, and you are, too, and even I know that he's not the very smartest man in the whole world. I mean, nobody is, right?" Then he threw handfuls of Lego pieces in the air and sang out, in a sing-song voice, "Dad-dy, you're com-ing home to-day!"

After lunch, I put finishing touches on the banner we were making. I sang my favorite Beatles song while I worked, humming the bars when I couldn't remember lyrics. I was excited. I just needed a little more orange to fill in here. There. *WELCOME HOME DADDY!* Our whole street would see it although the neighbors already knew Sam was coming home today.

"Madison! Conner! Come down and see the sign! I'm going to put it up now."

They charged down the stairs. "Oooh! Pretty, Mommy! What doeth it thay?" Madison was adorable in her raspberry coveralls and the white- and yellow-flowered sweater.

"Here, honey, let me fix this barrette. It's falling out." I knelt down and snapped it back on a lock of her golden curls. I kissed her plump cheek.

"Yeah, Mom. It looks great! Can I have an apple?" Conner reached toward the fruit bowl on the kitchen counter. "When are we going?"

"Sure, honey. Get three. Let's put Daddy's sign up and then we can leave for the airport."

I washed the paintbrush under the water tap. We went outside and the children watched as I climbed our ladder to tack the banner up over the garage.

I came down and stood back to look at my handiwork. "Daddy will love it, won't he?"

"Yeah, Mommy," they said in unison.

I glanced at my watch and replaced the ladder inside the garage. "Okay, kids. Time to get Daddy!"

Madison skipped over and climbed into the SUV, holding her stuffed giraffe. Conner climbed in the other door. He fastened his seat belt while I buckled his sister into her car seat. He shouted, "Let's go get Daddy!"

Traffic was light. I found a parking space close to the arrival terminal right away. We sat in the reception area outside of the security checkpoint. The kids kept fidgeting. I hadn't brought anything to read.

I repeatedly checked the Arrivals/Departures screens for information about Sam's flight. Conner asked if he could get a snack but that was when we saw Sam walk down the corridor. Somehow, we hadn't even heard the announcement that his plane had landed.

Sam turned his head searching for us.

"Daddy! There's Daddy!" Several people sitting nearby looked up and smiled at Conner.

I pushed closer to the barrier. Madison squirmed in my arms. "Here we are, Sam! Here we are!"

Slim and sinewy, Sam cut a fine figure at five feet ten in his desert fatigues. His high, heavy boots were the color of desert sand. My eyes lingered on them, and then squeezed shut against the image of a severed leg rolling slow-motion over and over, blown up into the sky, its boot still on the crimson-stained foot.

"Ith that Daddy? Ith that Daddy, Mommy?" Her question drilled home that Madison really did not know her father.

"Yes, honey, that's Daddy." I stroked her hair and pecked her cheek.

Sam broke into a huge grin and ran the last few steps. His backpack bounced and clinked against the loaded cargo-pockets of his uniform. He threw his arms wide. "Hi! You're all so beautiful!" He said between kisses, hugs and tears. "Oh, it's so good! So good!"

Finally, I pulled back and beamed, "You look good, too, Captain." I buried my head against his shoulder and breathed him in. My wet cheeks left dark spots on his tan uniform. "Oh, Sam! It's so good to have you home safe. I love you so much. Was it a good flight?" I wiped my face with a tissue and blew my nose.

"Daddy, Daddy, Daddy!" Conner hopped up and down. Sam grabbed him and hoisted him against his chest. Conner wrapped his legs around his father and held on tight.

"I missed you so much, my big boy." Sam kissed his son on both cheeks and then on his lips.

When he put Conner down, I kissed Sam again and again. Madison buried her head into my shoulder.

"Give Daddy a big kiss, honey. It's your daddy." I had to struggle with Madison as I pushed her toward him. She held her stuffed giraffe against her face. Sam reached for her and I tried to hand her off, but she clutched my neck. All of our wide grins and kisses and greetings appeared to confuse her. They seemed to have prevented the screamed protests that I felt were ready to erupt. Finally, she flashed an uncertain smile. Sam's pull and my push gradually broke her hold on me. She clasped her stuffed giraffe against her chest with both hands as she was passed over to Sam.

"Oh, Madison, honey. What a *big* girl you are! Give Daddy a kiss." His tears fell as he kissed her full cheek and tickled her chin.

"Kiss Daddy, Madison," I said again. She finally planted a loud, juicy kiss on Sam's mouth. "Let me get that picture!" They blinked at the flash.

"Let's go home," Sam whispered into my ear, his voice soft and thick.

Sam carried Madison in one arm while Conner skipped between us. The boy hung on to the bottom of his father's fatigue jacket all the way to the luggage-claim area. Madison held back in his arm, half-turned as she looked toward me. Sam kissed her cheek and ear and purred, "Mm," in her ear. I saw they would need time to get to know one another.

We talked over the muted roar of planes speeding down runways and the garbled announcements over the airport speakers. Sam and I gazed at each other. We hardly paid attention to Conner or Madison for a few moments. We even walked into strangers a couple of times—well, *almost* right into them.

Conner seemed embarrassed by our affection and annoyed by our clumsiness and apparent inattention to everything else. "Mom, watch out!" He was the only one, though, because it seemed that everyone in the airport was smiling at us.

"Welcome home, soldier!" A woman with silver-blue hair called from her seat. Several people walked over to Sam and said, "Thank you for your service, sir." A middle-aged, balding man saluted and extended his hand. "Glad that you're home safe, sir. I remember that day for me, too." Sam nodded and smiled back at the veteran.

Two men engaged him in brief conversation concerning where he was stationed and about the division patch on his shoulder. They said that they, too, had close ones serving. I stood off to the side when these well-wishers approached. Sam nodded and smiled. He thanked them politely and addressed each as "sir" or "ma'am." His eyes darted toward me when they detained him too long. I shook my head then. I felt a pleasant pressure in my chest and a shiver ran down my back as I watched strangers honor Sam—honor my husband.

Meanwhile, Madison's comical antics in his arms made me chuckle. While he engaged these strangers, she pulled her stuffed giraffe to her face, kissed its nose, and then quickly pushed it toward the stranger. Then, she pulled it back to her face, repeatedly, smacking loudly. Conner beamed and held Sam's right hand. He put his own right hand up to his brow in a salute several times. Finally, we moved on. Conner skipped an extra step to match his father's stride. I noticed that both of their tightly clutched hands had little pale spots on their fingers.

Despite his long flight, Sam wanted to drive home. He seemed to adjust right back to the busy freeway traffic. He drove and we talked. When we exited the freeway and got to our neighborhood his head turned side to side repeatedly. Sam marveled at the changed landscape in his hometown: a new strip-mall had gone up while he was away; our local hardware store had gone out of business. "What happened to Watson's? Gee, that's too bad." His expression became more solemn with every block. So much had changed in just one year.

When we approached our driveway, Sam saw our sign and laughed. "That's great, guys!"

He drove a little beyond the driveway and backed the SUV into the garage. I leaned over and kissed his lips. He turned off the ignition and just sat there for a moment. He scanned the large space, his tool bench, the cabinets and the ladders while I got out and unbuckled Madison from her car seat. Conner climbed out too. He pulled Sam's backpack out with him. Then Conner opened Sam's door.

"Come on Daddy! Come inside!"

Sam grinned. "Let me take that, Conner. It's too heavy for you, son." But Conner insisted on helping his father. The backpack was dragged along the ground.

Sam watched him struggle. He looked at me holding Madison. "He's really grown. Both of them have. They look great, honey. So do you." He leaned over and kissed and smelled Madison's head. "Oh, how I've missed being with all of you—all of us together. Let's go in, I'll get the rest of my gear out of the car later. I want to see inside again."

The brown-and-black shepherd next door ran and barked excitedly along the length of the fence. Marge Brown, our neighbor, came out to investigate. As soon as she saw Sam at the garage door, the heavyset brunette came over and hugged him. "Welcome home, Sam!"

"Hi, Marge. Thanks. It's so great to be home again. How are Ken and the kids?"

"Oh, we're fine, just fine, Sam. We won't bother you now. We'll see you soon. You will come over for dinner, okay? It is really wonderful to have you home again. You look great." She smiled at me and gave me a hug, too. "Hi, Conner. Hi, Madison." She gave us a final wave and went back into her house.

Once inside, Sam poked around in the kitchen. He opened cabinet doors and the refrigerator door. He picked up a package of cheese and some other things and examined their contents. He moved to the middle of the room and turned around slowly. "Did you repaint the kitchen, honey? It looks different. It's smaller than I remember."

Conner asked in a loud whisper, "How can a room get smaller, Mom?"

Madison pulled on her father's pant leg and chirped, "Did you bring me a prethent, Daddy?" Her little pink tongue protruded between her teeth.

"Yeah, Daddy. What did you get me?" Conner asked with wide eyes and parted lips.

"Madison, Conner! Daddy has just come home. That's present enough!" I immediately regretted my harsh tone.

"Aw, that's all right, honey. I love the way she talks." Sam's hazel eyes danced between us as he pulled out two small leather camels from his backpack. "Here you go! Now give me a kiss." He handed a camel to each of the kids and winked.

He reached again into his backpack and unfolded a silk headscarf. I curled my shoulders toward him and demurely bent my head. I felt the air puff as the tan-and-deep-red fabric settled onto my head. My cheeks crinkled into a broad smile. "Thank you, Sam. It's beautiful. I love the colors." I kissed him.

"Now, if you were in Baghdad, you could appear in public." We laughed.

Conner hugged his father's waist. "Thanks, Daddy! This is great!" He looked up into his father's face.

"You're welcome, kiddo. I thought that it would look good in your museum." He tousled Conner's hair.

Conner broke away. "I'm going to find a spot for it. I love you, Daddy. You're home for good and you're never going back. Yay!" He called as he ran up the stairs.

When Sam entered the den after his shower, I looked him up and down. He put on clothes that he had not worn in a year: blue jeans, a maroon turtleneck and a pair of soft leather slippers. "Look at you. You look normal again, honey. How do you like your new slippers? Do they fit okay? I bought them last month."

"Thanks, Sandra, they're fine. I feel wonderful." His gentle kiss lingered. Oh, it's been too long. I slid my palm along his cheek.

"How was the shower? Could you ever take one alone in military Iraq?" I poked his shoulder and chuckled.

"Awww, come on." We laughed and held hands. Then, I grabbed his neck and pulled his lips to mine.

The rest of the day was a party. We talked, joked and sat around the table and looked at pictures of Sam's friends—both soldiers and Iraqis. Conner told us that he used to think that the people who lived there only rode camels. Laughing, Sam corrected him: "No, they mostly ride in cars and trucks, just like us."

When he saw photos of Iraqi men, Conner asked Sam, "Why do men wear those stupid dresses, Daddy?"

"They dress the way they do to protect themselves against hot desert winds and blowing sand. It feels cooler to dress that way, too; those gowns are very loose, and air circulates and that cools them. We would wear those clothes if we lived there. The men's gown is a *dishdasha*."

Sam spent a lot of time with Madison that first day home. They needed to bond again; I didn't even have to remind him. They went up in her room and played with her dollhouse. I watched from the doorway. Sam was on the floor, lying on his side with his cheek propped up on his palm. Madison sat cross-legged next to him. They both could look into the house from its open back. She was describing what was happening with the family living there. Sam engaged her with questions about each of her "people." He asked her what they were cooking for supper that night. He looked over at me and winked. I had to stifle my laugh.

Conner came in and sat cross-legged on the floor beside them. He articulated the limbs and weapons of a couple of his toy soldiers while he made guttural sounds. At first I couldn't place what was different about him. Were those the same pants he wore to the airport? They were the same color, but…the pockets seemed a little different, like another one of his pair of pants. Hm, strange. No, maybe not.

I pushed away from the doorway. The sound of my family's voices and laughter followed me down the hallway to our bedroom. I think I heard Madison contracting Sam to put some additions on her little house with snippets about paint colors and how many more rooms she wanted.

That night, I made Sam's favorite supper: pasta with puttanesca sauce. I added a lot of anchovies, capers, kalamata olives, olive oil and plenty of garlic. I let Conner use a pastry brush to paint olive oil onto thick slices of crusty bread to toast. He did this so well that I even let him place thin slices of garlic on top and sprinkle fresh, grated Parmesan cheese over them. I slid the tray of bread into the oven and stood back to give my son a high five. "Awesome, dude!"

Conner's dimples deepened with his smile as he lowered his head. I could tell he was bursting with pride. He took a deep breath, looked up with a huge grin, and said, "Maybe I'll be a chef—maybe even a chef in the Army when I grow up, Mom."

"Yeah, honey. Daddy has just come home. I think we've had enough Army in this house, don't you?"

"Boy, that garlic smells good," Sam called from the den. "Now I know I'm really home."

I peeked at them through the doorway between the two rooms. Madison was on his knee. Sam was "stepping" her stuffed giraffe, Willie, around on the couch and over their legs. I heard their muffled conversation and laughter from the kitchen.

Since Sam's homecoming was a special occasion, we ate in the dining room. I set the table with my grandmother's china dishes, sterling silverware and crystal wine glasses. I lit candles. I didn't even mind that Madison spilled most of her food onto the linen tablecloth around her place setting.

The children watched us drink good Burgundy out of wide-bottomed narrow-topped glasses. Sam and I sniffed, swirled and tilted the glasses to inspect the "legs" clinging to the sides of the glass. We laughed and held hands. I was surprised that Sam had drunk most of the bottle by himself. I had just one glass. We made many toasts. Conner toasted us, too. "I'm glad that Daddy's home. Can I take a sip, Daddy?"

"No, Sam. Don't!"

Sam reached across and tilted his glass so that just Conner's lips were coated. Conner ran his tongue over them and scrunched up his nose. "Yuck!"

I laughed harder than I had in a long time.

CHAPTER 15

Sam was back at the office, back into his old routines. He had just picked Conner up at school. Both children went up to their rooms. We heard Conner's door slam. I smiled. "Did you hear that? He's been doing that, closing his door, I mean. 'I just want to be private, Mom,' he tells me as he closes the door right in my face. I don't mind. It's his step toward independence. He's growing up."

"Really?"

"Yeah." We laughed.

"I'm glad that I went to pick Conner up today." He sipped his coffee and leaned back in his kitchen chair. "So much came back, so many memories. And I got a chance to meet the teacher. I waited out front on the lawn. There were a few dozen other parents and a few grandparents, too."

I chuckled and touched his hand. "No, Sam. You're not in today's world. There are plenty of older parents; some even on their third and fourth marriages. A few of those 'grandparents' were probably the *parents* of some of these little kids."

His eyes widened. "You think so? Yeah, you're probably right. Anyway, I couldn't help remembering when I was a third-grader like Conner. You know, no one escorted their kids home from school in my day. I can't remember any of my friends ever being picked up. We walked home, and it was far. Here, we live less than a mile away. Why don't we let him walk or ride his bike to school?"

"I prefer to get him myself, Sam. Today's world…who knows? I read about crazy, horrible things in the papers and on the news. I will just drive him. So, tell me, what kind of things did you remember? I'd like to know."

He smiled and stared off and I started to imagine what reflections of his boyhood self were percolating up behind his glazed eyes.

"We talked about sports, we compared girls, we tossed stones at trees and lamp posts, we told jokes…I still remember, Sandra—I got this memory-flash of the day I told my mother about a girl that I liked when I was in, uh, I think it was fourth grade. I wrote a poem about her. I will never forget what my mother said. I was so disappointed: 'Girls in fourth grade aren't interested in boys, Sammy.' She shot me down like that a lot."

"I remember all those things you told me that she said; how she could be insensitive."

"That one still stings. It's stupid, I guess, but that's how I felt. I remember it happening. She was sitting in a chair in her pink housedress. Remember those things? I can't remember ever seeing her in slacks or pants.

"Anyway, today there was that long line of parked cars along the school curb. Some of them kept their motors running. I have to say that more than half were SUVs and minivans. Ah, America!"

"Yeah. And?"

"Those motors purred, Sandra, and I tried to think: what is this all about, you know? I mean this school, and all these beautiful kids. Here, where we are, we're all safe. But where I was—the kids in Iraq were beautiful, too. They sure grew up fast. Then I saw myself right back there—in Iraq. Sandra, I could see snipers firing on the construction projects, on our crews. We had to patrol garbage-strewn streets around those sites looking for buried explosives—IEDs. Everything there was potholed, shell-holed and bomb-cratered. It looked like hell. It *was* hell, honey." He lowered his head.

I reached for his hand. My eyes filled and my throat tightened. I tried to picture him in the middle of so much chaos and hurt and death.

He looked up at me. "I can still hear the rumble of our tank and troop-carriers roaring past. Men yelled in Arabic, our guys yelled in our military jargon...metal banging and slamming and clicking sounds would send me ducking behind vehicles and dirt and rubble mounds. You always had to be alert over there—watching, doing whatever you had to do to just stay alive and stay in one piece. I couldn't tell you all this when I was there, honey."

"I'm glad you didn't. I think I knew, though. I could sense how dangerous and terrible it was from the news and on the Internet. But I never watched TV news when the kids were around, Sam."

I heard the children move around upstairs. Sam tilted his head back and drained his mug. I got up and refilled it.

"Thanks. Everything felt so different in Iraq. I mean, I felt different: my hair, my skin and uniform were always caked in sand and dirt. Dust was always blowing; my lips were always dry and cracked. I'm not entirely comfortable being home yet, honey. Too many memories. Too many visions. It'll take a while until I can sleep the whole night through, too, I think."

I reached for his hand again and gave it another squeeze. "I know about PTSD, Sam. They talk about it on TV and I read about it. I know it can be terrible, honey. They say that a part of you never leaves that place. It's still with you the rest of your life. My dad's got it, too. And you're hurting, Sam. I can see it in you. You...we need...well, I want my old Sam back."

He straightened in his chair and drew his hand back. He glared at me. "I don't think so." He instantly softened. "Well, yeah. I think about it practically all the time. It's not that bad, Sandra. I'll get over it. In time, I'll get over it. The best thing is being home with you and the kids again." He pushed his chair back and started to get up. He clamped his jaw and pursed his lips.

"Come on. Sit down. That's what I mean. You get ticked-off so easily since you're home. You never used to be like that. Sit down. I want to hear what you have to say. Get it off your chest. Come on." I tapped his side of the table.

Our eyes met. I waited and felt my chest pound. He smiled, and, to my relief, sat down.

"That's it. Tell me more. I want to know, Sam."

"Anyway, on the days when the Iraqi parents thought it was safe to be on the streets, mothers dressed in *abayas* and even men dressed in their loose, ankle-length *dishdasha* gowns escorted their kids to school—their girls, too. You know, I showed you pictures of what they wear.

"Then, Sandra, as I was thinking about all of this the school bell rang and yells and shouts burst out of the opening doors. Teachers came down this winding walkway leading their classes toward us. I was searching for Conner. Hearing all that commotion from the kids' jabbering made me laugh, especially when I saw their school papers drop from those pudgy little hands. Such innocence! And they all were safe, too. Several of them hugged their teachers. That sort of tore me up, and then to hear their little singsong voices say, 'I love you, Mrs.—whatever!' and 'Goodbye!' Really, and then they skipped away. It was beautiful; all of that love, you know?"

I saw his eyes glisten. "Sandra, I have to admit that I got tears as I watched them. My mind spun with the images of our school kids compared with the Iraqi kids: the same faces, the same laughter, the same games." A soft, sibilant whistle escaped from his lips; he stared off.

"I know you can be a real softie, honey, and I love you for it, Sam."

He turned his head and came back to me. "Then I spotted Conner. He was laughing with another kid as they filed down the walkway behind their teacher. What's her name?"

"Mrs. Dorsey—Janet."

"Conner yelled when he saw me waiting there. 'Daddy! Hey, there's my Daddy! Yay!' I melted. It's been so long since I've been able to really talk about this kind of stuff, Sandra. Thanks honey."

I squeezed Sam's hand. "Thanks for what? For being human? Go on. Then what?"

"I wanted to find out how she thought Conner was doing. She said, 'Hello, Mr. Golden! Or, should I say Captain?' and we shook hands.

She told me it was good to have me back home and that I looked well, I told you that I didn't know her name. I just told her that I wasn't a captain anymore, that I had resigned my commission."

"So, did you ask about Conner? What did she say?"

"I did, and she said that he seems to be getting along better. I hope it's true. Conner was right there with us and she looked down at him when she said that. What else could she say with him right there? Then she asked me if I would talk to her class sometime soon and show pictures of the Iraqi people and of the country and of camels. I told her that I've got lots of photos. She said that she'll send a note home with Conner to arrange the visit. She was…yeah; I'd like to do it."

"I know she's very attractive," I chuckled and touched his arm. "Watch it, Sam."

CHAPTER 16

Subsequent weeks saw our lives settle into old routines. I hummed and sang a lot more, revitalized and unburdened by Sam's safe return. My family was whole again.

But not everything was as wonderful as I had dreamed it would be. I had anticipated that the family would have to make some adjustments when he came home. However, Sam was different, changed. His tone was often curt, and he was impatient. He lost his temper very easily—even with the children.

He drank more wine with our dinners. Before his last deployment, he would have one glass, rarely two, and that was occasionally. Since he had come home, he drank at least three glasses every night. Sometimes he polished off the whole bottle by himself, not expensive stuff. I didn't drink more than half or a whole glass with him. Moreover, he had started drinking the hard stuff, too.

I broached the subject one evening. We were in the den, I sat in the lounge chair, Sam sat opposite holding up the newspaper on the couch. The kids had gone to bed. "Sam, you've been drinking more than you used to. What's going on?"

"Aw, leave me alone, Sandra. I'm fine. It relaxes me." The newspaper hid his face.

"Honey, you moan in your sleep. Are you having dreams? Flashbacks? Tell me. You can tell me. I wouldn't be surprised if you did. Maybe I can help—"

"I'm fine, Sandra! Don't worry about it," his gruff voice barked from behind the newspaper.

"You know, Dr. Thomas offered to let me talk with him after he had started treating Conner. I missed you, and there were Conner's problems at school, and Tom needed me in the office and there was my writing...everything just piled up, Sam. I was truly stressed." I sat forward and clasped my hands. "I know those things were nothing compared to the danger you were in, but I was so stressed out. I never saw him as a client, but he helped to calm my nerves and fears a couple of times just by talking, talking over the phone. I am sure he would be glad to see you as a client. I know, I've read that—" Should I say it? Would he handle it in the right way? I had gone this far. We should get it out there: "PTSD gets worse and harder to cure the longer a guy lives with it without doing something about it."

Sam tapped the edge of the newspaper with his left index finger. He finally lowered it and I saw his clenched lips and his brows knitted with deep furrows. He enunciated every word: "Damn it, Sandra. No! I'll handle it. Let's leave it alone now, *will you*? Drop it. Just *drop* it." He sealed himself behind the paper again.

My chest and stomach tightened. He was running away. I wouldn't say any more just then. I would wait and see how things went. I leaned back in my chair and stared down. Damaged relationships were common among couples separated by this war. I knew that. I had read how combat confused ethics, how violence affected and troubled souls. I could not really know how bad it must have been for him. I could only imagine his rage when he witnessed terrible things and he was not able to do anything to help. Alcohol had become a refuge from those horrors.

I marveled at my son's close resemblance to his father during dinner one night. Conner had grown at least two inches while Sam was in Iraq. His thin face had begun to elongate and mature under his short haircut. Today, he was wearing a blue-plaid wool shirt and jeans, just like his dad. I had waited so long to see them like this.

Sam asked Conner about his experience with the psychologist. "What do you talk about, Conner?"

Was he fishing? Would he ask for help? I watched Sam, but his attention was on Conner.

"Lots of things, Daddy! Frank is nice." Conner shoveled a forkful of mashed sweet potatoes into his mouth. His cheeks puffed out like a chipmunk.

"Conner, don't put so much in your mouth at one time."

He gave me a perfunctory glance and kept speaking to his father. "I like talking to him. I can't wait 'til you meet him, Daddy."

I leaned forward. Both of my elbows were on the table and I watched my fork, suspended between my thumb and index finger, sway back and forth a few inches above my plate. Absently, I dragged the tines through a little pile of mashed sweet potato; the orange mass resembled a farmer's plowed field. I hung on their every word.

"Well, what do you say? What does he tell you?"

"We talk about school and Michael and all my friends and Mom and you. Frank has neat toys and models and stuff. We even played some chess. He's got a board, Daddy. I taught Frank the Dragon Ver... version of the Si...Sicilian you taught me. He didn't know anything about it." Conner beamed at his dad.

"You told him about the Dragon Variation of the Sicilian Defense? He didn't know it?" Sam grinned at me and looked back at Conner. "Good boy!"

Conner beamed as he nodded his head.

Across the table, Madison surrounded herself with pieces of golden fried-chicken skin and globs of sweet potato. The toddler was strapped into her booster chair, ferociously sucking on her sippy cup to get the last drop of chocolate milk. All of us jumped when she let out a sudden, loud burp. It bellowed and bounced off the kitchen walls. Conner and Madison shrieked with laughter. Sam laughed, too, and winked at her.

"Sam! Conner! Stop encouraging her!" I scolded as I leaned across the table to wipe sweet potato off my daughter's greasy mouth.

"Daddy gets to meet Dr. Thomas after your appointment tomorrow, Conner. Remember, Sam, tomorrow afternoon at four."

Several nods accompanied his penetrating gaze. "I got it on my schedule." He didn't smile.

I began to clear the table. "Okay, who's ready for dessert?"

After Conner's appointment, the kids stayed in the waiting room with Dr. Thomas' secretary while Sam and I were in his office.

I watched Dr. Thomas register my husband's bearing and confidence. Sam was a little taller. "Welcome home, Mr. Golden. It's good to finally meet you. You must be glad to be back." I noticed that the ends of his fingers turned pinker in Sam's grip.

Sam allowed a guarded smile as his eyes bore intensely into the other man's gaze. "You couldn't be more correct, sir. I had been dreaming of being home again. Thank you for caring for our son."

"You've both done a wonderful job with him, Mr. Golden. Conner is a very warm and loving child. Very bright, too."

"Thank you, sir." Sam's face broke into a broad smile and he slipped one hand into the pocket of his tan slacks. He cut a trim figure as he stood with one foot slightly forward. He wore a brown, V-neck sweater over a light-blue, buttoned-down shirt. His hair was growing out of his military buzz cut—dark, thick and curly.

I wrapped my arm around Sam's waist and gave him a little squeeze.

Dr. Thomas motioned to the sofa with a wave of his hand. "Let's have a seat, shall we?"

He settled into his weathered leather armchair and crossed his legs. Sam and I sat on the leather sofa opposite him.

"Getting right to the point, Doctor, what's going on with Conner? What's been happening with his schoolwork? I don't like that his school isn't satisfied with his work and that he's not progressing well."

I looked down at my shoes.

"Mr. Golden, I can tell you that my discussions with Conner have revealed a lot of anxiety in the boy. That's fairly common when a father is away in a combat theater. We have been addressing these issues. Conner has many concerns about you that he had tried to keep to himself, just shutting them all inside. When we began working together, I wondered whether we should ask a child psychiatrist or his pediatrician to prescribe an anti-anxiety medication. However, I concluded that would not be necessary. Medications are indicated for some situations, but I don't think that is the case here."

Sam leaned forward and rested his elbows on his knees. He stared down at his clasped hands extended before him. "Do you think Conner's schoolwork will improve now that I'm home?" He looked up at the psychologist.

Dr. Thomas sat back and tapped two fingers lightly on his lips. Then, he dropped his hands onto his lap. "Results of the psycho-educational tests that Conner completed do not indicate that he has any serious learning problems, Mr. Golden. That's excellent news, but I'm still not certain why his schoolwork is below grade level."

He looked at me. I exchanged a nervous glance with Sam.

"I do expect Conner's schoolwork to improve. He is very bright. His IQ is one-twenty-eight—far above average. Anything above one-twenty definitely is considered above average. I would like to continue to work with him and see if I can help him focus more in class. I believe that he is going to do fine. Try not to worry."

Sam nodded. He flashed a quick, courteous smile and rubbed his hands over his face. "That's a relief, but…" He sat up straighter and pressed his hands together in front of him as if in prayer. "Look, I'm really not familiar with psychology and, well, what you do. I mean, what do you do for kids? Conner's a little boy. He's eight! Kids goof off. They get distracted by all sorts of things. I certainly did. Won't Conner just grow out of this all on his own? How much longer do you think he needs to keep seeing you?"

Dr. Thomas's eyebrows rose and his tongue slid across his lower lip. "I'm sorry, but that's something that I can't say for certain."

Sam pinched the bridge of his nose with his left hand.

The psychologist waited. After a few seconds, Dr. Thomas leaned forward and cleared his throat. "Mr. Golden. Mrs. Golden. I believe I can help your son. I can teach Conner some simple techniques to help him relax and focus. I'll work with him to increase his motivation to pay attention at school. Why don't we just see how things go for a little while longer? We can see where we are in a couple of months."

Sam squinted and ran a hand over the top of his head. I saw that he didn't like Dr. Thomas' answer. He blurted, "So, you think that if I had been home last year, he might not—"

I sucked in a breath and felt a flutter in my chest. I tried to swallow the sour taste that rose into the back of my throat. I looked at Sam and reached for his hand. Despite myself, I had sometimes blamed Conner's problems at school on Sam's absence. But, I would never, ever say that! *Would* I? *Did* I?

Dr. Thomas narrowed his eyes. "As we've just discussed, kids get anxious, Mr. Golden. Your absence couldn't be helped. You are home now. That should help. We can work through Conner's anxiety and get him back on track with his schoolwork. Meanwhile, I'll always be available to you. Okay? One other consideration is that we can meet as a family during this period. Family counseling could be beneficial for you. Would you like to consider that?"

The psychologist's eyes darted toward me. That would answer my prayers. My lips parted as I took in a quick breath. We all sat in silence for a few seconds. Sam stared at the floor.

"That's something we can think about, isn't it Sam? I really think that we should consider this."

Sam looked at me with vacant eyes. Finally, he nodded, "Yeah." Then he turned back to Dr. Thomas. "We'll get back to you on that, Doctor."

I hesitated, suspended in frustration.

Dr. Thomas set his notepad aside and got to his feet. The leather furniture rubbed and creaked as we stood. He smiled and extended his hand. "We'll stay in touch."

Sam took the other man's hand. "Thank you, Dr. Thomas."

As he opened his office door, I heard Conner reading aloud from *Mother Goose Fairy Tales*. It had been lying on the reception table. Madison squeezed her stuffed giraffe against her chest as she leaned against her brother.

Dr. Thomas chuckled. "Now, that's a gorgeous sight."

Conner sneezed twice in quick succession. "Kleenex, Mom! Quick!" He shouted, his nose dripping.

"I hope you're not coming down with something, sweetheart." I removed a tissue from my purse and hurried to give it to him. "He was sneezing and coughing last night."

"See you next week, Conner. Feel better! 'Bye, Madison." Dr. Thomas called as we left.

Conner answered in a nasal voice, "See ya!" He wiped his nose with his sleeve and smiled.

"Ah, ah, ah. Not your sleeve, Conner. Use these." I pushed more tissues into his hand.

On the way back to our SUV Conner jabbered away about his appointment with Dr. Thomas. Sam looked down and patted his shoulder. He shortened his stride so that the boy could keep up and listened without comment. I walked beside them, holding Madison's hand. I could tell by his distant expression that Sam had gone into his own space. I felt a pang of unease.

I had always been careful not to worry him about stuff going on here while he was in Iraq. It wasn't fair to him. But, there were a lot of times that I was just so damned mad at him for being away from us. Why did he have to volunteer? Even in my moments of pique—and there were lots of them—I had been very careful not to take my frustrations out on Sam. But now…did I ever even hint to Sam that I thought it was his fault that Conner had problems at school? I wasn't sure. I knew I had gotten so mad about Conner. But, please, please, don't let me have ever blamed Sam for that.

My heart pounded as I buckled Madison into the car seat. I turned my head away and tried not to look at Sam. I was so conflicted about the changes in him and Conner's school problems. Then, without effort, my mind composed another intertwining poetic musing:

> *Birds winging wildly—*
> *Soaring high, singing—*
> *Volcano burst, gone.*

My body vibrated with an imperceptible shiver as I climbed into the SUV.

MARCH 5, 2007:
SOUTHERN CALIFORNIA

CHAPTER 17

I leaned on the side rails of Conner's hospital bed. My son sat propped up in it. Sam dozed in a chair on the other side. Madison was still asleep in the stroller next to him. That certainly made things less complicated. The haiku earlier today after the psychology appointment—no, it was yesterday, wasn't it? It was way after midnight now. *A volcano bursting*—then the convulsion? Why did I visualize that—and then? How prescient was that?

I couldn't detect any effects from the spinal tap that Dr. Choy just did. It was as if nothing had been done to Conner. He drank apple juice through a straw that I held to his lips. Sam opened his eyes and began to skim through a magazine. Conner, Sam and I all turned toward the sound of Dr. Choy's approaching wooden clogs.

He smiled and tousled Conner's hair. "Hello, Conner. You're feeling better now, I see."

Conner continued sucking from the straw in the container that he now held with both hands. He turned his eyes up at the doctor but he didn't respond.

"The spinal fluid is perfectly normal. There are no signs of meningitis or any other disease. His temperature is going down, too. It's one hundred degrees now, which is still a mild fever. Some Children's Tylenol should bring it down. You can take your son home now."

"Then, he's fine? Do you know what's wrong? Why did this, this convulsion happen?" I noticed that Conner was still glassy-eyed and didn't seem involved with what was going on. "I've been wondering if it was something Conner ate, Doctor. Maybe it's part of a growth spurt? I've heard people say—"

Sam nodded. "Yes, Dr. Choy, why did this happen?"

Dr. Choy shook his head. "Your son has an upper-respiratory infection that was caused by a virus. In other words, he has a bad cold. The seizure might have occurred because the fever lowered his defenses against it. But, no. Not a growth spurt, Mrs. Golden, whatever that means. Why it happened—why he had this convulsion—is the question. It could be epilepsy."

Epilepsy? Nothing—not a bomb's explosion—could have upset my world any more than what he had just said. Conner looked at us. It was hard for me to breathe. I clenched my fists. The doctor stood there and looked at me.

"Conner, we'll just be over there, honey. We will be right back. We can leave Madison here, but let's keep an eye on her, Sam."

Conner sucked on the straw, barely turned his head and watched us walk away out of the corners of his eyes.

I marched past the nurses' desk toward the conference room. A nurse looked up at me from her paperwork; the two men trailed me like a couple of sheep. I stopped at the doorway. Some volatile force coursed through me. This couldn't be happening. Was this doctor going to change Conner's life? Was this doctor going to change *all* of our lives? I turned around. My tongue pushed against my cheek and my face felt tight.

Sam stood next to Dr. Choy. They looked at me, their mouths slightly agape.

"How can Conner have epilepsy? He has always been a normal little boy! No one else in the family has epilepsy! You said Sam's brother's convulsion was not serious. Epilepsy is a terrible disease. This can't be right!" My hot cheeks stung with resentment. I shook my head and began to pace, taking several short steps to the right and then to the left to calm my pain and fears. I reached deep for control. I just couldn't—wouldn't—accept those words.

Dr. Choy's eyes darted from me to Sam and then back to me again. He looked uncomfortable. He was making those little puffs with his cheeks. I saw a bead of sweat above his lip and on his brow.

He rubbed the right side of his head with his yellow-stained fingers. "I didn't say that he has epilepsy, Mrs. Golden. Do not jump to conclusions. No. I only said, eh, that after this first seizure, we have to search for a cause of the seizure. Epilepsy is a very common cause. Obviously, there are other conditions that induce seizures, too."

I stopped moving. "Like what?"

Sam edged closer and turned to face Dr. Choy.

"The tests that we did tonight show no signs of any other serious disease, er...ah...that might have caused the seizure." Dr. Choy turned his head and coughed into his hand. "Excuse me. Maybe the cold—his febrile illness—caused it. However, we will need a neurologist's expertise to decide. I am going to order an EEG. That's the electroencephalogram—you know, the brain-wave test—to see if there's any seizure activity in your son's brain. I'd like the neurologist to have the results by the time of Conner's appointment."

I shook my head and looked at Sam. My mind whirled. I didn't understand much of what the doctor was telling us; the only words I heard were 'epilepsy' and 'seizure activity.' Did I give this to Conner? Did I do something to him? I had smoked a joint at college—only one! But, that was almost twenty years ago. Surely, no, that couldn't be it. That was crazy.

Sam looked at me. Then he took my hand. I shook it off. He said something—finally. "How's this EEG done, Dr. Choy?" Sam wrapped his arm around my waist. I pulled out and moved a few steps away as Dr. Choy watched. I ignored Sam's hurt expression.

He said to Sam, "That test involves having some wires placed on the scalp with a special cap. Conner will just lie on a bed in a dark, quiet room while his brain activity is recorded. It doesn't hurt at all. In fact, he will probably sleep through the test. The neurologist's office will contact you to set up an appointment once they receive my referral."

Dr. Choy's voice had become thick and raspy. He cleared his throat and coughed softly into his fist; then, he coughed deeper and louder. "Excuse me. As I said before, I've already started Conner on a medication to prevent any more seizures." His cheeks puffed again after almost every sentence.

"*What* medication?" I drew a deep breath.

"Dilantin. It's a very effective anti-seizure medication. Dilantin has been around for a very long time—around seventy years. It should prevent Conner from having more seizures. I'll write a prescription with directions how he should take it. You can fill it at any pharmacy."

"If we give him this medicine, what will it do to him?" I demanded. I shook my head. How could this be happening to us? Just hours ago everything was so different, so good. I looked at Sam. I couldn't tell what he was thinking, what he was feeling. His face was expressionless. Was he even listening to the doctor? Was he with me?

"Well, Mrs. Golden, there are a few possible side effects that you'll need to watch out for: a skin rash, some drowsiness. Sometimes it affects the blood and the liver—"

"Side effects." I shook my head and narrowed my eyes. "That's why I try to never give my kids medicines, even Tylenol, unless our pediatrician says that I really should. That's how we are in this family." I was not in control. I did not understand what had happened to my son. I grabbed Sam's arm and looked up into his inexpressive eyes.

He didn't look at me. His head was down; his chin almost touched his chest. My husband looked exhausted. I felt alone.

"I'm prescribing Dilantin to prevent any more seizures from happening. I can't guarantee that he won't have another one, though. No one can. We'll have to wait for the EEG and for the neurologist to—"

"Wait. They still could happen with this medicine? Can't you give him a different medicine, one that is safer and that will work better?"

Dr. Choy shook his head and smiled at me. "Mrs. Golden, do you know that aspirin commonly causes bleeding in the stomach? We hear about it on TV all the time. People take penicillin to cure pneumonia, but that same medicine can cause a potentially fatal allergic reaction. One out of ten thousand surgical patients suffers a serious complication from the anesthetic alone. It can even kill them. You see, *all* medicines are associated with possible side effects. I emphasize *possible*. People drive cars, yet we all know that driving has risks: we may never get home alive. That's the kind of a risk we're talking about, Mrs. Golden."

"Sure, I know that, Doctor. Please don't patronize me. No. I'm sorry. It's just—I'm so—Ahhhh! This is just crazy! So much has happened. Now I have to be scared and live in fear that this will happen again, or that this strong medicine will hurt him!"

Sam's expression softened. He wrapped his arm around my waist; this time I let him. He asked, "So, Doctor, ah, you think that we should have Conner take this, this Diltin or—"

"The medicine is *Dilantin*, Mr. Golden. And, yes, I do think it is necessary. Look, I have to tell you these things. I am not going to tell you that there's nothing to worry about. You would not believe me if I did. You brought Conner to the hospital because you were very worried about your son. Now, I'm doing everything I can to help him."

I blinked; I blinked a lot, and fast, too. The floodgates would have unlocked at any moment if I didn't. Sam squeezed my hand.

Dr. Choy moved a step closer. "This is not the end of the world, Mrs. Golden. Conner might never have another seizure."

"So, how long will he have to take this medicine?"

"I can't answer that. Just keep Conner on it until he sees the neurologist; it will be up to the specialist to decide."

"What if he needs it…is it possible that he'll need it for months? Years? Will he need it the rest of his life? God!"

"I can't answer that. The neurologist might even stop it when you see him, depending on what he thinks caused the seizure."

Here was hope. "Really! He might stop it so quickly?"

"Yes. He might."

I stared at the far wall. No more seizures! It was possible. Stop the medicine! It was possible. Maybe…

The doctor pulled a small prescription pad from a pocket on his scrub shirt and started to write. "Our pharmacy in the hospital is always open, so you can pick up this medication before you leave. Conner should take both capsules every day. They're different sizes. Give him the one-hundred milligram capsule—the bigger one—before bed and the thirty-milligram capsule—the smaller one—when he wakes up in the morning. The directions will be on the bottles. Start giving it to him at bedtime tonight. Here you go."

Sam and I exchanged a tentative glance.

Dr. Choy replaced his pen into his shirt pocket. I took the prescription.

"If Conner develops a rash, stop the Dilantin and call me immediately. The neurologist will order blood tests to monitor for any problems. Also, Dilantin can make the gums swell—"

Dr. Choy must have seen me grimace. He suddenly directed his attention toward Sam and continued his spiel. "To minimize this, Conner should brush his teeth twice a day and floss at least once a day. The fewer particles that could irritate his gums, the better. If drowsiness remains a problem, give me a call and I'll make some dosage adjustments until the specialist takes over. I am sending the referral to the neurologist in my medical group: Dr. Hal O'Rourke. I believe Conner's pediatrician knows him. Dr. O'Rourke is very competent and experienced. You should be getting an appointment with him in the next week or two. His office will call you to schedule the EEG. Would you like me to fax over our records to your pediatrician?"

"Yes, please. I'll call him in the morning, too." I looked down at my watch. "It is morning, isn't it?"

"You should tell Conner's school about his seizure. Inform them that he is on Dilantin but that he does not need to take it at school. The school nurse should be apprised so she can help to educate the staff. They need to know that Conner has had a seizure so they can be prepared if he has another one."

My eyes squeezed shut. I saw the image of my son's thrashing body—the blood, the urine-soaked pants, or worse—in his classroom—in front of everybody—at his friends' homes. I opened my eyes. Sam had been watching me. I stared past him. How would I tell the school? Would Conner be different in their eyes, now? Maybe it would never happen again. By some miracle, maybe it would just never happen again.

"Do either of you have any questions before I discharge Conner?"

"No. Thank you for all of your time and for what you've done for our son," Sam said and extended his right hand.

"Yes, Dr. Choy. You've been wonderful. I am sorry if…I'm sorry. Thank you."

"I know, Mrs. Golden," Dr. Choy said, softly. He puffed his cheeks, smiled and shook my hand, too. "You both look exhausted. Take Conner home and get some sleep."

Sam went to the pharmacy to fill the prescription. I helped Conner out of his hospital gown. He was pretty much awake now. There was a red spot on the sleeve where his IV had been. A Band-Aid covered the puncture site. I got him back into his pajamas. They smelled of urine, but the yellow stain was almost dry. I would throw them into the washer as soon as we got home. An orderly helped Conner out of the high hospital bed and into a wheelchair. Madison was on her side in the stroller, still asleep.

Eight years ago, I was in another hospital. I was twenty-eight and pregnant for the first time. Was that too old? Did that have something to do with Conner's brain and this seizure? No. Twenty-eight was not old. So, why did Conner get this? My pregnancy had been good; labor had lasted ten hours. Conner had been a glorious baby: chubby with full, rosebud lips. Such a beautiful boy, everybody had said. But, now?

I turned around, ready to go. Conner fiddled with the brake lever on the wheelchair. I was exhausted.

The orderly pushed the wheelchair across the E.R. to the exit door. I followed with Madison's stroller. Conner marveled at his unique transportation. With wide eyes, his cupped palms skimmed over the rolling rubber wheels.

Sam appeared with a small, white paper bag in his hand just as we got to the emergency department exit doors. "How are you feeling, Conner?" He bent down and kissed his son's cheek.

"Hi, Daddy. Look at this neat rolling chair."

Several nurses watched us leave. One told us to call if we had any questions. I smiled back. Dr. Choy was nowhere to be seen, but I was sure I could hear him talk to a patient behind a curtain next to the bed where Conner had been just a little while ago.

CHAPTER 18

Both children slept all the way home. Madison dozed in her car seat while Conner was stretched across the back seat strapped in the seat belt. Madison whimpered softly a couple of times. When I turned my head to check them I saw her eyelids twitching.

I clutched the paper bag that contained the medications. "What do you think, Sam?" I asked softly. "We give him this pill twice a day? How long do we do that? And all those side effects. We need to talk to that neurologist right away!"

"We'll call the pediatrician in the morning and see what he thinks about all this. And stop worrying about side effects, will you? Dr. Choy said they're not common. We've taken all kinds of pills ourselves and nothing bad happened. All of those antibiotics we've taken and things, and those pain pills after I broke my arm. What about your birth control, huh? You're all right on them." His voice got louder. "Don't worry so much!"

I hissed back, "You know what? Mothers worry! That's what we *do*! I'm not so sure you're even that concerned, anyway. You sure didn't say much back there in the E.R."

Sam snapped his head around and narrowed his eyes at me. I immediately regretted what I had said. "Damn it, Sandra! What do you want me to say?" He lowered his head to glance into the rearview mirror.

"Shh! Not so loud. I'm sorry! I'm sorry! I shouldn't have said that, Sam. That was really mean of me. I know you're worried, too."

"Of *course* I'm worried. What do you want from me, Sandra? God *damn* it! I'm doing everything I can! What more can I do?" Sam sighed. "Dr. Choy says that Dr. Jackson knows the neurologist. Maybe he can get us in quicker."

"I'll call him first thing." I looked out my side window and bit my lip as we drove on. I felt his eyes on me—that noncommittal, distant stare that I couldn't read—like the one before I ticked him off. I had detected that look a lot ever since he got back two months ago. He rarely flew off the handle before. Well, I did provoke it. It had been a terrible night.

I leaned my head back against the headrest. The SUV's tires sang as our vehicle skimmed over the road. I liked that wet sound. It had rained while we were in the emergency room. The shiny streets reflected shafts of yellow light that poured from street lamps onto the black, wet asphalt. Beams from headlights reflected off the mist like tiny shimmering diamonds.

My thoughts turned back to Sam's deployments: his friends, the horrors and, yes, some laughs that he must have had. He told me a few things, but he really didn't talk about what happened over there. I knew that war changed people. I had heard that some guys in other units killed themselves months after they got home. Others got hooked on drugs and booze. I didn't think Sam did that stuff—well, maybe the booze.

Conner. I turned around to look at him. What would happen now? Doctors and then more doctors? There was bound to be more strain on all of us. It was up to me to keep us, this family, together.

As we drove by a local diner Sam said something.

"Hm? What?"

"Doughnuts and coffee to go. That sign over there."

The orange neon sign had just flickered on as we stopped for a red light. I saw two cars parked in back. In the lamplight, misty ribbons of steam rose off their hoods and two figures moved around through the shop window. They must have been opening for the morning coffee and doughnut crowd. Actually, coffee and a lemon-cream doughnut would really hit the spot right now…

We pulled into our driveway. Sam pressed the door opener on the visor.

"No! No! I don't want to!" Conner moaned while Sam unbuckled the boy's seat belt as he lay on the back seat. He pushed his father away with small, clenched fists as Sam lifted him into his arms.

"Be careful! Don't press where the needle was."

"I know." It sounded like a snarl. He didn't look at me. Then Sam whispered, "Hey, Conner. We're home, son. You can go to bed now."

Conner opened his eyes and lifted his head. "Home, Daddy? Why?" He dropped his head back onto Sam's shoulder and closed his eyes in sleep-drugged confusion.

I stripped the almost-dry sheets and blanket off Conner's bed and pulled off the bloodstained pillowcase. Sam, still holding Conner on his shoulder, appeared in the doorway. He stared at the pillowcase. Was he wondering the same things? What happens next? Did Conner have epilepsy? Would he grow up and be able to do normal things?

"Just about done," I whispered. It sure was smart to have those plastic mattress protectors on all our beds. I flashed Sam a superficial smile and pulled on a fresh pillowcase, sheets and a cover. "Done."

I went downstairs to the washing machine and stuck everything in. I would try Choy's milk trick if the stains didn't come out. Dr. Choy—I had given the poor guy a rough time, I guess.

When I got back upstairs my husband was still cradling Conner in his arms. Sam's head was bent over, his wet cheek pressed against Conner's. It was as if he was in no hurry to put our son down. We exchanged a wan smile. I held out my hand. When he took it, I saw that his eyes were filled with tears. I wrapped my other arm around him and held him close. Right then my love for Sam was as much as I had ever felt. But, I had come to realize how much he needed me and how much he needed my direction.

"I never want to let him go," Sam sobbed softly.

CHAPTER 19

My eyes fluttered open. I looked over at the clock. Had I only been asleep for an hour? It would be morning soon. Careful not to disturb Sam, I slid out of bed and padded softly down the hall. I paused to check on Madison. Her breathing was regular. Then I crept into Conner's room and looked down at him. His chest moved peacefully up and down, and each breath whistled. I smiled, exhaled and felt my chest relax.

I tiptoed out of his room and hurried to the study. It was time to do some research. I turned on the small light beside the computer, pressed buttons and closed the door. I tapped my steepled fingertips together and waited for the computer to whir to life.

I googled "seizures." What the—! There were thousands of hits. I clicked "seizures" on a medical reference site: "Seizures are symptoms of a brain problem. They happen because of sudden, abnormal electrical activity in the brain. Seizures can have many causes, including medicines, high fevers, head injuries, brain tumors, alcohol and certain diseases. People who have recurring seizures due to a brain disorder have epilepsy. Ancient cultures associated epilepsy with the sacred and the divine, with deities and demons, and with magic. So-called 'primitive' societies even today still hold these beliefs."

Since the lab tests showed no other disease, Conner's convulsion was probably caused by the fever. I felt comfortable with that. That was how it happened. "...They generally last thirty seconds to two minutes." I leaned back and looked at the ceiling, trying to absorb all this information. I stretched my arms over my head. How could this be happening to my Conner?

I groaned and read on: "...Some people have milder seizures that are called 'partial seizures' and 'petit mal' (absence) seizures, and 'focal seizures' and fever (febrile) convulsions." I was riveted by the descriptions of convulsions: "...generalized tonic-clonic seizures." Conner had this. It fit Conner.

It was becoming hard to concentrate on all of these new terms. I pressed another key and skimmed the section about Complex Partial Seizures: "...the most common type...any age...loss of awareness, staring, chewing, swallowing and other movements...strange thoughts and smells and tastes." Conner had a convulsion, and it was nothing like *that*.

The next topic held me. "Is epilepsy inherited?" Apparently, some kinds of neurological problems were passed through families and could cause seizures. I sucked in my breath. Sam's brother had a seizure as a baby! Did Conner inherit something from Sam that caused this seizure? Or, from me? No, not me. No one in my family ever had a seizure. I knocked my knuckles on the wooden desk. My eyes skipped around the page on the monitor. All that scientific jargon about genes and chromosomes and...There was too much information and not enough answers.

A site titled "Coping with seizures and epilepsy" caught my attention. "...not a mental illness...a brain disorder...moods, feelings of self-worth..." God, how depressing! Epilepsy changed everything in a person's life. How did people live with it? How did they function?

I scrolled down. My jaw dropped as I caught my breath; a subheading gripped me. "Sudden Unexplained Death—people with epilepsy have an increased risk of dying for unexplained reasons. This condition is called sudden unexplained death in epilepsy, or SUDEP...They are usually found dead in their beds without apparent cause...It is not clear if it is the sequel of a seizure...that affects the heart or breathing."

God! But that was epilepsy. Conner didn't have epilepsy. He only had one convulsion caused by the fever. I gritted my teeth; my shoulders and temples tightened.

The words on the screen started to swim away. I was so tired. I shut the computer down and stared at the blank screen. The sky was getting lighter. I yawned, stretched and switched off the lamp. I went to our bedroom.

Sam had rolled onto my side. I gave him a gentle poke; he pushed over.

CHAPTER 20

Conner was still asleep at noon. Madison sat at the kitchen table with us and gulped chocolate milk from her sippy cup.

Sam held up half of a peanut-butter-and-jelly sandwich for her to bite. "Where did we go yethterday, Daddy?"

As he started to explain, I jumped up to answer the phone. "Oh, thank you for calling back, Dr. Jackson. I want to tell you what happened to Conner last night…"

After I hung up I said to Madison, "Hey, kiddo, how about watching a *Barney* DVD?"

The toddler grinned and clapped her hands. "Yay!"

"Would you pour some coffee, honey? I'll get her started on the DVD, and then I'll tell you what Dr. Jackson said." I returned to the kitchen a few minutes later. In a low voice, I said, "The pediatrician was very complimentary of Dr. Choy. Apparently, Dr. Jackson works with him a lot. And with Dr. O'Rourke, too, that neurologist Conner's going to see. Anyway, he agreed that we should continue to give Conner the Dilantin since Dr. Choy had already started it. But he said that the neurologist might change the medication, or even stop it—please, God."

I sat down and poured cream into my coffee. After I had watched the steam rise and swirl above my blue-and-white mug, I took a cautious, noisy sip. "Just like Dr. Choy said, Dr. Jackson thinks that we should tell Conner's teachers what happened. You know, so they'll be aware of, well—in case anything happens at school."

Sam nodded. "So, Dr. Jackson thinks it could happen again too, even though all of Dr. Choy's tests were normal and he's on the medicine?"

"Well, no! I mean, it shouldn't." I put my cup down too hard and some coffee sloshed onto the table. I stared at the spilled drops and then pushed them together with my finger. "That medicine, the Dilantin, should prevent any more of those seizures, he said."

"But, Sandra, until we see the specialist—until we know exactly what's going on—I mean, could Conner have another convulsion?"

My eyes bored into his. "Yes."

"Mommy! Mommy! I'm hungry!"

We sprang from our chairs. "Madison, we'll be right back, honey!"

Sam took the stairs two steps at a time in front of me.

Conner was sitting up in bed when we got to his room. "It's so late, Mom. What about school? My tongue hurts real bad. I hurt all over! And I got a bandage on my arm. And there's one on my back! How'd they get there?"

Sam and I exchanged a glance. Sam sat on Conner's bed. I knelt on the floor and wrapped both arms around my son. I closed my eyes and squeezed him. I didn't know how to tell him about his convulsion, or even if I *should* tell him. No, of course, he needed to know. Still short of breath after my rush up the stairs, between gasps, I asked, "Do you remember...what happened...last night, honey?" Conner shook his head.

"You remember...how bad your cough was...last night, and your nose was all runny? Do you remember?"

"Yeah..."

"Well, you got a real high fever and your cold...made you shake all over. It made you bite your tongue, too. That's why it hurts, honey. Here, let's see it." I stuck mine out reflexively.

His swollen tongue—pink, but for a bluish, ragged gash along its left side—jutted out between his teeth. "Ooooh! It *hurts*."

"I know it does. But, the doctor said it'll get better in a day or two, honey."

"Doctor? I was shaking? Why? What doctor said?"

"We took you to the hospital last night because you were shaking, honey. You stopped after a couple of minutes." I looked at Sam. He nodded. "You had a brain scan—a CT scan, the doctor called it—and some other tests."

"Oh. I don't remember. A brain scan! I had a brain scan, Mommy? Oh, boy! Wait 'til I tell the other kids. I know about them from TV! I remember that doctor guy, Beth's father. He came to my class and showed us pictures. Can I have breakfast?"

"Of course you can, and you can stay home from school today, too." I laughed and squeezed him tighter. "How's about chocolate-chip pancakes with lots of syrup and some chocolate milk?"

"Yeah! Let's go!"

I remembered the headache Dr. Choy said could happen after the spinal tap. "How do you feel honey? Does your head hurt?"

"I feel achy, Mom. But my cough is better, isn't it?"

"Yes, it is, honey. But does your head hurt?"

"No. My tongue hurts. Can I have those pancakes and chocolate milk?"

That evening I stood in the doorway of the kids' bathroom and watched Sam tell Conner about the anti-seizure medication. "Conner, the doctor said that you need to take these Dilantin capsules or you could start shaking again." Sam forced a hesitant smile, gauged Conner's response and his expectant face, and continued, "So you need to swallow these capsules. You have to take one of these smaller ones with a drink of water every morning. Then, you have to take this bigger one—this one with the red stripe—every night before bed. We're going to start with the bigger one."

"No! It's too big, Daddy. I won't! I can't swallow that!" A vein throbbed in Conner's neck and his eyes brimmed with tears. He kicked the lower cabinet door under the sink. "I won't do it!"

"Conner! Stop that right now! I am not going to argue with you about this! You're going to take this medicine," Sam ordered. "Here's a glass of water. Put the capsule in your mouth and swallow it with some water. It will go right down. Open up."

It was difficult to watch them, but I didn't butt in.

I saw Sam's hand tremble as he placed the capsule on our son's swollen and discolored tongue. Conner wrinkled his nose and took a sip of water from the glass. He immediately started to gag.

"Here! Swallow, Conner! Hold your head over the sink!" Sam's attempt at self-control was pathetic. He was about to lose it.

Conner retched a couple times and spit the capsule out with the water. He sobbed, "I can't swallow it! I'll choke!"

Sam grimaced. "Come on, Conner," he said as he retrieved the capsule from the sink. "You can do it. Try again." The boy began to cry even harder and kicked the cupboard again. "Stop it! Stop kicking!"

He grabbed Conner's arm. Sam's face blazed with fury.

I unfolded my arms and moved forward. "Hold on, Sam! Sam! Stop!" Conner's screams muffled my protestations.

"Ahhhowwww! You're hurting me! Stop it, Daddy! Stop it! You're hurting me!"

"Sam! Sam, enough! Let me try. You wait downstairs. Conner and I will get it down. Go ahead. I'll be down in a minute."

Sam dropped Conner's arm and shook his head. "Okay. Yeah, I'll go downstairs. I'm sorry, Conner." He handed me the capsule, turned on a military heel and left.

Conner sobbed, "*Owww.* Daddy hurt my arm, Mom!"

"He didn't mean to, honey. He didn't mean it. Come on. I'll help you take it."

"I won't t-take it! It's n-not fair!" He screamed between sobs. "Why do I have to t-take that pill? It's too big! I'll ch-choke!"

"I know, Conner. It's hard to do new things sometimes. But it's very, very important that you swallow this pill." At that moment the tune from *Mary Poppins*, "A Spoonful of Sugar," sprang into mind. "Do you think that if I put it in some ice cream, or maybe chocolate milk, you'd be able to swallow it? I think it would be a lot easier. Let's try that, okay?"

Conner's demeanor immediately softened. I flashed him a smile. I should have asked Dr. Choy to give us a liquid form of the Dilantin if there was one. Conner would have to swallow this tonight, but if he couldn't get it down I would call Dr. Choy.

He sobbed a couple of times and wiped tears with his pajama sleeve.

"Let's go to the kitchen and put the capsule in some chocolate ice cream." I took his hand and we went downstairs.

"Did he take it?" Sam called. He was sitting on the couch in the den, holding a glass half-filled with an amber liquid. An open whiskey bottle was on the coffee table. "I'm sorry that I grabbed you, son. Forgive me, Conner?"

"Yeah, Daddy, but you squeezed my arm real hard," he answered as he wiped his nose with the sleeve of his free hand.

"He's going to take it with chocolate ice cream." I said with a grin and began to sing, "A-spoonful-of-sugar-la-da-da-da-da-da." Conner sat in his usual seat at the kitchen table. He had a sheepish grin. I got the ice cream out of the freezer and scooped some into a bowl. Sam walked in, the newspaper clenched in one hand and the glass in the other.

I put a large spoonful into his mouth as he mumbled, "Whipped cream?"

"Whipped cream! What a great idea, Conner! Sure." I took the can of whipped cream out of the refrigerator and shook it. "Here's what we'll do: swallow that chocolate spoonful, and then we put the Dilantin capsule on your tongue. You open wide, I'll squirt the whipped cream into your mouth and you swallow it right down. Okay?"

A broad grin appeared and he nodded.

"Open wide." I put the capsule on his tongue, tilted the can and depressed the nozzle. A white mass hissed and billowed as it squirted into his mouth. His cheeks puffed out. He swallowed.

"Open." I peered in. "It worked!" I looked at Sam. We all laughed.

"Hey, can I try that?"

"Open up, Daddy," I said, as I squirted the whipped cream into his mouth.

Conner squealed with laughter.

"That's a great technique, guys. Ice cream and whipped cream whenever you need it, Conner."

Conner beamed. "Yeah, Daddy, that way I can eat the medicine."

"Okay, honey. You did great. Now, floss and brush and get into bed. Daddy will come up to tuck you in after me. Let's go."

I turned and glared at the glass in my husband's hand. "Put that away." I mouthed the words and followed Conner upstairs.

CHAPTER 21

"**H**urry, Conner. We'll be late!" I leaned against the railing downstairs. It was two days since his convulsion. Today was his first day back to school. I barely heard any sounds and murmurings from the street or even from inside my own house as I inventoried my challenges—our family's growing problems. It was obvious that things had not been easier since Sam came home.

Conner hopped two-footed down the stairs. "Okay, Mom! I'm ready. I can't wait to tell everybody what happened!" He stopped on the bottom step and looked at me. "Mom? Mommy? I'm ready. Let's go!"

Echoes and then words crept in. Uh-oh. "Okay. You want to tell everyone about the...the seizure? Really?" I pushed my body away from the railing. He didn't seem to be tired or to have any of the side effects Dr. Choy had mentioned. Conner even took the Dilantin with the whipped cream without any fuss this morning.

"Oh yeah! I had a CT scan. Boy. Wait 'til I tell everybody. They'll think it's so cool!"

His grin and his twitchy eyebrows compelled me to return his smile. I sighed and followed him into the garage. "Bye Sam. 'Bye Madison. I'll see you later."

Prior to today, my mind had barely registered this short drive to his school despite having done it so often. Now, something compelled me to see every detail that had formerly been only vague and familiar. I wanted the past to regain me, to go back to that time before Conner's convulsion had forced its ugliness into our lives. This feeling—illogical and an impossible attempt, I knew, to make these past few days disappear—reminded me of that passage from Fitzgerald. How long ago was it? My college roommate, Kathy, and I read and re-read and talked about Fitzgerald's last lines in *The Great Gatsby*. Something about how we were all constantly going against currents yet still getting swept back into our pasts. That was exactly how I felt now, what I wanted now. And these streets—dependable sights of my former world—were my anchor to that past: the scooters and bikes that were in driveways and that laid on lawns. And that large yellow dog, with its long pink tongue that dangled from the side of its mouth as it watched from a front stoop most mornings, a fashionable brown-and-blue-striped handkerchief tied around its neck like a cravat. That sight always made me smile. He was obviously a member of some warm family. A calico cat perched atop a brick pillar; mothers chatted and pushed covered strollers that enclosed infants and toddlers bundled up against the crisp early-March air.

But today I would tell the school about Conner's...Conner's trouble. I swallowed hard.

"Mom, why are you going here? We should have turned back there!" Conner's yell pierced me from the back seat.

I had missed our turn. "Oh, wow, I'm sorry. I was just in my own little world, honey." Several minutes later, we coasted to a stop. The crossing-guard—a bald, older man with white stubble on his chin and a paunch protruding comfortably through his open, luminous lime-trimmed vest—stood in the middle of the crosswalk. He smiled in recognition and held up the red stop sign.

I stared. He looked suddenly decrepit and frail. I made myself smile back before I turned my head to watch the boys and girls crossing in front of me. Their sweet, clear-eyed, cheery faces chattered away as they passed in front of my SUV. I drummed my thumbs on the steering wheel. How many of these youngsters had seizures? One in a hundred,

Dr. Choy had said. Had any of them gone through that tortured jerking and groaning and biting and wetting and...?

The guard walked back to the curb and waved us on.

I raised my hand in acknowledgment and then pulled into the school parking lot around the corner. "Okay, we're here. I'll go in with you. I need to talk with Mrs. Dorsey."

"What for, Mom?" Conner unclipped his seat belt and climbed out of the SUV.

He had become very conscious of referring to me as "Mom" instead of "Mommy." I had pangs of regret every time he used that more mature moniker, but he still called Sam "Daddy." That was sweet.

"I told you. Dr. Choy said that I should tell Mrs. Dorsey about—about what happened a couple nights ago. Hey! Don't forget your backpack!"

He reached for his pack. "Who is Dr. Choy?"

"He's the doctor at the hospital who took care of—"

Conner was no longer listening. He had spotted two of his friends standing by the flagpole and had run to join them.

I sighed. Sparrows flew off branches above me in a dark, chirping wave when I slammed the door. I trudged after several groups of chatting, laughing children heading into the school. I smiled when I spotted my son with his friends; then they disappeared into their classroom. The corridor was empty. I stood and stared where he had just been.

I turned around and was confronted by a collection of staff photos that was displayed on the wall. All of those smiling expressions assaulted my emotions and exaggerated my insecurity. I recognized several faces from that SST conference months back. The reflection in the glass showed tired and puffy eyes. My short, auburn hair hung limp around my neck.

I squared my shoulders and approached the administration desk. A secretary with too-black hair and who appeared to be in her mid-fifties was rifling through a drawer in a filing cabinet behind a desk. She turned and looked at me. Our eyes met before her attention returned to the cabinet. The other secretary sat at her desk. She was younger and pretty, with a mane of flowing red hair. A small diamond ring sparkled on her left hand.

The younger woman looked up. I cleared my throat. "I'm Sandra Golden, Conner Golden's mother. I'm here to meet with Mrs. Dorsey."

"Do you have an appointment?"

Her manner unsettled me. She barely smiled and her eyes were unreadable. "Uh, yes, I do. I know I am early. I just dropped my child off. She's expecting me. She said that she'd meet with me after her first-period class."

The redhead handed me a stick-on "visitor" tag. "Please sign the visitor book. You can wait right over there."

I took a seat in the reception area and placed my purse next to my feet. I smiled when I saw a two-year-old issue of *Junior Scholastic* on the table. I flicked through it. I remembered the subscription I had during junior high. The next thing I knew, Conner's teacher was behind me telling the secretaries that she would be in the conference room with the parent of one of her students.

I sat up, rubbed my eyes and rose to greet her. "Oh, Mrs. Dorsey, I must have dozed off."

We shook hands. She gave me a strained smile. I glanced down at my soft, brown leather jacket over my pink blouse, tan slacks and brown slip-on shoes. I felt a little haggard; she must have seen that. I pulled in my stomach.

"Let's go where we can talk. Mr. Backus, our art teacher, is taking over my class this period. How are you? I was wondering what was up when I got your message. It sounded important." We walked through the administration area to the conference room.

The teacher opened the door. A set of fluorescent bulbs automatically flickered on and flooded the room with cold-blue light. I recognized it as the room in which I had met the Student Study Team.

Mrs. Dorsey closed the door behind us and pulled out two chairs. We sat next to each other at the corner of the conference table.

I shivered and rubbed my hands together. I was glad I had worn my jacket.

"I'm sorry that the room is so cool, Mrs. Golden. It's like this when no one has used it for a while."

I nodded and smiled. I leaned forward and blinked rapidly as I began to tell Mrs. Dorsey why Conner wasn't in school yesterday. My voice was low and tremulous as I described his convulsion, the E.R. visit and his anti-seizure medication.

I registered the genuine shock in Mrs. Dorsey's voice when she finally spoke. "Mrs. Golden, I'm so sorry! Certainly, I will keep an eye on Conner. Our school nurse will, too. It's really good that you let us know," she gushed. "We appreciate it. I mean, I have taught other children with epilepsy before, and we—"

"Conner does *not* have epilepsy, Mrs. Dorsey. *No one* said that he has epilepsy! He had a seizure. That is *all!* The doctor said that it's not epilepsy." My stomach churned; I tasted sour coffee in the back of my throat. I glared into her green eyes. How dare she say that Conner had epilepsy! I couldn't let Conner get that label: "epileptic." I would not let anyone even think it. It had come to this.

I was suffering and, oddly, it was a shameful feeling. I shouldn't have sunk to such depths. I couldn't help how I felt then—illogical, but it was the truth. Illness had come to my family. It was going to be up to me to be strong and to support my son.

Mrs. Dorsey touched my arm and lowered her head. She said in a near-whisper, "No, of course not, Mrs. Golden. I'm not—I'm not a doctor. I am sorry. I didn't mean—"

I exhaled, suddenly embarrassed and guilty for my outburst. She truly was sweet. "No, no, *I'm* sorry Mrs. Dorsey. You did not deserve that. I'm not—I shouldn't have—it's just—" I bent my head into my cupped hands as uncontrollable sobs racked my body.

Mrs. Dorsey put her hand on my shoulder. "I'm sure everything will turn out all right for Conner. Please don't cry. Please, Mrs. Golden. You'll see." I looked up and saw tears welling in her eyes. Dark spots appeared on the emerald-green scarf around her neck.

Mrs. Dorsey grabbed a wad of tissues from a pink box on the table. She gave some to me and kept the rest. We blew our noses, leaned back in our chairs and looked at one another. Then we laughed, both dabbing our eyes and cheeks. For these moments, the shared emotions melded us.

I said softly, "Look at us! Thank you, Mrs. Dorsey. I am so sorry. I have to go, now. I'll talk to you later. Thank you for your concern about Conner." I stood up. I had to get out of there and be alone.

The teacher reached over and placed her palm over my hand. "No apology necessary. I understand. Again, I appreciate your telling me what happened to Conner," she added as she looked up at me. "We'll keep an eye on him." Then she stood.

I grabbed my purse and hurried out of the room.

CHAPTER 22

T he following week I returned from an early-afternoon errand with Madison and received the call I had been waiting for. I phoned Sam in a flush of excitement. "Honey? Sam? The neurologist's office just called. Conner's appointment is on Friday after school. Isn't that great? I think—I hope—Conner will be able to stop taking those pills then."

"That would be great, but we don't know if the doctor will stop them—not for sure. We shouldn't get our hopes up prematurely, Sandra."

Why did he always have to do that? Why did he always have to smother my confidence, my optimism? Why couldn't he just agree and be hopeful, too? "I know, Sam, but Dr. Choy told us that all of Conner's tests were normal. Even *he* said that the neurologist probably would stop the Dilantin. Remember? He *said* that. I remember it. Don't you?"

I was holding on, clinging to my very own one-person "lifeboat." I knew that this was illogical, wishful magical thinking, but I would not let go of these hopes.

"No, Sandra. He said—whatever. Fine. We will clear everything up on Friday. That will be good for Conner. It'll be good for all of us."

This was not what I wanted or needed to hear: his typical pessimism. He would say it was his *realism*. "We're having steak for dinner. 'Bye." I hung up.

"What are you doing, Mommy?" Madison padded down the stairs to find me circling the kitchen like a merry-go-round. I had been singing and clanging pans together, preparing to bake.

"I'm going to make a special dessert for tonight, honey—a surprise for Daddy and Conner. Chocolate biscotti! Do you want to help Mommy, little one?"

I hummed and twirled as I opened cupboards and brought out more ingredients. I grabbed a bag of gourmet-chocolate nuggets and a bag of walnuts. "We all love my chocolate biscotti, and there's just enough time to make it before our men get home. Do you know what, precious one? Conner should be able to stop taking those pills in two days. *Two days!* Won't that be great, sweetheart?"

I whirled like a dervish. I glided and spun from the refrigerator to the cupboard to the cutting board and back again as I poured and measured, mixed, kneaded and chopped the ingredients.

I tied an apron around Madison's little waist. She knelt on a chair at the kitchen table and pushed a rolling pin back and forth over an empty cutting board. She hummed with me, too.

I put the tray of biscotti into the oven. The essence of chocolate filled the kitchen. I telephoned my parents to tell them about Conner's upcoming appointment and reconfirmed that no one else in our family ever had seizures. Then I called Kathy and Marge, my two closest friends, to share my excitement.

"Yes, Conner should be able to stop taking those pills in two days. I really hope so, I pray so. It's what I've read on the Internet. We'll finally get to the bottom of this whole nightmare, and that should be the end of it."

When Sam and Conner came home, I hugged and kissed them and hurried them off to wash for supper. Everyone loved the meal.

After we put the children to bed, Sam and I lingered over wine, talking on the couch in the den. It had been a good day—until now. I drank more than usual, a second glass just so he couldn't drink the whole bottle by himself. He wanted to start a second bottle. "No, Sam. We've both had enough. You, especially. Please! You need to cut back. You never used to drink this much."

His lips curled with a defiant glare. I froze. No arguments now, please…

He got up and brought out another bottle from the cabinet. Then his eyes darted swiftly between the bottle and me while he seemed to consider the situation. Slowly, he articulated each syllable: "I'm not *ready* to cut back, as you say."

"Oh Sam. There's so much happening with our family. I'm starting to think that we might not survive this."

"Aw, c'mon. What are you talking about? It's not that serious." He began to cut off the cover over the cork.

I sat forward and looked up at him. "I'm telling you how it is, Sam. Now I'm going to tell you something else—something about me. I admit it. I've buried what's really happening. I know that's what you think. Nevertheless, I just had to. I'm so worried about Conner and for all of us. No one has yet told us why he had that convulsion. Not really. I've swallowed what Choy and Bob Jackson fed me—that the neurologist will agree with what they both told us. That he could stop the Dilantin. What if this neurologist finds something terrible in Conner's brain even if the tests were normal? I've read about all kinds of terrible diseases on the Internet. Doctors make mistakes; it happens all the time. Everybody knows that. I need you with me now. Now, especially…" I felt drops roll down my cheeks and wetness ooze from my nose as I stared up into his face. I pulled out a tissue from my pocket.

His expression softened. "I—I—Okay, honey. Conner will be all right. You'll see. He's a strong kid." He lowered himself onto the couch next to me with the dark bottle still in his hand. He laid the corkscrew on the coffee table. "I'm sorry. I hear you. Yeah. Okay. No more, tonight. I *have* been trying to cut back, honey. I have. It's hard." He stood the bottle on the coffee table and put his arm around my shoulders. I curled into his chest as he pulled me toward him.

"Oh, Sam."

"Come on, honey. You're so wound up with all these suppositions: they'll stop the medicines; he'll be on them forever. Just ease up and go with the flow. Isn't that what you've always said? It'll work out. Come on, Sandra. Remember Mark Twain? He was right. He'd 'crossed many a bridge that never was there.'"

I looked into his eyes and managed a weak smile. "So, now *you're* the one glossing over the problem and encouraging *me*? Nice."

⚬✖⚬

Sam snored softly in his sleep. I tossed, turned and then gave up. Quietly, I rose in the darkness and slid into my slippers and bathrobe. I tiptoed down the hall. Madison's and Conner's still forms and the sounds of soft, regular breathing comforted me.

The study doorknob felt cold as I closed it. I switched on the desk lamp. It illuminated the sheets of notes I had already made on my seizure research.

I drummed my fingers on the desk as I looked out into the cold, clear, indigo March night sky. I loved the color the sky was now. An occasional wind buffeted the windows. I shivered and wrapped my robe tighter around me as the computer screen came to life. The desktop screen showed my favorite picture of the kids taken last summer. They smiled in their vegetable garden out back. I clicked on the Internet Explorer icon. It was time to find out about Conner's neurologist.

I typed "Hal O'Rourke." The screen filled with pages of references for those key words. I scrolled down until I found a link for the neurologist's website. The homepage displayed a photograph of a smiling, avuncular, clean-shaven middle-aged man. He wore a white doctor's coat over a blue buttoned-down shirt and a bright blue, red and yellow-striped bow tie. I smiled. One didn't see bow ties very often. I leaned in.

Dr. O'Rourke was a full professor of neurology. He had been in practice for more than twenty-six years. He had done a tropical-medicine fellowship in Papua New Guinea as a medical student. I wondered if there were cannibals and headhunters over there. Conner would be intrigued by this. He and his friends were always watching TV shows about exotic animals and people who lived in jungles.

The next page showed several pictures of Hal O'Rourke as a young medical student in a primitive world doing medical things and tramping around tropical forests. In one photograph, he posed with a large white parrot on his arm. In another, he held a huge hypodermic needle stuck in the side of a native lying on a table in a mud-floored, jungle operating room. I squinted at the monitor. I was horrified to see that there were no screens on the windows. People leaned through them to watch. I guessed that was how they lived there. I would be dead in a week without modern conveniences.

The bibliography of Dr. O'Rourke's research papers went on for several pages. I read a list of his research articles. They were about headaches and other unfamiliar medical conditions published in medical journals.

What followed was a little astonishing: a section called "Shakespeare and Neurology." It listed Dr. O'Rourke's articles about that great dramatist. If he was doing all of these other things—and this literature research—did he have enough time to be a really good doctor? Did he know enough about seizures? According to the article, Dr. O'Rourke had studied every neurological symptom that had ever been mentioned in Shakespeare's works.

The English major in me was immediately fascinated. As I continued to read my confidence in this neurologist returned. Othello and Julius Caesar had epilepsy. King Lear had delirium and "an epileptic visage." Juliet's nurse got migraines. Shakespeare even described how alcohol's damage to the liver affected thinking. A character in another play had double vision. Others were incontinent and a few were demented. I laughed quietly. This was wild.

The last page listed awards and some lectures he had given at medical conferences around the world.

My gut instinct—a mother's instinct—spoke to me. My Conner would like him. Dr. O'Rourke could be the man to make everything all right again. He had been doing this for a long time, after all. One more day and then we would get some answers.

My eyelids drooped and my head started to nod. I leaned back and closed my eyes. Once again, haiku images coalesced:

Huge waves roaring in—
Crashing over jagged rocks—
A swimmer reached home.

CHAPTER 23

I rarely remembered my dreams, but the images that woke me the night before Conner's neurology appointment were a nightmare: a horse was chasing me, and no matter how fast I ran I could still feel its steamy breath on the back of my neck. I slipped and fell into an open pit and suffocated at the bottom.

My eyes sprang open. My pillow was damp. I gasped for air and understood: the images represented Conner's crisis. My mind whirred with questions: what would the neurologist find today? What would he do? Could Conner have a brain tumor, after all?

I couldn't let go of the deep terror I had felt ever since his seizure. Moreover, it wasn't just Conner's seizure; it was *our* seizure. *My* seizure. I clasped my sweaty hands on my chest and stared at the ceiling.

I could no longer fight that other memory that was starting to haunt me: Sheila Braun lived next-door to me for a short time when I was in high school. She had epilepsy. She even had to stop driving. I remembered how she sobbed as she told me that she was afraid to have children because she might pass it on when she got married—*if* ever she got married. I remembered our horror as she showed me awful pictures of epileptics in asylums from a long time ago. I cried with her. I hadn't thought of Sheila in years.

❧

I moved robot-like all morning. I stared at the wall and then out the window. I walked toward the bathroom, stopped, shook my head and turned back to the kitchen. A couple of times I opened the refrigerator and just stood there. Then I closed it without taking anything out. I had to make sure that I had thought of all the questions I was going to ask the neurologist that afternoon. I wandered back to the sink and leaned against the kitchen counter. I clicked my fingernails against my coffee cup and stared out the window.

"Sandra, are you okay?"

I looked at Sam. "This is making me crazy!"

"Sandra—"

"I'll be right back." I bolted out of the kitchen and rushed upstairs.

A moment later I was at my desk, pen in hand. I reached for the paper with the questions I had written down days ago. I chewed the end of my pen and reconsidered my questions:

1. *Will Conner ever be normal again?* The doctors had warned us that he could have another seizure. Now he was taking those pills with all of those side effects. Would the medicines change him from the sweet little boy that we all knew?

2. *Will people treat him like a freak?* Ever since Conner's seizure, Sam and I had become very cautious around our son. I would gladly have kept Conner home from school or even home-schooled him until he had the appointment with the neurologist. Even Sam had started to coddle the boy: he didn't let Conner play touch football or soccer or even ride his bike with his friends. That wasn't like Sam. I was worried that other children would make fun of Conner now.

3. *Could Madison have a seizure?* I had read that seizures could run in families; that epilepsy was sometimes passed along genetically. Sam's brother had one. Was it possible that seizures were contagious, like a cold?

4. *Does Conner have epilepsy?*

I took a deep breath and leaned back in the chair. Getting answers to these questions would help me get a sense of control over this new craziness in my life. But would I actually gain control of Conner's situation? Of that, I had no such delusion.

When I returned to the kitchen, Sam was sitting alone over his coffee. He seemed mesmerized by the shadows cast from the window blinds. The stripes just missed the morning paper spread out in front of him.

"Sam? Are you all right?"

"I'm trying not to focus on the appointment. If you must know, it's all that I can think about." He lifted the steaming cup to his lips. He leaned back in the chair and stretched his legs out. He stared straight ahead.

I wrapped my arms around his shoulders. "Yeah, I know. Me too." I took the chair next to him.

"Conner had such a good day on Monday. The kids had been joking and giggling all throughout dinner. Sandra, do you remember how Conner began making those grotesque faces while he tried to knot that cherry stem with his tongue? You know, inside his mouth. The kids laughed so hard, gobs of their hot fudge sundaes sprayed out of both their mouths. Remember? Chopped nuts, whipped cream, ice cream and all. And when you scolded them, it just made them laugh harder. You couldn't help laughing, too. That was so great."

His smile faded. He turned the pages of the newspaper without looking down. "After today, do you think we will be able to laugh like that again?"

He stood up. "Okay. Gotta go. I have to visit the new construction site. I'll be home by two; don't worry. I won't be late. I'll say goodbye to the kids." He kissed me and left.

Sam came home on time as he had promised. I approached Conner's bedroom; his door was closed. I tried to remember how old I was when I began to shut my door against my parents' intrusion. He didn't answer my knock. "Conner, are you ready? It's time to go." He didn't respond. "I'm coming in, honey." I opened the door.

"I don't want to go," he protested. He sat cross-legged on the floor and didn't look up at me.

"I know, honey. But Daddy and I will be with you. It'll be all right. We want you to be able to stop those medicines if you don't need them, and only this neurologist can decide that. He needs to talk to you and find out why that seizure happened."

"I don't want any needles!"

"I know. You've said that. You know that whenever you had to get a shot or a blood test, it wasn't so bad. That's how life is, Conner. Things usually are not as bad as you expect them to be."

Conner began to hit the floor with both fists. "I'm not going! No! You go!"

Sam called from downstairs, "Let's go, people! We don't want to be late. Mrs. Hall just drove up to stay with Madison."

"I'm not going!"

Sam bounded up the stairs and loomed over his son. "Conner, let's go. Get up. Right now, son!" He scooped the boy into a standing position. "'Atta-boy!" Conner offered no further resistance—not when his father was in this mood.

We settled into the SUV and buckled up. Sam appeared calm and in control, but I saw that his breathing was fast. When he turned his head to back out of the driveway, he glanced at Conner. I turned, too. Conner stared out his window. His fingers were pressed against his mouth, and I saw his lips move silently behind them.

Sam relaxed his grip on the steering wheel. He flexed his fingers a few times. I looked straight ahead, but I sensed his eyes on me, his mind working. Other than a soft cough into my hand a couple of times, no one uttered a sound.

He placed his hand on mine. I moved my hand away from his and onto my lap. I saw him shrug out of the corner of my eye.

Conner announced that he would count all of the blue cars that we passed. "That's a good idea. Can I help?" I twisted around in my seat and reached for his hand.

"No, Mom." He snatched his hand away. After a few moments, he said, "I'm going to count crows now." He had counted fifty-eight of the birds perched on telephone wires and utility poles by the time we arrived at the medical office building. "I thought if I counted a hundred crows before we got here, Daddy would turn around and drive me home."

"Oh?" I said. We had stopped the car. Sam opened Conner's door and waited for him to get out.

Conner screwed his face into a scowl. "Oh, *man*," he groaned. Sam bent over and released his seat belt. Conner slowly swung his legs over the edge of the seat. I saw his widened eyes bore into his father's.

"Come on, son."

Conner shuffled away from the vehicle. At first, he tried to drag behind Sam and me. Then we each took one of his hands and approached the main entrance.

People were coming and going through the big brass and glass doors. Some of them were even kids. I looked down at Conner. The way his eyes followed kids who were exiting, I could imagine how he wanted to be one of them.

"I have to go to the bathroom," Conner announced when we got inside.

"Okay. Me too. Let's go." Sam, still holding Conner's hand, led the way. I scanned the directory and made a note of Dr. O'Rourke's suite number. Then I leaned against the cool granite wall. There was an odor—not unpleasant, like mothballs that I remembered from my childhood. Whatever happened to mothballs? Were they still around?

As I watched people pass, an occasional gaze fixed onto mine. But one of us looked away before any dutiful acknowledgment was prompted. A few individuals with casts on their limbs were pushed in squeaky wheelchairs. Others swung casted legs and thumped rubber-tipped crutches as they hobbled by. Several elderly people pushed walkers that scratched and scraped along the hard floor as they shuffled down the corridor. One or two had shaking hands and heads. Many walked with stooped postures and leaned heavily on companions or on canes that ticked rhythmically on the dark marble.

My eyes fell on a youngish man pushing a child in a stroller. A woman, probably his wife, walked beside him. The girl looked too old to be in a stroller. Then I noticed twisted arms up on her chest and that she drooled and stared straight ahead. I looked back at the adults' somber faces. I shut my eyes. The broken conversations and the other sounds that echoed in the corridor hammered my ears.

"You okay?" Sam asked.

I opened my eyes. "Of course." I flashed a weak smile and pushed my arm under Sam's as we entered the elevator. Conner turned his head all around at the unfamiliar clanging and humming sounds as its old doors closed.

The car ascended, and I regarded his distorted reflection in the shiny brass door. Conner looked taller and skinnier. His arms were slightly extended; each of us was holding one of his hands.

"If my arms were wings and you let me go, Mom, I would fly home now." His chin quivered.

"I know, honey. I know." I smiled and gave his hand a squeeze.

The elevator stopped and its doors squeaked open. Conner tugged back but we just gripped his hands more firmly. The gold painted words on a shiny, dark wooden door—Hal O'Rourke, M.D., Neurology, EEG, EMG/NCV—loomed before us.

"This is it," Sam said and opened the door.

The waiting room was quiet. It smelled sweet, not like the sour odor of Dr. Jackson's noisy pediatric office. Dark-green cushioned chairs lined the pale walls. A tan tweed carpet with brown flecks fit the quiet mood. Floor lamps in each corner created a soft glow, and a tall vase filled with purple silk irises sat prominently on a low corner table. Several rows of news and entertainment magazines lay neatly on another low table in the middle of the room.

I turned Conner away from the wall displays of brochures titled *EEG* and *Epilepsy*. I would pick them up when we left.

A slim, elderly man sat hunched in a wheelchair. Short white stubble covered his face. His head was mostly bald, but long strands of limp, white hair hung over his ears. He drooled slightly, and both hands shook more than his head.

"Gee, why's that old guy shivering so much? It's not *that* cold in here," Conner whispered loudly.

I whispered in his ear, "Shh, Conner. He's sick. That's why."

There were several bright-yellow stains on the front of the old man's wrinkled, open-necked white shirt. I saw the top of his white undershirt at the opening. An oversized black belt was pulled so far around his thin waist that the end of it hung down out of the loops of his dark-blue trousers. He wasn't wearing socks, and his ankles were fat and white against his scuffed black shoes.

A younger man sat just behind the trembling man's wheelchair. He was reading *Time* magazine. Both turned to look at us. The younger man smiled and quickly retreated into his magazine. The elderly man looked at Conner as we walked by.

"Hi there, sonny," he croaked in a low, hoarse voice. His cracked lips broke into a smile that revealed a row of crooked yellow teeth. His breath smelled stale.

"Hi." Conner mumbled. Conner looked away and moved closer to me. Sam and I nodded and smiled at him.

"Let's sit over here, son." Sam put a hand on Conner's shoulder and guided him to a chair across the room.

I walked over to the receptionist's desk. I detected the sweet, citrus scent of her perfume.

The slightly built middle-aged woman looked up from her computer. Her short silver hair waved behind one ear to expose a lapis lazuli earring. Deep-blue eyes peered out from her long, pale thin face that embellished her cheery smile. Glasses on a sparkly neck chain lay on the tan sweater that covered the woman's flat chest. Her unusually narrow nose, placed too far above her similarly thin lips, fascinated me. I would not say she was pretty, but her demeanor, posture and confident air fashioned a striking woman.

"Hello. May I help you?"

"Yes. Our son, Conner Golden, has an appointment this afternoon."
I looked down at the nameplate on her desk. "One of my grandmothers
was named Hannah. I've always liked that name."

"Thank you." She smiled broadly. "So do I." Hannah turned back to
her computer screen. "Ah, yes, here you are: Conner Golden. The doctor
is right on time. Let me give you these registration forms to fill out for
our records. And these are for the insurance company." She handed me
a packet of papers attached to a clipboard. "Do you need a pen?"

I shook my head. "No thank you." I sat down next to Conner and
began to fill out the forms. After a moment, I sensed that I was being
watched. I looked up. Hannah's kind eyes were on me. We exchanged
a perfunctory smile and looked away.

Meanwhile, Conner kept stealing glances at the old man. "I have to
tell Michael about that funny old guy shivering," he whispered.

Sam tapped Conner's thigh and frowned. "Shh."

Conner slouched in his chair and watched his legs swing in unison.
The tips of his soft shoes repeatedly scraped the carpet.

"Stop that, Conner," Sam quietly admonished.

He turned toward his father. "Daddy, what's the doctor going to
do?" Conner sat up straighter and gripped the armrests.

"I really don't know. I guess he is going to talk to us; check your
ears and eyes and all that stuff. You know." Sam looked down at his
son and smiled.

"No shots, though! I'll run out of here if he wants to give me a shot."

There he goes again with those shot worries, I thought.

Sam wrapped his arm around Conner's shoulder.

CHAPTER 24

Conner squeezed my hand as we followed Hannah to Dr. O'Rourke's office. I glanced at the framed art reproductions that adorned the corridor walls; several looked familiar. As soon as we entered his office, I detected the aromas of cinnamon, apple and coffee, but I couldn't see any lunch leftovers or candles or anything.

"This is Conner Golden, Doctor." She then turned toward us, nodded and with a face-lit smile announced, "Mr. and Mrs. Golden." Hannah then indicated the neurologist with her open palm. "And this is Dr. O'Rourke." She left and pulled the door closed behind her. My heart quickened.

The man whom I recognized from the website smiled, stood up and came around his desk to greet us. He was several inches shorter than Sam and only an inch or so taller than me. The doctor's bow tie was not the same as the one in his website portrait. This one's butterflied wings were deep red and arrayed with narrow, bright blue and yellow diagonal stripes. His temples were gray; the rest of his head was covered with dark, medium-length hair parted on the left. The crown of his head had a neat, round bald spot that reminded me of the tonsure that monks wore in paintings from the Middle Ages. The corners of his light-blue eyes wrinkled with a warm smile. A slight paunch pushed aside the edges of his unbuttoned knee-length white coat.

Dr. O'Rourke smiled even more broadly as he extended his hand to Conner. Our boy pressed against his father's torso. Sam smiled and gently pushed Conner out in front of him with his palm. Our child's eyes widened as he looked up at the neurologist with a guarded expression.

At Sam's encouragement, he extended his arm and shook the doctor's hand. He reached for mine with his other hand and looked down. His small palm was icy-cold.

The doctor leaned forward and regarded Conner's hand. Several of the fingers were stained with blue and red ink that I couldn't remove from his recent art project. "Hello, Conner. I'm Dr. O'Rourke. It's very nice to meet you. I see that you've been doing some painting."

Conner looked at his right hand, which was mostly enveloped in the doctor's. Then he cast a sideways glance at the doctor and flashed a shy smile.

"I'm so sorry, Dr. O'Rourke. I couldn't wash off all of the ink from Conner's hands. My son is into mythology, and he likes to draw and paint Greek and Roman and Egyptian characters."

Still leaning over Conner he exclaimed, "Mythology! Hey, now! Wow! And you are only in the third grade? You're eight, right?"

"I'm eight and a half." Conner cocked his head and grinned with widened eyes. Sam and I both smiled at our son's brisk retort.

The neurologist nodded several times and looked up at us. His broad grin exposed a small chip off his left lower-front tooth. "That's a pretty sophisticated subject for a third-grader. You must be really smart."

The small talk was helping our son get comfortable with this man in the white coat. I saw him turn his attention to the certificates and pictures on the walls and to the books on the shelves as we chatted.

"Do you also know the Scandinavian stories and the Native American mythology tales too, Conner?" Dr. O'Rourke cocked his head, raised his eyebrows and waited for his young patient's response.

Conner grinned with growing enthusiasm. "Oh yeah. I know pretty much all of them. They're on my computer. I have tons of mythology games. I play with Zeus and the Titans and the Greek Underworld. There's some stuff about the Vikings too, but not much about the American Indian ones." Conner waved his hands and shifted his weight from foot to foot as he described his favorite mythology games to the neurologist.

I smiled and felt a bursting feeling in my chest. Sam had a proud grin.

"That is *wonderful*, Conner." The doctor indicated three matching dark-green cushioned chairs in front of his desk. "Please! Everyone have a seat. Why don't you sit here, Conner," he pointed to the middle chair. Dr. O'Rourke lowered himself into a cordovan-shaded leather armchair behind his large mahogany desk.

"I've been reading Dr. Choy's notes, and I've had a look at the results of all of your lab tests, Conner. I'm pleased to say that everything seems normal." He smiled at me and then at Sam. "That's great news. Let me explain more about the records that I've seen."

Even though the doctor's friendly and confident demeanor was reassuring, I couldn't relax. My jaws clamped and my hands pressed down in my lap. There was some pressure in the sides of my head and I breathed quickly.

The neurologist placed both hands on the desk and leaned toward us. Sam leaned forward, too—he clasped his hands between his legs. I was aware of my rapid breathing; I tried to control it. I exhaled and sat back in my chair. I crossed my legs. Conner's brows furrowed, which added to his cautious, serious expression.

"Conner, do you want to see pictures of your brain on the CT scan? They're really interesting." Dr. O'Rourke angled the computer monitor so we all could see the images. "Have you studied the body and the brain in school yet?"

"No." Conner stood up and leaned against the desk.

"That's right. Get close so that you can see," Dr. O'Rourke said.

Conner propped his elbows on the desk and cupped his chin and cheeks in both palms. "Gee! Wow! My brain! It looks just like on TV shows, only this is *way* cooler. That's really *me*? That's really *my brain*?"

I looked at the black, gray and white images on his computer monitor.

The neurologist smiled at Conner. "Yes, it is. This is your brain. Here are your smelling nerves, your eyes and ears." His index finger showed us where Conner's balancing center was and the muscles that made his eyeballs move. Then he explained how thinking, speaking, comprehending, remembering, moving, seeing, touching and feeling happened in specific parts of the brain as he indicated them.

He indicated the cerebrospinal fluid that surrounded the brain and filled the chambered ventricles. "Dr. Choy obtained some of this fluid from your lower back when he took care of you in the emergency room, Conner. It was a very important part of your examination, and it was entirely normal."

Conner reached behind and touched his lower back. His eyes widened and his mouth opened as he turned toward me. "That's why I had that Band-Aid on my back when I came home from the hospital, right Mom?"

I nodded and touched my son's shoulder. He turned back to the doctor.

Sam leaned closer to the screen.

The neurologist sat back and propped his elbows on the armrests. He steepled his fingers under his chin. "Everything in your brain looks normal, Conner. Now, let's find out how it's working."

Conner stiffened. "You're not going to give me any shots, are you?" I saw him glare at a small red ball that was on the tip of a long, thin pin protruding from the lapel of the doctor's white coat.

I touched Conner's neck. I wondered what the neurologist did with that long pin in his lapel. I counted three pens and a small flashlight in his left breast pocket. A thin handle with a pointed end protruded from the side pocket of his white coat. I glanced over the framed diplomas and certificates on the walls. I got a sense that they were staring down at my son, and modern medical science and all of its mystery were about to scrutinize him. My hands were cold.

"Conner, right now I'm going to ask you some questions about how you're feeling. Then we will all go into the exam room, and I'll check you out there. Your parents can come too; there won't be any shots or blood tests." He smiled at Sam and me.

I appreciated how Dr. O'Rourke reassured our boy. Still, Conner anxiously snapped his head around to look at his father. Sam nodded back. Then he glanced down at the spot where his IV had been. The bruise on his arm was mostly faded and had turned a pale bluish-yellow. He rubbed his arm and looked at Dr. O'Rourke.

Sam glanced over at me. We were poised to say something or to touch our son to reassure him. However, there he was, listening and seeming to understand everything the doctor said.

"Now, do you remember the night that the seizure happened?" The doctor looked down at the papers on his desk. "When was that, about a week and a half ago?"

I nodded. "Uh-huh."

Conner tilted his head and frowned. "I didn't feel good."

The doctor looked at me. "Mom, can you tell me what happened?"

I described that evening: Conner sneezing and coughing in his sleep, his high temperature, hearing the strange noises coming from his bedroom, finding him jerking all over the bed, the wet sheet and blanket, all that blood in his mouth...

"My tongue got bit. It still hurts!" Conner blurted. He opened his mouth. "Thee?" He lisped as he protruded his tongue.

We all looked at the almost-healed blue laceration.

I heaved a sigh to slow my breathing. I put my cold fingers under my thighs to warm my hands. "Then there was that rush to the hospital and Dr. Choy."

Dr. O'Rourke glanced again at the hospital notes in front of him on his desk. The neurologist smiled and drew a deep breath.

Before he could continue I sat forward and interjected, "Doctor, I, uh, *we* were hoping"—I flashed a glance at Sam's querulous face—"Uh, we were hoping to stop the Dilantin as soon as possible. Do you think that we can?"

"We'll see, Mrs. Golden. Dr. Choy did a thorough job screening Conner for causes of that seizure. I see that he put Conner on Dilantin. That medication *may not* be necessary. Your boy is a bit old for his convulsion to be secondary to just a fever, though. Let me find out a bit more. I need more information."

I beamed at Sam and squeezed his hand. *Yes!* He was confirming what I had learned from the Internet. The neurologist just said what I had been praying for. I leaned back in my chair.

But, he said that he would investigate further. That was when I pictured a detective with a baying hound that scurried right and left over the ground smelling out prey. So there it was again. Something wasn't right for these doctors. Dr. Choy had said something like that about the convulsion and Conner's older age, too. What wasn't Dr. O'Rourke telling us? I got the feeling that he was taking care not to terrify my already-shaken family. I don't exactly know why—I felt some ominous undertone.

Dr. O'Rourke asked, "Has Conner ever passed out or fainted in the past?"

"No. But, you know, I wanted to ask you: Sam's brother had something similar when he was an infant. He had a fever then, too. That was the only time it happened though. Right, Sam?" Sam nodded. "I've heard that seizures can run in families. Is that true? God, I hope not…" My voice trailed off.

"They can."

I clasped my hands and leaned forward. Then I sat on my fingers again.

Dr. O'Rourke turned and addressed his patient. "Conner, have you ever blanked out when you're thinking about something?"

"Uh, like…what?"

I looked at Conner. Sam did, too. Why did Conner say that? I got this uneasy feeling that Conner somehow understood what the doctor was hinting at. Sam's mouth dropped open. He looked at me; his eyes narrowed.

The neurologist cleared his throat and leaned forward over his desk. "I mean, let's say that you're thinking about something, or watching a movie or a TV program, or someone is talking to you. Does it ever seem as though you suddenly missed what was happening? Like your mind went blank all of a sudden. I don't mean daydreaming; everybody does that. When you daydream, your mind is still thinking of something—like you zone out—but you know it. Let's say something is important to you and you are really paying attention."

Dr. O'Rourke stole a quick glance at Sam and me. Then he looked back at Conner and continued, "And then, all of a sudden, the scene in the movie or on the TV screen has changed, and—" He clapped his hands once. "Suddenly you don't know what happened, even though you were following the story really closely. Has that ever happened to you?"

Conner leaned forward in his chair and dug his fingers hard into the edge of the doctor's desk. I saw white at their tips. "Well, um, sometimes I get these, uh...you know, I get this funny, this *ding* feeling. I don't know, I—I—and then something else has happened and I don't know what."

What? Sam and I looked at each other. My jaw dropped. My body tightened and my voice was loud. "What do you *mean*, Conner? What *ding* feeling? What are you *saying*? When does this happen?"

He turned toward me. "A lot. When it happens at school Mrs. Dorsey gets mad at me."

"Mrs. Dorsey gets *mad* at you? What do you mean? Why? What happens?" I grabbed his arm.

I looked at Dr. O'Rourke. He sucked in his cheeks and his lips pursed as he slowly nodded his head one time. His eyes moved down to my hand that gripped Conner's arm. Otherwise, he maintained a placid expression as he watched us.

"She asks me if I...um...if, uh...I need more time to do my tests. Like that spelling test. She said I needed more time...um...to finish."

"Did you finish? Did you need more time? Which was it?"

"I—I don't know. I don't know!" Conner's chin quivered.

Dr. O'Rourke picked up his pencil and held it poised over his notepad. "What you're telling us is very helpful, Conner."

I released Conner's arm and leaned back in my chair. As my legs straightened, my shoes kicked the bottom of the neurologist's desk. What was he saying? None of this made sense.

Dr. O'Rourke licked his lower lip. "How often does this happen, Conner? This ding?"

Conner shrugged. "I dunno…I dunno. I don't!"

"Well, what would you say? Does it happen every day? Does it happen every few days, or every few weeks or months?"

"I dunno. A couple of times, I guess."

"Did it happen today?"

"No." Conner sniffled.

"Did it happen yesterday, Conner?"

"No."

"Does it happen a lot?"

"It doesn't happen every day…I think." He shuddered and hiccupped back a sob. He looked at me. Tears started to roll down his cheeks. His chin trembled. When I leaned over to wrap my arm around his shoulders he sobbed louder. "I'm scared. I'm scared, Mom!" He wiped his cheek with his sleeve.

I stared out and couldn't move for a moment. I was in slow motion. Everything was in slow motion. I took some tissues out of my pocket and began to wipe his tears. My ice-cold hand shook. "Don't be scared, honey. You're doing fine."

My gaze darted between Conner and the doctor. Sam stared at our son; his cheek muscles rippled.

"Yes, you *are* doing just fine, Conner. This is very good, very helpful." Dr. O'Rourke kept his gaze fixed on his patient. "Now, do you ever imagine that you smell something that's not really there, that nobody else can smell? Do you ever get a taste that just came into your mouth without eating anything?"

Conner gave a tiny nod.

"Is it a smell or a taste, Conner?"

"I think I smell something…um, uh…but I don't know what it is."

"Well, is it like something bad, Conner? Like, burning rubber? Something like that?"

"Yeah!" Conner's face brightened. He nodded vigorously. "That's it! That's what it is. It smells like the things Daddy burns in the yard at work." Animated now, he scrunched up his nose and his body rocked back and forth as he nodded. "It's gross," he added.

I couldn't believe what I was hearing. I looked at Sam. What was Conner talking about? Why had he hidden this?

The neurologist continued, "And then what happens, Conner?"

"I don't know!" Conner wiped his nose on the cuff of his shirtsleeve.

Dr. O'Rourke turned to me. "Have you ever witnessed one of his ding spells? Have you talked with his teacher about them?"

"I don't even know what Conner is talking about. I've never seen anything like that!" I looked at Sam. "Have you? He's never said anything about them to me."

"No. I've been away so long. I served in the Army in Iraq this past year, Doctor. I just got back two months ago."

Dr. O'Rourke held his gaze on Sam. "I see."

"The school had him evaluated by a school psychologist because he wasn't completing his class assignments," I volunteered. "Everybody thought his problem was stress from, you know, because his father was deployed in Iraq. I arranged for him to be treated by a psychologist, Dr. Frank Thomas. Conner has already seen him a few times."

Conner lowered his head and curled his fingers in his lap.

"I know him." The neurologist nodded.

"Could these spells be causing him to fall behind in school? You know, it turned out that his teacher from last year thought he could do better work then, too. They had no idea why he was not. And now, you're saying that these things...these things could have...could have been going on for a whole year, Doctor?" I turned to Conner. My eyes narrowed and my voice got louder. "Conner, these have been happening for a year? Or more? Why didn't you say something, honey? Why didn't you tell us?"

"Sandra." Sam reached for my hand. I snatched it away.

I pressed my lips together and shook my head. "I don't believe this!"

"Conner, when did these dings start?" The doctor asked. His voice was gentle and even. I looked at my lap and tried to organize my thoughts. Dr. O'Rourke continued, "Do you remember when you had the first ding, your first one?"

"I—I don't know."

"Well, did they start a month ago? A few months ago? Before Christmas? Did they start last year, when you were still in second grade? Or, even before that? When do you think?" He smiled at our son. "Take your time. You're doing very well, Conner."

"Last year...um...I think, when I was in second grade. Yeah... ahh...second grade. I think..."

"And what do you mean by what you call 'dings,' Conner?"

"They're dings because...uh, uh...I guess, because they feel like, uh...like little dings. You know...I don't know."

The doctor nodded and regarded him for several seconds. "What does a ding feel like?"

"Um...I get this funny thing...I think it's down here." Conner looked down and touched his shirt right over his belly button. "Then I get scared...but I don't know why because there's nothing around to make me scared. You know. Then I smell that bad thing. And then...I don't know! I don't know!" He sniffed and wiped his nose with his sleeve.

Dr. O'Rourke directed a quick gaze at us and then back at Conner. "How long do the dings last, Conner?"

"I don't know!" He started to sob again. I flashed a weak smile at the doctor as I wiped my son's cheeks and put the tissue into his hand.

"Have you ever fallen down when a ding happens? Do they ever happen when you're standing up?"

He sniffed. "No...um...but, yeah, sometimes I fall when I'm running or playing a game."

Dr. O'Rourke smiled at him. "Do you think you fall because you're having a ding?"

"No." He snorted and wiped his nose with the tissue. "I'm just playing and...uh...I trip on something or somebody tackles me. But, sometimes I drop things...you know...when I have a...um...a ding."

"Oh, Conner. Why didn't you ever tell me you were having these things?" I tried to smother the panicked tone in my voice as I brushed a lock of hair out of his eyes. "Honey, have you had these dings at home? Have I ever been with you when they happen?" I turned back to the neurologist, "I can't recall seeing *anything* like what he's describing, Doctor."

"I don't know when they happen, Mommy." He sniffed again and rubbed his nose with his sleeve. "I don't."

The office was quiet now except for his sobs. It shimmered with the vibrations of our fear and pain—a pain that pierced and gripped me completely—an agony that I would carry and remember for the rest of my life. Whatever happened to my son would change—no, it had already irrevocably changed—our lives. Just weeks ago we were having the happiest of days: Sam came home from Iraq; we pulled into our driveway with him; neighbors welcomed him home; he put on his old clothes; the gifts he gave us; that wonderful first dinner with candles...

"Has Conner had any problems with bed-wetting?" Dr. O'Rourke asked me.

"Hm? Oh, ah...bed-wetting?" I looked at Conner. This was not the time to shelter him—not here in this office. "There've been a few times, and he's had a few accidents in his pants during the day. On laundry days—a few times I've found yellow stains on his underpants. They smelled like he had wet them."

Conner moaned, "Mo-om!" and looked up at me, his eyes pleading.

I placed my palm on the top of his head. "Honey, I'm so sorry. I don't mean to embarrass you, but this is important. The doctor has to know."

"Conner, do you lose your urine—your pee—during these spells?" The doctor asked softly.

"We-ell..." Conner looked at me.

I nodded. "You can answer the doctor, Conner."

He said, "Um...yeah."

"Do you know that you're going in your pants and you can't stop it? Or is it that all of a sudden you're wet and you didn't know that you were going?"

"I-I d-don't know that I-I've done it until I-I've d-done it," Conner stammered through his sobs.

"Have you ever pooped in your pants?" Dr. O'Rourke's voice was so low that I could barely make out what he said.

Conner gulped down a sob.

The neurologist cast a quick glance from Conner to us. "Has he had any bowel movements in his pants?"

"No, thank God." I shook my head.

"Has Conner ever bitten his tongue or lip when he's sleeping? Have you ever found blood on his pillow, Mrs. Golden?"

"Only on the night of his seizure, Doctor. I've never seen blood any other time."

"So it seems that he hasn't had any other convulsions in his sleep that you and Mr. Golden had not witnessed."

I shook my head and looked at Sam.

Dr. O'Rourke smiled at his patient and asked, "Conner, have you ever noticed any weakness in your arms or legs when you have a ding? It can be before the ding or after it, or at any other time."

"No." Conner shuddered.

"Good. What about tingling feelings? Have you ever had any tingling—you know, like the pins-and-needles you get if you hit your funny bone in your elbow—anyplace in your body when you have a ding?"

"Uh...no. I don't think so."

I wanted to know more, as I listened to their exchange. Yet, I feared more bad news.

"Conner, have you had any headaches or double-vision? You know, like seeing two things instead of one thing. And, do you ever have any trouble seeing out of one eye? Or numbness, like funny feelings that stay there on your face?"

"My face itches, sometimes." Conner scratched his cheek.

"Well, yes. That's normal. What about any funny or tingly feelings on your face when you get your dings?"

"No."

"What about swallowing or hearing problems? Do you ever hear strange noises or voices when there's no one talking and no one else around during your dings?"

"No." Conner shook his head.

"Which hand do you write with, Conner?"

"Um, my right hand." The boy held up his left hand, looked at it and quickly replaced it with his right. He turned toward me and gave me a tentative smile. He asked abashedly, "Is this my right hand, Mom?"

"That's good," Dr. O'Rourke said with a wide grin. He looked at me. "He is right-handed, correct?"

"Yes. He seems to write and draw with his right hand, Doctor."

I looked at Sam. So, he finally spoke up.

"Since he writes with his right hand, the middle section of the left side of Conner's brain is where his language center resides. In other words, it's his dominant side. That suggests that there's no serious structural problem in that part of Conner's brain, especially since he had a normal CT scan. You see, the left side of the brain is dominant for most people. If you or your son reported that he had speaking or comprehension problems—that is, difficulties understanding speech—it could be a clue that his seizures came from that left-sided language area. However, he will need an MRI—a Magnetic Resonance Imaging scan, with—"

"What's that? No! Will there be needles?" Conner leapt to his feet. Sam and I immediately reached up and touched his shoulders.

"Sit down, son." Sam tilted his head in the direction of the boy's seat.

Conner dropped hard onto his chair. He elevated his shoulders, opened his mouth and squinted at the neurologist. His voice quivered, "Will there be needles? Will there?"

"The MRI scan is just like the CT scan you had at the hospital. But, this time you'll be in a tunnel." The neurologist moved his gaze from Conner to Sam and then to me.

"Conner wasn't awake when he had the CT scan, Doctor O'Rourke. He was still asleep after the seizure."

"Oh. Okay. I see." He nodded and turned back to his patient. "Well, Conner, there shouldn't be any needles, but I can't promise. That will be up to the radiologist. That's the doctor who does the MRI. The radiologist will be evaluating the images as the scan is being done. If the doctor believes that more information is required, then an intravenous line may be started to inject a special dye, but—"

Conner pouted and crossed his arms over his chest. His swollen, red eyes welled up again.

"No. Wait, Conner! That won't be done unless it's absolutely necessary." Dr. O'Rourke reached across the desk and touched our child's hand. "The MRI shows the brain structures a little differently from the CT scan. It can give us additional, more detailed information. We—the doctors—need to be certain to rule out any problems.

"Look, Conner. We are going to become a team. From now on, we are going to be working—like playing—together, for a long time. I am going to be your coach. You are the star player. I will give you your rules and your plays. Your mom and dad will be like our team trainers. I'll tell you what the team will do."

I liked that metaphor. It should capture Conner's cooperation. Brilliant. I smiled at my son and touched his back.

Dr. O'Rourke watched us momentarily, then continued, "I know this can all be confusing, but usually we don't find any cause of epilepsy."

CHAPTER 25

*E*pilepsy! All my denial—my protective armor—shattered. But of course, something had been undercutting this realization for months. Why had he been wetting his pants at his age? And the times when I thought he was not paying attention and maybe he seemed confused. Dr. O'Rourke's interview…Conner's secrets…all his hidden spells…these *dings*…over a year. Oh, God. Oh, my God.

"Epilepsy? So, that's it. This is *epilepsy*. Oh, God!" I leaned back and stared at the ceiling.

Conner had been watching me. He grabbed my hand and gritted his teeth, his eyes wide with alarm. I put my other hand over Conner's and patted it several times. Sam wrapped one arm around Conner and blinked hard. He reached across our boy's body to cover Conner's and my hand with his.

The doctor furrowed his brow as he ran his tongue over his upper lip. "Mr. and Mrs. Golden, we say a person has epilepsy when he has had more than one seizure. Conner's dings are all seizures. It seems like he's had many of them, a great many of them." He looked at Conner.

Conner stared back.

My mouth was so dry. I squinted and gazed above the doctor's head. My preliminary presumptions surrounding Conner's convulsion dissolved in tangled confusion. My temples throbbed. I looked at

Conner and lowered my head. Conner has to be protected now. I stifled a sob.

I lifted my head and looked into the neurologist's eyes. My husband stared straight ahead. I took a deep breath. "I didn't want it to register, Doctor. I'm sorry. Yes, you and Conner were talking about his dings— or whatever he calls them—those little seizures; apparently there have been lots of them."

Dr. O'Rourke swiveled his leather chair to the side and crossed his legs. He kept his gaze on me as he tapped his pencil softly on his desk.

Conner watched me, too. He opened his mouth but kept silent as I turned away.

I looked at the floor and then I closed my eyes and said, "He's been having these things for over a year? Right in front of me? How could I have missed them? How could I not have seen them?"

I had known that Conner's convulsion weeks ago could completely change our lives. I just didn't know how. I didn't want to know. It was deep in that chamber where I kept secrets, repressed secrets. Conner looked at me again. "Mom! What?"

"Oh, honey." I wrapped my arm around his thin shoulders. Sam clenched his fists in his lap.

The neurologist spoke in a slow, deliberate voice. "Your son's seizures are different from the grand mal seizure, the convulsion that brought him to the hospital. Conner's seizures are caused by abnormal electrical brain activity. They probably originate in just one part of his brain— that would be in his temporal lobe—less likely in his frontal lobe." He paused for emphasis. "Convulsions affect the whole brain. Anybody witnessing a convulsion would recognize that type of seizure. However, Conner's dings—as he refers to them—can be harder to recognize… they affect just one part of the brain. What's so difficult for many people to accept is, as I just said, a cause for epilepsy is often never identified."

"You *mean* that, don't you? You don't know why they're happening?" The hostile tone in Sam's voice surprised me.

"Look. My patients say, 'Dr. O'Rourke, there are men walking on the moon. Don't tell me in this day and age that you can't say why the seizure happened. How can that be?' Mr. Golden, there are just so many things that we do not understand, especially when it comes to the brain. Medical knowledge humbles us. The more our experience and research teaches us, the more we appreciate how little we actually understand. We do not even know how we think or what thinking really is.

"The EEG should document where in the brain these seizures are originating," he continued. "However, a normal EEG does not mean that there is no seizure disorder. 'Seizure disorder' is another term we use that means epilepsy. An EEG can still be normal if the epileptiform discharges do not happen while the test is being done. And that's common."

I lowered my eyes and dug my fingernails into the edge of my chair. "What about the Dilantin?" I leaned forward and looked up. "Does Conner still have to take it? I guess so, huh? But I was, uh, we were so hoping, praying, that he could stop taking it today…"

I saw Conner's puzzled expression. Sam's eyes locked onto Dr. O'Rourke, but the neurologist focused on Conner.

"Let's discuss treatment options after I finish—" Dr. O'Rourke coughed into his fist and cleared his throat. "Excuse me. After I finish your son's physical examination. I want to get a more complete picture of what's going on before I make any decision about medications."

He asked him a few more questions to affirm that his mental functions were intact. "Spectacular," Dr. O'Rourke said with a broad grin. Conner knew the date, where he was right at that very moment and his home address. "Conner is very well-oriented to date and place. He even knows who the president is. Not everyone can tell me that— even adults, believe it or not."

Our boy beamed.

The neurologist demonstrated that Conner could also add and subtract, count and spell simple words backward—all accomplished appropriately for a third grader. His memory and his ability to draw, write and name objects the doctor held up were normal, too. "You're very smart for an eight-year-old."

"I'm eight and a half, Dr. O'Rourke."

The neurologist scrunched his eyes shut, grimaced and slunk down in his chair. "That's right. You already told me. Eight and a half. Sorry." He straightened up and winked at us.

He asked me about Conner's past illnesses, immunizations and symptoms in other parts of his body. He also wanted to know about my pregnancies. "Has he ever exhibited any unusual or disturbing behaviors?" His eyes darted between Sam and me.

"No. He's always been a normal child." I looked at Sam. He nodded several times.

Conner sniffled and looked up at me.

"Very good. Do any diseases run in the family?"

"No, Doctor," Sam answered in a solemn voice. "None that we're aware of, anyway." We looked at each other. I raised my eyebrows and shook my head in agreement.

Dr. O'Rourke's face became very serious as he asked, "Do you smoke, young man?"

Our son twisted in his chair and laughed. "No-oooo. The sy…the sychilist at school—the first icky one—she wanted to know if I was *married*. That was *funny*."

"He's referring to the school psychologist who first attempted to do testing on him in the school, Doctor. Apparently, she and Conner didn't get along. That's what both of them told me, anyway. That's sort of how we got to Dr. Frank Thomas." My grim expression softened into a smile.

"Oh." He said to me and then turned back to Conner. "So you don't smoke. That's what I like to hear." The doctor stood up. "Okay, family. Let's go across the hall to the exam room so I can check Conner over."

He walked around his desk and put his arm across our boy's shoulders. "Don't worry, Conner. I won't be giving you any shots today. I'll just be checking your eyes and things."

We shifted in our chairs and began to rise. Conner said to Sam, "I have to go to the bathroom, Daddy." His voice had become tremulous again.

"Can't you wait until the doctor's finished, Conner?" I asked with a sharp tone.

"No!" He practically shouted and cast a sidelong glare at me. He hitched up his pants and hopped a few times.

"Okay. Let's go." Sam took him by the hand.

I sat down again. "I had no idea that Conner's been having these things, Dr. O'Rourke—and for so long?" I leaned forward. "I've gone to the Internet and just about every...but, I never suspected this." I licked my lips and hesitantly asked in a softer voice, "You really think he has epilepsy, don't you, Doctor?" My throat and chest were tight. Of *course* it's epilepsy. He just *rammed* it down our throats. I was so blind.

Dr. O'Rourke went behind his desk. He stood there with a hand on the back of his leather chair, fixed his gaze on me for a moment, and then sat down. He rested his palms on the desk. An inch of light-blue shirtsleeves protruded from beneath the sleeves of his white coat. I noticed *"HO"* embroidered in dark-blue thread on the left cuff. I did not expect a physician to be so fashion-conscious as to have a monogram on his shirt. I didn't know why I was surprised; look at his bow ties. I looked for cufflinks, but saw none. The scene was so surreal that for a moment I wondered if I was living it or merely watching myself and the doctor in a silent movie.

"Look, Mrs. Golden, we've discovered a lot today. I am probably as surprised about this diagnosis as you are. I did not expect this history of covert, hidden seizures based on my review of the hospital records. I believe that Conner has a form of epilepsy called 'complex partial epilepsy.' Its newer term is 'mesial temporal lobe epilepsy.' Look at it this way: your son has been suffering; that is why you are here. That is the reality. Now that we have identified what is wrong we can do something about it. We can help him."

Dr. Choy had said virtually the same thing to me at the hospital. Did they all read the same script?

The neurologist arched his eyebrows. "I expect that Conner will do fine, Mrs. Golden. I understand how upsetting this is for you right now, believe me. But, you're all going to be fine."

His words morphed into distant sounds. I forced a weak smile and stared at the framed documents on the wall. Then I asked again, "Are you sure? Are you *absolutely* sure that Conner has epilepsy? It couldn't be something else?" I groped for an admission of doubt. "No, no. Of course...It's just that—" I stared out the window.

"I'm sure, Mrs. Golden. His history is classic: the auras—which are the warnings of the seizures and the smells that he told us that he gets—his confusion, losing control of his bladder. All of those phenomena are textbook symptoms."

Everything that this neurologist said would be a part of our lives—always, forever. So, this would be my lot in life. I remained motionless. I felt so hollow.

Dr. O'Rourke swiveled his chair around to face the computer on the desk extension. Thuk, thuk, thuk—the keys spoke as he typed. His eyes skimmed the screen, but occasionally I saw him glance at me as I juggled my pain and anguish.

When Conner and Sam returned to the office, Dr. O'Rourke ushered us across the corridor to his exam room. The fluorescent lights flickered on as soon as he opened the door. Conner turned his head from side to side before he entered the room.

I remembered that I had read how flickering lights could induce seizures in some epileptics. Was it better to say "people with epilepsy"? What should they be called? Was Conner an "epileptic"? Or was he a "child with epilepsy"? I squeezed my eyes tight, and my body shuddered.

Closed vertical blinds blocked out most of the late-afternoon sunshine that tried to stream through a single window. A rack on the back of the door proffered a selection of brochures on different neurological diseases and various popular magazines and children's periodicals. There were a few copies of *National Geographic,* too. A low shelf held several rubber dolls, a Barbie doll, a few toy soldiers and several small action figures similar to the snap-together ones Conner had at home. I wondered if the doctor put them together himself. He must have many children as patients; maybe one of them did it.

Conner was immediately drawn to a colorful diagram on the wall: a gray, wrinkled brain attached to the spinal cord with yellow nerves projecting to all parts of the body.

The neurologist tapped the boy's shoulder. "Take everything off down to your underpants, Conner. Shoes and socks off, too." Dr. O'Rourke looked at me as he said that and I nodded. "When you've undressed put on the folded gown that's on the exam table. I'll be right back." He smiled and left the room. The door shut behind him with a loud click.

I sat on a green plastic chair and waited for Conner to undress. I recognized several framed photographs on the walls that I remembered having seen on the Internet. The first picture was of a very young Hal O'Rourke in Papua New Guinea. Another large frame had a newspaper article about his interest in Shakespeare and neurology.

Sam moved closer and inspected the pictures, too.

What was the doctor doing now? Where did he go? Paperwork? The bathroom? Dr. O'Rourke had discovered things that all the other doctors had missed. Why didn't Dr. Choy or Dr. Jackson or Dr. Thomas—even the school psychologists—why didn't they figure out what was wrong? What about his teachers? Why did it take so long? And me—his mother! I was the worst of all. I closed my eyes and shook my head at my stupidity. Well, Dr. Choy did mention that it could be epilepsy, but I wouldn't entertain that diagnosis then. That was preposterous.

CHAPTER 26

Conner shuffled over to a shelf. His lithe, four-foot frame was draped in an over-sized adult patient gown that floated around his ankles. He wore it open in the front rather than in the back.

He picked up a plastic, multi-colored model of the brain. He turned it over and sideways, and then started to pull apart its components. A piece fell onto the thinly carpeted floor.

"Don't do that, Conner!" I said sharply.

Sam turned and winked at him. "Aw, I'm sure that's what it's there for, Sandra. He's okay."

When the doctor returned I saw him focus on Conner's underpants. We exchanged glances and grins about the tan-and-olive camouflage motif. Conner had begged for them because they were military like his dad. I bought him a dozen.

Sam and I sat beside each other along one wall. I started to get up. "Would you like me to reverse the gown, Doctor? Conner insisted on tying it in front."

"No, no. It's fine. Okay, Conner, let's see you just walk back and forth, normally."

"Like this?"

The neurologist nodded. He evaluated Conner's arm swings, balance and how he walked. "Perfect. Now, walk on your tiptoes. Like this." Dr. O'Rourke rose onto the balls of his feet and demonstrated what he wanted Conner to do.

"Good. Now, walk on your heels like this." The doctor rocked back onto his heels as he leaned forward and elevated the toes of his shiny, black shoes to take a few awkward steps. Once again, our boy mimicked him. I covered my mouth with both hands to conceal a smirk at their awkward postures.

"Fine! Your legs are equally strong. Now, I want you to walk as if you are on a tightrope. Put one foot in front of the other and touch the heel in front with the toes on the other foot. Keep the feet real close together."

Conner took five perfect in-line steps.

"You've got great balance."

"This is easy, Dr. O'Rourke!" Conner beamed.

The neurologist returned Conner's broad, toothy grin. "I knew you'd like this part of our visit. Now, hop up and down on your right leg like this." Dr. O'Rourke put his hands over the side pockets of his white coat to prevent papers and tools from popping out as he hopped a couple of times. Conner imitated him. "Now switch legs. Excellent!"

"Okay, now put your feet together like this so that they touch ankle to ankle, side by side." The doctor stood with the side of each of his shoes touching the other. "Yes, just like that! Now, stand like that and don't move."

"This is so easy!" Conner exclaimed. Sam smiled at him and then looked at me.

The neurologist nodded. "Now, stay just like that and close your eyes. Don't move."

Conner stood ramrod straight and squeezed his eyelids extra tight in that exaggerated way that little kids do. A few seconds later, the doctor said, "That's great, Conner. Your balance centers could not be better. Now turn around so I can check your back."

He lifted Conner's gown and bunched it up around his shoulders. "I don't see any spinal curvatures or birthmarks that sometimes accompany degenerative nervous system diseases that are associated with epilepsy."

That was good to hear. All doctors should interact with patients and their families: educate us, for crying out loud! Dr. Choy did that, too.

"Okay, now climb onto the exam table, young man." He felt Conner's wrist pulses and then inspected Conner's hands and fingernails. "There can be telltale clues of diseases here."

Then he picked up a thin, cloth measuring tape and wrapped it around Conner's head. "Your head circumference is fifty-three centimeters." He looked at a chart and declared, "Normal head size."

"Oh, that's good!" I felt my heart thump and then, just as suddenly, a sharp gloom settled over me. I had become so distracted by their interactions that for a precious few moments I had actually forgotten why we were here.

Conner looked at us and giggled. He seemed to be enjoying himself.

The doctor smiled and began to wrap a pediatric-size blood-pressure cuff around Conner's left upper arm.

"No! That gets too tight!" Conner yanked his arm away.

"This is a very important part of the evaluation, Conner. It's a small cuff made for children. I don't think I'll have to make it *too* tight, and the pressure will only last for a few seconds. I promise."

"Let the doctor do it, Conner," Sam commanded.

Conner cast a sober glance at his father and slowly extended his arm. He grimaced every time Dr. O'Rourke rhythmically squeezed the large black bulb that slowly tightened the cuff around Conner's arm.

The doctor placed his stethoscope in his ears: "Seventy-eight over fifty. That's fine!"

Dr. O'Rourke moved the stethoscope to the boy's chest. "No heart murmurs." Then he moved the stethoscope over both sides of the boy's neck. "No abnormal 'whooshing' sounds here, either. That suggests no blockages in the arteries leading to the brain. I wouldn't expect to hear any in a child."

Conner nodded and looked into the neurologist's eyes. Dr. O'Rourke smiled at him.

"I appreciate how you're explaining what you're doing, Dr. O'Rourke. It's like we're all in medical school." I laughed and gave Sam's hand a gentle squeeze.

Finally, the neurologist placed the end of the stethoscope on top of Conner's head and closed his eyes.

"I've never seen a doctor do *that* before—listen over the *top* of the head, I mean. Do you hear something up there?"

"I'm just being thorough, Mr. Golden. If there's an abnormal blood vessel or increased pressure inside the skull, sometimes we can hear a telltale sound."

"Well, did you hear anything?" Sam and I exchanged a worried glance.

"No, and that's normal. I *shouldn't* hear anything."

This examination was turning out to be quite a performance. My doctor never did any of these things.

He told Conner to lie down on his back. Then, he quickly moved his hands over Conner's belly as Dr. Choy had done, stopping here and there, pressing softly and moving his hands again. Conner looked uncomfortable once or twice, then erupted into giggles. "That tickles!"

"If an abdominal organ is enlarged, that could be a clue of a neurological-associated disease. Conner is normal." He pulled out the waistband on Conner's undershorts and took a quick look at his privates. "No evidence of a developmental or genetic disturbance here. Okay, you can go ahead and sit up now, Conner."

The neurologist walked over to a shelf and picked up a dark vial. He shook it a couple of times, unscrewed the cap and sniffed. He returned to Conner, who was swinging his dangling legs over the edge of the exam table. Our boy appeared quite comfortable being the center of attention.

The neurologist gently pressed Conner's left nostril closed and waved his other hand with the open vial under his right nostril. "Can you smell this?"

Conner jerked his head back and contorted his face. "Ahhhh! Nooooo!" He covered his nose and mouth with his hands.

"No, Conner. You don't have to do that," Dr. O'Rourke reassured him. "This one's a good smell. Can you tell me what it is?"

Cautiously, Conner bent forward and took another sniff. Before he could answer, Dr. O'Rourke repeated, "Can you smell that?"

"Yes."

He tested the other nostril.

"It's good," Conner pressed. "Is it gum?"

The neurologist turned around and held the vial under my nose. I sniffed. "It smells like something, uh…is it, uh, some spice? No. Cloves! It's cloves."

"Right! That's what it is." Then he placed it under Sam's nose.

"Yeah. It smells good. You're right, son. It did smell like chewing gum."

The neurologist replaced the cap and placed the vial back on the shelf. Then he picked up a handheld eye chart. Conner tested twenty-twenty in each eye.

"Good job. Now, keep your right eye closed and look into my eye."

The doctor stood three feet in front of Conner. Dr. O'Rourke closed his own left eye and pointed to his open right eye. "Keep looking right here in my eye," he instructed. The neurologist stretched out both of his hands to the sides. "Look only into my eye, Conner. I want to out find how well you can see out of all of the corners of your left eye." Dr. O'Rourke wiggled a finger off to the side and had Conner say "now" when he saw the movement.

After the exam the doctor explained, "You did great, Conner! The fact that he sees my fingers move when they're off to the sides means that the visual nerve tracts between Conner's eyeballs and the visual cortex at the back of his brain are working well. All of that function takes up a lot of space in the brain. My visual field testing suggests that there are no hidden abnormalities where these pathways are. That's very important."

I sat back and shook my head. My mind churned with his explanation and trying to visualize what he was talking about. I had never seen a neurologist at work, and I was so proud of Conner's mature cooperation.

"He's doing great, Sandra!" Sam whispered.

The neurologist switched off the overhead lights and lifted a cylindrical instrument off its perch on the wall behind Conner. "You're doing very well. Now I am going to shine a light into your eyes so I can check the area where the retina and nerves are. Keep looking straight ahead and try not to move your eyes. Just stare at the *X* on that wall. Keep looking at it even if my head gets in the way."

The doctor aimed a beam of light at Conner's right pupil and moved within a couple inches from our son's face. As Dr. O'Rourke peered through the instrument, he told us he could see where the optic nerve entered the back of Conner's eye and the little veins pulsating around it. Then he examined the other eye. "There's no sign of abnormal pressure inside Conner's head," he announced and replaced the cylindrical device on its wall holder.

"That's a relief," I sighed. Sam and I looked at each other. We chuckled. Conner's face had a quizzical expression, but he smiled, too.

During this neurological evaluation, I thought that Dr. O'Rourke had evolved from being just a medical specialist to now being a powerful member of our family. We were literally in his hands. He had the power to guide all of our futures. For this little while—and possibly for years to come—Conner would be his charge, too. I wondered how long he would be around and when he would retire.

The neurologist removed a small flashlight from his breast pocket and twisted the end to activate its bright white light. "Just keep looking at that *X* on the wall behind me, Conner," he instructed.

Conner squeezed his eyelids closed and turned his head away. "That's too bright! *Ow*! It hurts!"

"I know," Dr. O'Rourke commiserated. "It's very bright. Try not to close your eyes or move your head, though. This will take just a second." He aimed the light at one pupil and then at the other. Then he swung the light quickly back and forth several times between Conner's eyes. "Good. That's all normal."

"Doctor, I'd like to ask you, everyone sees doctors shining lights into pupils on those medical shows. I have always wondered about that. They make it seem very important. What does it tell you?" Sam asked.

The neurologist turned to us as he replaced the switched-off light to his coat's breast pocket. Conner watched Dr. O'Rourke with disinterest as Dr. O'Rourke started to speak. Conner looked at the wall and back at us and then back to his neurologist. Then he made little bubble-bursting popping sounds with his lips as he looked down at his swinging feet.

"The pupil normally gets smaller when a light shines into it. If it doesn't constrict—if it doesn't get smaller—we suspect that something's wrong, but we need other information from the total neurological examination in order to isolate the problem. The pupil might get smaller to light if there's something wrong in the pupil itself or with the optic nerve and retina.

"Now, Conner, follow my finger with your eyes. Don't move your head, just move your eyes." The doctor moved his finger to the far right and then left, up, down and in toward the tip of Conner's nose.

Conner's eyes followed the doctor's finger. I put my hand over my mouth to hide my smirk when Conner looked cross-eyed at the tip of his nose. "Good. Okay, Conner. Now, smile real big and scrunch up your eyelids tight, like you have soap in them." The doctor gently attempted to pry Conner's eyelids apart, but he couldn't. Next, he broke a wooden tongue depressor and touched different parts of our Conner's face with its sharp point. "Does this sharpness feel the same all over?"

Conner nodded. "Uh-huh. It tickles, it doesn't hurt."

Then Dr. O'Rourke rubbed his fingers together near one of Conner's ears and then the other. "Hear that?"

"Yeah."

Dr. O'Rourke pulled out his pocket flashlight again. "Great. Now, open your mouth and say 'Ahhhh.'" The doctor peered in. "Now, stick out your tongue and move it from side to side. Good! His throat and tongue muscles are moving normally, Mom and Dad."

The doctor returned the flashlight to his breast pocket. "Okay, lift up your arms and hold them out straight in front of you. Good. Now, close your eyes and keep your arms right there. Don't move." Dr. O'Rourke stood still and watched Conner's hands for about five seconds. "I'm looking for downward drifting of either arm, which could indicate a subtle weakness. There is none. Conner's fine.

"Now, young man, open your eyes but keep holding your arms up. Let's see how strong you are." The doctor pressed down on Conner's outstretched arms. They both grunted, "Grrrrrrr." Conner's grin contorted into a grimace.

"You're a very strong boy!"

Sam smiled and gave Conner a thumbs-up.

"Now, I want you to relax your arms and make them go limp like a noodle." Dr. O'Rourke rapidly twisted, bent and straightened Conner arms, one at a time, in several directions. It looked like they were shaking hands. Then, he knelt and slid his palm under Conner's sole and thrust Conner's foot upward. He repeated the maneuver on Conner's other foot. "I'm searching for tightness and involuntary jerking of his foot," he told us. "All of these maneuvers tell me that his motor functions are working well. There is no tightness or involuntary jerking of these muscles. That's normal."

He stood and removed a rubber-edged, round-wheeled hammer with a long handle from the waist pocket of his white coat. "Now, I'm just going to test your reflexes, Conner." When the corners of Conner's mouth started to turn down, Dr. O'Rourke added, "This won't hurt."

He tapped the tendons on Conner's elbows, wrists, knees and ankles. Conner's eyes widened. His foot and entire leg jerked way up when the doctor tapped his knee, and Conner burst out in a full-throated laugh. Sam and I laughed, too. That reflex trick never ceased to amaze me. We had done that to each other as kids.

The doctor squatted again; his white coat tented on the floor around him. "This will tickle, so try not to move." He slid the pointed end of the reflex instrument's handle along the side then across the ball of Conner's sole. I remembered Dr. Choy doing that in the emergency room, too.

"*That tickles*!" Conner's big toe curled down. Sam and I laughed again.

"That's great. A normal reaction."

He grabbed a two-pronged metal fork from the shelf. When he struck it with his palm I heard a low hum. Then he placed the vibrating thing on Conner's left knuckle.

"Okay, Conner, let me know if you feel any vibration or buzzing."

"I feel it. Ooh!" Our startled boy snatched his hand back. "That feels funny!"

The doctor struck the instrument again and placed it on his patient's toes. "I can feel that, too!"

"Now, do you see what I'm doing?" He took hold of one of Conner's fingers and wiggled it up and down. "Do you feel that?"

"Yes."

"Good. Now, shut your eyes and keep them closed tight. I want you to tell me which way your finger moves. Keep your eyes closed! Are you ready?"

Conner nodded and squeezed his eyes closed again. He looked so cute; he was trying so hard.

The neurologist held Conner's index finger and moved its tip upward. "Which way is it going? Up or down?"

"Down. I mean, *up*." Conner opened his eyes.

"Yes. But keep your eyes closed." Dr. O'Rourke moved the finger again. He repeated the test with a finger on Conner's other hand. Then, the doctor knelt and performed the test on his patient's toes.

"You're doing magnificently. You gave the correct answer every time."

Conner tilted his head to the side. I wiggled my fingers at him.

Dr. O'Rourke broke off a wooden stick from a cotton swab and gently touched Conner's feet and hands with the sharp end. "Does that feel the same all over?"

"Uh-huh."

"Good. We're almost done. Now, point your index finger and touch my fingertip with your finger. Good. And, touch the tip of your nose with that same finger. Great!" Conner repeated the exercise several times.

"Your coordination and balance centers are fine. Okay. We're all done. Go ahead and get dressed. I am going to talk with your folks in my office. Just hang out here for a few minutes, and then I will come back to get you. There are books and some models and toys you'll like to keep you busy." He nodded at Sam and me, and held the door open for us. The corners of Conner's mouth dropped again.

"Should we be leaving him alone like this?" I asked.

"He'll be okay here. We will be right across the hall, Conner. I will come get you in a few minutes. Remember, we are a team now: you and me and your parents. I will leave the door open a little bit. My secretary knows that you're still in here. You can look at the books or play with the toys. Check out that brain model. I'm going to show you what it does in a few minutes."

Conner looked at me. I stared down at his plaintive face. He said, "Okay, Dr. O'Rourke. Yeah, I'm on your team. But, hurry." I was relieved when he flashed a weak smile at the doctor.

I gave Conner a little wave and walked the few feet to his office.

CHAPTER 27

I hesitated at the door. Just moments ago I had found the safety I needed—that brief, diverting, and even comical relief while I watched my son interact with the neurologist. But now...Conner has *epilepsy*!

I stepped into the office and sank onto my chair. I heard the door close. Dr. O'Rourke's thoroughness, his humanity and Conner's cooperation during the examination had been so heartening. But it had been a mirage. What was there to be encouraged about? This was not what the Internet had said! Nothing suggested that he had epilepsy! A miasma of fear and disappointment settled over me.

I lowered my head. Sam reached for my hand; I moved it and rubbed my cheek. I couldn't see him to be that helpful for me. I was worried—for him—for us.

The neurologist sat down behind his desk and regarded us as we sat stiffly across from him. He had already changed our lives. What more would he tell us?

Dr. O'Rourke cleared his throat. "Well, we learned that Conner's spells—what he calls 'dings'—have been happening quite frequently over the last year. It sounds as though he first started experiencing them when he was seven. His description of what happens is classical for complex partial seizures. These events, as I've already told you, are also known as temporal lobe or psychomotor seizures, uncinate seizures and in the more current nomenclature, limbic seizures." He drew a deep breath. "There's no question: Conner has epilepsy."

I stared over his head and saw a montage of images from my son's life: Conner's birth; his first birthday with chocolate cake smeared over his laughing face; Sam teaching him how to catch balls and to ride a bike; his convulsion…And dying?

Sam turned and wrapped his arm around me. He gave my shoulders a slight shake. "Don't!" I whispered, and his arm dropped away. Dr. O'Rourke averted his eyes.

"This condition is actually very common. One percent of the population has it: that is three million Americans and more than fifty or sixty million people in the rest of the world. It can affect absolutely anyone. It affects celebrities, politicians, scholars and even champion athletes.

"So far, the testing that we've done shows no serious cause. There is no indication of any tumor or cancer, or abnormal blood vessel or infection—conditions that are known causes of epilepsy. I want Conner to have an MRI scan because it could show brain structures, blood vessels and areas of scarring—known as mesial temporal lobe sclerosis—more precisely than the CT scan. The MRI will help to ensure that we're not missing anything serious."

Sam cleared his throat. "Why didn't Choy do the MRI scan right from the beginning, two weeks ago? We would already *know*. Now he needs a *second* scan, and more radiation?"

"Conner was admitted late at night, Mr. Golden. The MRI scanner doesn't operate twenty-four-seven. The emergency doctor on duty would have had to call in the technician specialist to do it. If the CT is normal and the other tests are, too, then an additional MRI scan often isn't done. Dr. Choy did not suspect that Conner had epilepsy at that time, so he didn't order that scan. The MRI scan is very safe. There is no radiation exposure."

He swiveled around in his chair and reached for a life-sized model of a head on a bookshelf behind him. Then he placed it on his desk and removed the top of the gray "skull." There was a plastic "brain" inside, complete with a network of red and blue blood vessels painted on its surface.

The doctor disassembled the model and held one-half of the brain in his hand. "This is the left cerebral hemisphere." He removed a large piece from the plastic model and said, "This lobe on the lower portion is the temporal lobe. It lies beneath the temple part of our skull, right here." Dr. O'Rourke touched his fingers to the side of his head. "The type of epilepsy that Conner has probably comes from this region. It's the most common form of epilepsy overall, and it's very common in children."

We both leaned in.

"You said that you've been doing research about seizures on the Internet, Mrs. Golden. I recommend that you go back to your computer and look up the terms 'temporal lobe seizures' and 'mesial temporal lobe epilepsy.' You will be able to read about everything that I'm telling you. Look up 'complex partial seizures,' too. The more you understand Conner's condition, the more comfortable and the more confident you will feel about helping him deal with it. Here, I'll write them down for you."

He pulled out a fat black pen from his shirt pocket. I heard a soft, hollow sound as he unscrewed the cap. A fountain pen! I hadn't seen one of those in years. Its golden nib made scratching sounds as the doctor scribbled on a notepad and handed the paper to me.

I cleared my throat and crossed my legs. "I know what you told us, but...such a common condition. It's just hard to accept that modern medicine doesn't know. Maybe more tests. Just to be sure, Doctor?" I looked at Sam. He nodded with a half-smile.

The neurologist bent forward and pressed his hands on the desktop. "Honestly, Mrs. Golden, if the MRI is normal I don't think we'll ever know why Conner has epilepsy. Medicine has come a long way since the ancient Egyptians and Greeks first wrote about it three thousand years ago. But, again, the cause in any individual can still be a mystery."

Sam asked in a low voice, "So what do we do now?" His voice sounded weak, pathetic. I touched his hand.

When Dr. O'Rourke leaned back, I noticed damp palm prints on the desk. He was a specialist. He must have diagnosed epilepsy and changed lives hundreds of times. He was a father, a family man. I surmised that the several photos on the wall were of his children; the picture of a woman's smiling face displayed on the side of his desk must have been of his wife. I looked into his eyes. It could not be easy to diagnose epilepsy in a young, apparently healthy child. Moreover, he really seemed to like Conner; anyone could see that this was hard for him to do.

"We can't cure epilepsy, but children *can* outgrow it. Sometimes, the epilepsy just stops on its own. Otherwise, we can usually control it with medications."

"*Really*? It can go *away*? Just like *that*? On its *own*?"

"That's definitely possible, Mrs. Golden. I've seen that happen in lots of patients; children, especially."

"But how do we know if—when—it'll go away, or if he'll have another seizure? Isn't there any way we can tell?" Sam demanded. His eyes, hard with fear and disappointment, didn't waver from Dr. O'Rourke's face.

I wanted to nudge him. Didn't he hear what Dr. O'Rourke just said? That sharp edge…There it was again; he had been so mercurial ever since he came home from Iraq.

Dr. O'Rourke swallowed and looked at me and then back at Sam. "It seems that Conner's seizures happen mostly when he isn't engaged in activities with other people. Or, if the dings—uh, his seizures—happened when other people were around, they weren't recognized." He shifted in his chair. "It was only when the fever precipitated the convulsion—his grand mal seizure—that you even knew he had a seizure. And that was a different type of seizure from what he usually has."

"Mrs. Golden, you mentioned that Conner is having learning problems in school—

"His teachers would have noticed them. They should have. But maybe they did. Yes, they did. I *know* that they did. They saw them, but…nobody recognized…nobody knew what was happening. Yes. That's it. It is so obvious now. At a school conference I attended last fall, about Conner's school performance, both his current teacher and his second-grade teacher from last year said that sometimes he didn't seem to hear them. They said Conner sometimes didn't pay attention, too. That was when he could have blanked out." I bent over and pounded a fist into my palm. "That's *it*, isn't it? That's why Conner's not doing well at school! And they wanted to move him back a grade."

I felt energized as I contemplated this new scenario. Maybe I really could have some control. *I* would make sure Conner was going to be okay. We—Sam, me, the doctors, the teachers—would monitor him. Everyone would watch him now. My crossed-over leg bounced rapidly up and down.

I placed both feet on the floor, sat forward, leaned over my clasped hands on the neurologist's desk and looked into his eyes. "Now that we know what's wrong, you can help him, Doctor! You know, his teacher told me that Conner hadn't finished many of his assignments in class, like spelling tests. Some time ago, she said that on one of them—yeah, that must have been the spelling test Conner was talking about—he didn't write half of the words that she called out. She thought Conner was stressed and anxious, and she presumed it was about Sam being in Iraq. We all did. But, if he was having seizures all that time and no one knew what was happening…that would explain things, wouldn't it?"

Dr. O'Rourke nodded. "Yes, it sounds like seizures have been affecting his school performance for quite a while, Mrs. Golden. When one occurs, his mind stops. Everything stops for him. He becomes confused; he blanks out and becomes unaware of his surroundings. He told us that he was able to tell when his seizures—his dings—start. He said that he perceived—uh, he said it was a funny feeling, didn't he? Something in his stomach, he said. Then he would feel afraid. And he would imagine that he could smell something foul, like the odor of burning rubber. That kind of olfactory hallucination is a classic symptom. If the person perceives a taste, it's a gustatory hallucination. We think these hallucinations originate in abnormal irritated cells in the temporal lobe."

The neurologist sat up straighter. He clasped his hands together on his desktop again. His voice became more emphatic as he warmed to his subject. "Conner's symptoms are typical of this form of epilepsy. Some people even chew and make swallowing movements and lick their lips with their tongues. You could see that."

My tongue clicked from the top of my mouth when I said, "You know, I just remembered. A few months, ah, no, three or four months ago, one of Conner's friends was over for a play-date. The boys were playing videogames on the game console downstairs while I was up in my office. Michael—his friend—said that Conner was acting weird. He said that Conner had been eating something, chewing, while they played. But that couldn't have been true; there were no snacks around. I never let the children eat in the den. Conner knows the rules. I remember thinking that their conversation was odd, but I just dropped the subject. Do you think that Conner had a seizure that day? I'll have to talk to Michael."

The neurologist nodded. "It sounds like it."

"Why didn't the school notice what was going on in the first place?" Sam's eyes flashed but his voice remained controlled. "They should have seen what was going on! They've been happening for so long. Jesus!"

"I just said I thought that they did see his seizures, Sam. And the doctor said they can be hard to notice. They didn't understand what was happening to Conner, Sam." I felt like now I was on Dr. O'Rourke's team. It was Sam—angry and disappointed—who had to be conciliated.

"Well, Mr. Golden, inappropriate staring into space during class may be a tip-off to epilepsy. Unfortunately, these symptoms can be difficult to recognize. It is easy for a teacher—for anyone—to miss what is going on. It would be easy to mistake it for daydreaming."

"The school district made Conner take all those tests—"

"Yes. But remember, Mrs. Golden, those tests were not intended to diagnose a seizure. Neuropsychological testing might have uncovered these lapses in Conner's attention but only if he had a seizure at that time. There are so many variables when it comes to epilepsy. Now you appreciate how classroom teachers need to be alert to children with a condition like Conner's."

"But, if they couldn't tell that something was wrong with our son a few months ago, how do we know that Conner will be able to function at school, now?" Sam challenged. He shook his head.

"Well, I think that you now know what to tell his teachers to watch for. You are not the first family with this story of missed seizures in classrooms. Young children, especially, have difficulty describing what is happening to them. Complex partial seizures are very confusing for anyone, especially for young patients.

"Federal and state laws mandate that schools provide special support for children whose epilepsy interferes with their academic success." Dr. O'Rourke looked first at Sam and then at me. "Now that we know what's going on, I predict that he will do fine. He shouldn't need any kind of special support at school."

The neurologist took a deep breath. "I need to make a few remaining points clear before we bring Conner in. I'm going to be truthful and hopefully not too blunt, but these are things that you need to know. You may have noticed special warning messages on the cases of his videogames. Videogames with flashing lights are known to precipitate body jerks or even grand mal seizures. However, these stimuli typically do not affect the type of epilepsy that Conner has. So I don't think you need to restrict his playing those games unless, of course, you observe they're associated with his seizures."

"Yeah, I've seen those warnings. They never meant anything to me before this. But, how are we supposed to know he's having one of those dings of his if we don't see it?"

"Mrs. Golden, you'll know a ding—one of his seizures—is happening if Conner suddenly gets confused and stops talking, and he stares inappropriately. Ask his friends if they have ever witnessed anything like that. If you see something suspicious, test his awareness level. For instance, ask Conner to put his right hand on his left ear or something like that. Those kinds of instructions require intact awareness. If Conner is in the midst of a seizure he won't follow the command, or he will do it incompletely. When he comes out of the seizure he won't recall hearing you tell him anything."

Dr. O'Rourke watched us process what he had just told us. "Seizures can last several minutes. Once the seizure starts, Conner may be incoherent for a while. He might get up from a chair and aimlessly walk around. Patients can lose their urine at this time, too. You both need to encourage Conner to tell you if he gets that funny feeling whenever it occurs."

"But he never seems to know he's wetting himself or doing any of that stuff," I said softly. I thought about the yellow-stained underwear and wet pants I found under Conner's bed the day Sam came home from Iraq. So, Conner did change out of the pants he had been wearing in the morning. I hadn't imagined it. I had let it go as something that happened in kids when they got excited. I guessed that he must have hidden his wet clothes because he was embarrassed to have an accident at his age. He had a ding while he was alone in his room. Oh, God, Conner. I am so sorry.

"That's typical, Mrs. Golden. When a seizure ends, the person enters a period of confusion: the 'postictal confusion' period. It's when the disrupted brain function slowly starts to normalize. It lasts minutes or even longer. Conner won't remember anything that happened during the seizure."

Sam frowned and waved his hand in front of his face. "Isn't that dangerous? I mean, you just said Conner doesn't know what goes on during a seizure."

I glared at Sam as this new reality crystallized. I knew my annoyance with Sam was irrational, but now…Conner could really be in danger after all. I pictured a myriad of possibilities: falling downstairs or onto sharp things, coming off his bike, being hit by a car…

Sam nodded. "It's true, Sandra. Doctor, when Conner has a seizure, isn't it possible that he could really hurt himself, bump into things, fall down the stairs or even walk into traffic? That's what you're telling us."

"That's right. Sometimes, not often, complex partial seizures last hours or even days. That is called 'status epilepticus.' It is a state of prolonged seizure. If we did an EEG during such an episode, it would show continuous seizure activity. Even these can be missed. People in this condition can walk, eat and even speak some words, but they are not truly cognizant of their surroundings. Casual observers might think the person is just a little out of it, or 'ditzy,' as they say. The condition could be mistaken for a psychiatric problem, too. And, just as you said Mr. Golden, he could walk in front of cars without knowing it."

I gasped. "And what about that sudden death condition, uh, suddenly dying that I read about on the Internet? Where people are found dead…just found dead."

"You read about SUDEP, Mrs. Golden. Sudden unexplained death in epilepsy."

"That's it. Yes."

"It is very uncommon, like one in a thousand. We don't know much about why this sudden death happens. Rarely, a patient is found dead, usually in bed. Often, there's no blood from biting a lip or tongue, and there's no loss of the urine or bowels as evidence that the person died during a convulsion. It may happen because of some abnormal brain message to cause the lungs or the heart to dysfunction." He paused and looked as us for a moment. "You certainly are doing your research. It's beneficial for Conner and for your whole family to have as much information as you can. SUDEP tends to occur in people whose epilepsy is poorly controlled—those with many seizures, usually convulsions. Some of these unfortunate people are very lax in taking their medications. Or, they abuse alcohol or they don't get enough sleep. That's why we encourage our patients to follow a healthy life-style in order to minimize this rare occurrence."

He shrugged his shoulders and held his hands in supplication toward me. "I'm highlighting these possibilities to prevent as much as possible any of these things from happening." Dr. O'Rourke pressed on, "Conner should never take a bath or even a shower unless the bathroom door is unlocked and someone is at home if he collapses. Mark Twain's adult daughter had epilepsy, and she drowned in her bath. An acquaintance recently told me of a family that had to break down the locked bathroom door upon hearing thrashing. It was too late. The teen with epilepsy drowned in the tub. People could drown if they block the shower drain. I have had patients—and I know of others—who have experienced this tragedy in the shower: at least five people. They drowned face-down in only two inches of water. I investigated shower drains that were elevated to prevent their bodies from blocking the drain. I wanted to recommend them to my patients and to teach my students to do the same. It sounded so simple. I even called plumbing supply stores and plumbers. They all told me it is against local building codes because people could trip and fall. That kind of design would be too dangerous for the public."

He continued, "These warnings are so important for you to keep in mind. You can see all of the possible scenarios. Conner should never go swimming alone. It is critical that if he does go swimming, everyone with him must be aware of his diagnosis in case he has a seizure while he's in the water. In addition, they must be physically capable of pulling him out, if necessary. But this is really no different from the safety precautions that you would take with any young child."

"My God, Doctor!" Tears rolled from my eyes as I pictured what the neurologist was telling us.

"Please don't get me wrong. Your son can still lead a pretty normal life. He just needs to follow common sense. He can ride a bike—with a helmet, of course. Everyone should do this anyway—but no riding in traffic. If his seizures are well controlled, Conner will be able to get a license to drive a car when he's old enough. However, his epilepsy might keep him out of the military if the seizures don't stop by the time he's a teenager. And he might not be allowed to pilot a plane."

Dr. O'Rourke watched our charged reactions. "Conner's a smart boy, and epilepsy shouldn't interfere with his intelligence. He can go to college, medical school, law school…he can do just about anything that he wants. As I have already mentioned, many accomplished and famous people in all walks of life have epilepsy: Alexander the Great, Julius Caesar…so many other notable people and leaders had epilepsy. The Russian author Dostoevsky had it, as did some of his most memorable fictional characters. I know several physicians, neurologists even, and scientists who have epilepsy. Who knows? Perhaps people will one day include Conner Golden on that list of notable personages."

"What about medicine? Conner will need medicine, right?"

The neurologist nodded. "I was coming to that, Mr. Golden. Conner will need to be on anti-seizure medications for years—possibly all of his life."

I had expected him to say that. I was surprised, though, that I now felt no resistance to the idea. I supported my elbow on my crossed-over knee and rested my chin in my palm.

"Doctor. You just said he could lead a pretty normal life! How can Conner be normal if he has to take medicines the rest of his life? How can anyone be normal like *that*?"

Dr. O'Rourke's eyes widened; he swallowed. "Mr. Golden, epilepsy can be totally controlled in half of the patients. If we get him on the right medicine at the right dosage, your son will have total control of this condition and he won't have any more seizures."

"Half? Only half? And what's that *right* medicine, Doctor?" Sam leaned forward with narrowed eyes.

"Honey, please. We're upset." He turned his head quickly toward me. "So much has happened this afternoon. Dr. O'Rourke is *going* to tell us."

Sam worked his jaw with his eyes on me but I was not sure that he saw me or even heard me. He scratched the side of his head. "I'm sorry, Doctor. This has really gotten to me. I mean…the implications…"

"Mr. Golden, finding the most effective treatment for Conner will be a process of trial-and-error. I will start him on a medication called Keppra. It is a very promising treatment for Conner's type of epilepsy. If necessary, I'll increase the dosage until all of his seizures stop or until he can't tolerate the side effects."

"Side effects…" I crossed my legs and sighed.

"There could be some alteration in his personality and drowsiness. Some people have trouble concentrating. Skin rashes and liver or blood abnormalities may develop. If Conner's seizures continue, I will switch him to another medication or add medicines until all of his seizures stop. One thing that he should never do is stop taking the medicines on his own—especially not suddenly, not all at once. Doing so could worsen his condition and even be dangerous."

"Those are some side effects, Dr. O'Rourke!" I shook my head and reached down. My hand felt icy-cold on my calf. I put both feet on the floor.

"We can successfully deal with them if they occur, Mrs. Golden. Anti-seizure medicines are absolutely necessary for this condition. However, twenty to thirty percent of patients with epilepsy only get partial control of their seizures. That means they may have one seizure every few months or once or twice a year even taking the best anti-seizure regimen fitted to their needs. Finally, the remaining twenty percent of patients have what we call 'uncontrolled' or 'intractable' epilepsy. They do not respond to any of the medications. Sometimes neurosurgeons can remove those abnormal areas of the brain from where their seizures emanate."

Brain surgery? On Conner? I was dumbfounded.

Dr. O'Rourke added, "That treatment can be curative. We're certainly not considering anything like that for Conner."

It had started to sink in for me—epilepsy could be survived.

"But, Dr. O'Rourke, Conner's convulsion—he was shaking all over and bleeding. It looked like he could have died. It could happen again?"

"That was a grand mal seizure, Mr. Golden. It was a true convulsion, what most people think of as 'epilepsy.' Your son had a convulsion because his brain's defenses against a seizure were lowered by the fever." He added, "By the way, sleep is another time when the brain's defenses against seizures are somewhat lowered, but lack of sleep and getting over-tired is an even worse trigger. Make sure Conner gets enough rest every night."

The neurologist pulled a form from a drawer and began filling it out with his big, black fountain pen.

"Speaking of sleep, I'd like you to bring Conner in for the EEG at the beginning of next week. My secretary will schedule it. This will be a 'sleep-deprived' EEG, so make sure your son stays up as late as he can the night before. That will help to ensure that he will sleep during the test. It will give us a better chance of capturing epileptiform activity."

"So, the EEG will show when he has a seizure?" Sam asked.

The doctor signed his name with a flourish at the bottom of the form and looked up. "If seizure activity occurs during the EEG, the test will pick it up. Still, epilepsy patients' EEGs are often normal because the seizure does not happen at the time of the test. And to answer your previous question, Mr. Golden, yes: I'm afraid that a grand mal seizure can certainly happen again."

"It's hard to imagine how anyone can live through those seizures, Doctor. To go through that again …" I said quietly.

"Convulsions are much more dramatic in appearance than they are dangerous, Mrs. Golden. They stop on their own. They usually end within two minutes. People typically hold their breath during the convulsion, which can make them turn blue. It does look very scary if you have never seen it before. If it lasts longer than that—like five or more minutes, which is unusual—call nine-one-one and get help immediately because that lengthy seizure can be dangerous."

More dangerous? More dangerous than what we have already? I bit my lip.

Sam was on the same wavelength. "Why is that more dangerous than the convulsion he had a couple weeks ago? How could it be worse?"

"You see, Mr. Golden, a convulsion that lasts longer than a few minutes deprives the body of oxygen, especially the brain. Prolonged convulsions are harder to stop. These extended convulsions are dangerous forms of status epilepticus. Conner's complex partial seizures—his dings, as he calls them—do not interfere with breathing, you see. They are not as dangerous. Almost always, convulsive shaking gradually stops and leaves the person exhausted. The person is confused for a while. That's the postictal state. Then they sleep. They often have a headache after these seizures, too. They'll return to the way they were prior to the seizure and just carry on with their lives."

"It was so terrible; really scary. He turned blue," Sam said.

"And he wet the bed, too."

"Losing bladder and or bowel control is very common. Tongue biting is typical, too, because all of the person's muscles tense up, including muscles in the jaw. Don't stick anything in his mouth during the seizure; it's possible to break teeth by biting on a hard object. Definitely do not stick your finger in Conner's mouth or you'll be bitten. There is nothing you can do if he bites his tongue. No one has ever bitten off or swallowed their tongue. His tongue will be sore for a few days, but it will heal. You see that Conner's bitten tongue is already healing. If his tongue is not in the way of his teeth at the start of the convulsion, then it won't be bitten."

"This is all very helpful, Doctor. But, what should I do—" Sam looked at me. "What should we do if—if he has another convulsion like that? I can't just watch him being tortured. He could die! You said so."

Sam blinked rapidly and reached for my cold hand. My husband was crying. I squeezed his hand and continued to catalog in my mind everything Dr. O'Rourke had said. I pictured Conner's tortured shaking and the blood in his mouth.

"No, no, Mr. Golden. It is very unlikely he would die. The prolonged convulsions—the ones that last longer than a few minutes, like five minutes and more—those are the dangerous seizures, and they are uncommon. Teach everyone who could be present if your son should have a convulsion how they can help. They need to know how to turn Conner onto his side while he's shaking so that any saliva or vomit that might accumulate will drop out of his mouth. You do not want that material to go down his throat and into his lungs; it could lead to serious pneumonia. They need to know not to fight his thrashing limbs. They should let him jerk until it stops by itself. We don't want any unnecessary injuries to him or to the observers. Warn them that his mouth could get bloody from biting his tongue or lip. Reassure them that it is not a serious wound. I know people sometimes freak out if they see blood. Do the best that you can to educate them. They need to try to prevent his falling onto hard or hot objects, and especially not into water. Just ease him to the floor and let the convulsion run its course. Nothing can be done to...stop it at...that...point."

I could hear the doctor's voice weaken as he continued to speak. He needed to take a breath; he barely finished that last sentence.

Dr. O'Rourke picked up his pencil and tapped it on the desktop. "Reassure them that Conner will be as good as new in a few hours after he sleeps it off."

The doctor cleared his throat. "The medication I'm going to prescribe for your son should prevent the seizures, but I have to prepare you for the possibility that any of his dings—I like Conner's term." He stopped, smiled and shifted his gaze between Sam and me a couple times. "If that's what he wants to call them, I'm okay with that—any of his dings could turn into a convulsion. In that situation, Conner's usual seizure activity—his loss of awareness—would spread out from where they started in his temporal lobe to his entire brain. If that happened, we call it a 'complex partial seizure with secondary generalization.' Sometimes these secondary-generalization types respond to a different anticonvulsant or anti-seizure medication. We'll just have to wait and see how he does on the Keppra."

"Will my son ever be able to get married and have children like everyone else? Will he be like normal people?" This worry had preoccupied me the entire past hour.

Dr. O'Rourke folded his hands on his lap, leaned back in his chair and regarded us for a moment. "Mrs. Golden, of course he will. Look, hopefully, today was the Golden family's worst day. I am pretty confident that the Keppra will control further seizures. Everything should get better now. You'll see, Conner should be a normal eight-year-old—uh, eight-and-a-half-year-old, as he already has told me more than once." He chuckled. "And I stand corrected. His future isn't as bleak as you imagine. I doubt that he's the only pupil in his entire school with epilepsy."

Memories of that day almost two weeks ago flooded back: I had watched the passing group of children in front of my car on the way to school. Dr. Choy had said the exact same thing and I searched for that illusory child who might already have had a seizure.

"As I told you before, just about one percent of the United States' total population has epilepsy. An additional eight to ten percent of the population—otherwise normal people, as far as we can determine—will experience a single seizure during their lifetimes and never have another. In fact, that one seizure usually occurs and—"

The office door clicked open.

CHAPTER 28

D r. O'Rourke stopped talking. Sam and I twisted around in our chairs. Conner was grimacing and crying. He yelled, "Mommy, Mommy! I have to go to the bathroom right now! I mean it! Right *now*!" He was dressed but he wasn't wearing any shoes. His cheeks and eyes were red and tears streamed down his face as he squeezed his thighs together and pressed his fists into his groin.

"I'll take him. He had some diarrhea the last time he got panicked like this." Sam got up quickly and took Conner's hand.

Dr. O'Rourke followed them to the door. We watched them disappear around the corner. "Your little guy looked pretty upset. Your husband should keep him company for a while and calm him down. Then I'll talk with Conner and explain what's going on." He closed the door and sat back down behind his big desk.

"Why didn't I see it?" I pounded my balled fists against my thighs. "How could I have been so stupid? Stupid!"

"There's no way that you are responsible for any of this, Mrs. Golden. You didn't see his seizures. Conner didn't even understand what was happening to him. I told you, those kinds of events can be very mysterious, very hard to describe. The thinking process becomes so confused that the person doesn't even know how to tell anyone what is happening to him. I have seen it many times in adults—some very articulate people, too. And Conner is a young child."

"Yes, but—I'm such an idiot!"

The doctor held up his palm. "Please. No one working with him recognized his seizures, even the medical professionals. This is not uncommon in my experience."

"But Dr. O'Rourke, I'm his mother. I should have—I'm so angry. Oh, Conner..."

"I've had school nurses refer children to me after teachers became suspicious about students' lapses in attention, but even then it took many months to determine exactly what was going on. This happens over and over, Mrs. Golden. I am sure that you would have noticed the change in his behavior if you interacted with Conner when he had had a ding. I venture to guess that no one actually witnessed it when it happened. You could not have done anything differently—no one could have.

"I recently evaluated a nineteen-year-old girl whom an orthopedist referred to me for numbness in her hand after she injured her arm. She left my office with a diagnosis of epilepsy, albeit, a different type than Conner's. It was totally unsuspected. How could that happen? You ask. She had short blank outs lasting ten or fifteen seconds, up to forty or fifty times every day. This had been going on for most of her life. She thought everyone had them. She thought it was *normal*. She was unaware of these brief losses of concentration, so she never complained about them. She said that she had a reputation for being 'ditzy' and for not paying attention or not hearing what people said sometimes. Don't be so hard on yourself, Mrs. Golden."

"Yes, but...I could count off many times, many incidents that, looking back, seemed suspicious. They probably were his dings. I mean, knowing what to look for, now...his teachers, even the one last year, said Conner didn't always pay attention in class. Several months ago, Conner didn't answer me when I called up to him. When I got to his room, his handheld video console was on the floor, and he seemed confused. He was just standing over it. He could not really explain how he dropped it or why he didn't answer me. He got very upset when I questioned him about it, and I accused him of being careless. And then there was that time his friend, Michael, said he was acting weird and chewing on brownies when there weren't any for him to eat. Oh, God..." I buried my face in my hands.

"Mrs. Golden, I want you to get Conner a medical bracelet to identify his condition. He should wear it on his wrist. If he needs medical assistance outside of your home—for instance, while he is on school trips or on vacations—a medical bracelet would let people know he has epilepsy and how to contact you. The bracelet really helps when ambulances or emergency rooms get involved, because the information on the bracelet gives medical personnel a head start on giving the appropriate care."

"Doctor, I don't know. It sounds like a good idea, but then the whole world will know what's wrong with my son. There's such a stigma—"

"Mrs. Golden, I understand. These are modern times. Heart patients' and diabetics' lives are saved by people knowing *instantly* what's wrong when an unknown person collapses: there's the diagnosis right on the patient's wrist. Immediate life-saving care can be given. I strongly recommend the bracelet for him. Hannah will give you a form to order one when you leave. They are inexpensive. I also want you to know that there are epilepsy support groups for parents and patients."

He opened a desk drawer and began to fumble in it as he continued to talk. "You might find it helpful to share your concerns and problems with other parents who are going through the same thing that you are dealing with. Hmm, I thought that I had their card. Hannah will give you information about how to contact the Epilepsy Foundation and other epilepsy groups when you leave."

"I—I just want my son to have a normal life, to be a normal boy and to grow up and be a normal man." My voice caught in my throat as I contemplated those immortal longings that any mother would have had for her child. "I just need to know if my son will grow up and be able to marry and to live a normal life."

He rolled his chair back and rubbed his crossed-over knee with his hand. He smiled. "As far as Conner getting married and having children, Mrs. Golden, of course he'll be able to do that. He could very well grow out of his epilepsy. I told you that."

"When? How will we know if that happens?"

"We'll begin to suspect that the epilepsy has become inactive—in other words, that it has 'cured' itself—" He flicked two fingers on each hand to indicate quote signs. "—when Conner hasn't had any seizures for two years. If he hasn't experienced any warning aura symptoms, well, that will be very encouraging. If, after those two years, his EEG is also normal, I will consider tapering your son off the medications. None of this will guarantee that he will never have another seizure, but it will be a very hopeful sign. Remember: we cannot know for sure if he was seizure-free during that period because the medication was working effectively or if he would not have had one anyway even without the anti-seizure medications. That's just an unknown."

"In a few years Conner will be old enough to drive. I've heard that people who have seizures shouldn't drive. You said it, too. Isn't that right?" I pressed my hands on his desk.

"Six states—including ours, California—require doctors to report people who have seizures to the health authorities: Obviously, if those drivers black out while behind the wheel they would endanger themselves and everyone else on the road. A person can still get a driver's license if his seizures are controlled by medications. Department of Motor Vehicle officials decide what it means for seizures to be 'controlled.' It usually implies that the person has been seizure-free for six months up to one or two years on the medications.

"I'll take him off the Dilantin today and replace it with Keppra. It has fewer side effects. Keppra—or Levetiracetam, its other name—does not require testing for the drug levels. Your little guy should be happy about no blood tests. Now, I think it's time that I explain some things to my patient and settle him down." Dr. O'Rourke gave me a hesitant smile and stood too. He hitched up his pants with both hands. "I just heard Hannah talking to your husband. I believe he took Conner into the exam room. I'll bring Conner and your husband back in now." He moved toward the door, opened it and took a step into the corridor.

I reached for his arm and stood up. I said in a soft voice, "Dr. O'Rourke, wait! I don't know…this is very difficult for me, for us. I feel so…I'm devastated." My mournful tone immobilized his face. He stiffened. I lowered my head. My breath caught in my throat.

"Mrs. Golden. Please, listen to me. Look at me."

My chin quivered. "I—I'm so sorry. I don't have a normal son anymore, do I, Doctor?" I heard myself say it. How could I have said that? I wanted my baby back the way he used to be!

Dr. O'Rourke stepped back into the office. He closed the door, took my hand from his arm and gently guided me back into my chair. "Please, Mrs. Golden. Sit down."

The doctor wrapped his white coat around his hips and perched on the corner of the desk. "Mrs. Golden, I told you, most people who have epilepsy have their symptoms well-controlled. There's that chance that Conner will outgrow it. Really! He might never have another seizure."

"Senator Ted Kennedy had epilepsy. He *died*!"

"Senator Kennedy had a brain tumor; that's why he had epilepsy. The tumor was irritating his brain. Most people with epilepsy do *not* have brain tumors. Conner's brain scan was normal. I expect the MRI to confirm that. I told you, we usually never find the cause of epilepsy."

"What about Madison? What are the chances our three-year-old daughter could get it?" I sniffled and dabbed at my nose as her face appeared behind my eyes.

He shook his head. "Inheriting epilepsy is not usual. It is the minority of cases. I wouldn't expect your daughter to develop epilepsy just because her brother has it."

"And how do I protect our little girl from Conner's seizures? If she sees one of those convulsions it would scare her to death!"

"She's three, you said?"

"Yes, that's all. She's very young."

The doctor cupped his chin in his palm and tapped his lips with a straightened index finger. His eyes never left my face. "You're going to have to use your best judgment, Mrs. Golden. If she witnesses a convulsion, I agree, it could be very frightening for a young child. Nevertheless, this is the time to start familiarizing her with the situation. She can be very helpful to you. She is more apt to see his complex partial seizures, the staring ones. Conner probably cannot be relied on to tell you about every seizure because he will not be aware of them himself.

The passage of time will be your teacher. Epilepsy support groups are very helpful in this regard—the sharing of experiences."

He stood and looked down at me. "Okay, I'll bring Conner and your husband back in now." I followed him across the corridor.

Dr. O'Rourke rapped lightly on the door and walked in. I waited at the door. Conner was sitting on Sam's lap, enfolded in his father's arms. His head rested on Sam's shoulder and their chests moved in unison.

Sam looked up and smiled. "I thought that we'd just wait here awhile, Doctor." Sam nodded at me; I smiled back.

"Are you feeling better now, Conner?"

"Yeah, Dr. O'Rourke. I was scared." His wide eyes stared up at him. "You left me alone."

"I'm sorry you got scared. We were just across the hall. Why don't we go back into my office? I want to explain what's been happening to you." He held out his hand to Conner.

Sam gave Conner a nudge. "Go on, son."

The boy jumped off his father's lap and grasped Dr. O'Rourke's hand with his ink-stained fingers. It seemed that a special bond had come alive in their clasped hands. Dr. O'Rourke's calm and confident demeanor seemed to reassure my son. Conner smiled widely at the neurologist; his wide eyes seemed filled with admiration.

We crossed back to his office. Sam took the middle seat beside me. He patted his knee, and Conner climbed onto his father's lap and faced Dr. O'Rourke across the desk. Conner flicked his tongue out between his lips twice, and then a third time. I saw him rub his bitten tongue along the sides of his teeth. The room was quiet. I brushed a lock of hair off Conner's brow.

"Conner, I've just been explaining to your parents what has been happening to you. You are a wonderful patient, by the way—very helpful and smart. I think we are going to get on famously. We're going to be a great team. Right?"

"Right!" He grinned broadly and nodded several times. He looked over his shoulder at me and scratched the back of his neck. I watched as he hung on Dr. O'Rourke's every word as the neurologist disentangled our little boy's confused past year.

The doctor angled his computer monitor so Conner could see the images. He tapped on the screen. "Take a look at these CT scan pictures of your temporal lobes. This is where your dings come from, Conner." The neurologist reached across the desk to touch my son's temple above his left ear. "This is where your temporal lobe is in your head."

Conner widened his eyes and rolled them far up in their sockets toward his left temple, trying to see where his neurologist touched him. He moved his left hand to the area and blinked rapidly. "Won't that other tem...temple lobe on the other side stop...um...the dings? Will that other one stop...um...me from wetting my pants?" He glanced at me with anxious eyes and turned back to the doctor.

"Ah, I knew you were real smart the minute I met you!" Dr. O'Rourke winked at me and at Sam. "That's a great question. But, no, the other lobe doesn't stop the dings."

He cleared his throat. "The name of the condition that causes your dings is called 'epilepsy.' Have you ever heard that word, Conner?"

Conner shook his head. "No. But I don't like the dings to happen. I don't want anyone to know that I...uh...wet my...my pants. I can't help it. My friends will think that I am a baby. I'm not a baby! I don't want it to happen anymore. Please stop it from ever happening, Dr. O'Rourke." The corners of his mouth sagged as he turned toward me and tears welled in his eyes. I reached over and rubbed soft circles on my son's back with my palm. He shifted on his father's lap and looked at the doctor. I lowered my head and closed my eyes.

When I looked up, Dr. O'Rourke had a serious expression. He told Conner, "I'm going to stop the Dilantin—what you are taking now— and start you on a different medicine called Keppra. I can't guarantee that your seizures, your dings, won't ever happen again, Conner, but it is a very good medicine to help prevent them. I think it will be better for you. Best of all, it doesn't require blood tests. How does that sound?"

"Yay! No needles!" Sam moved his arms from around Conner's waist and rested them loosely on Conner's shoulders. "So, um, this medicine might not stop my dings all the way then? They could still happen...like...like at school? Then Mrs. Dorsey will get mad me again! Will these dings go away when I'm big? I want to be a videogame developer when I grow up. Can't you take my brain out and...like... switch it, like...you know, like I have seen brain operations on TV? Can you do that?"

Dr. O'Rourke looked into our eyes and replied, "No, we'd *never* do that, Conner." The doctor shook his head and pressed his lips into a thin line. "I can tell you that most people who have seizures like your dings *do* get better as long as they take their medicines. This means that you can't *ever* skip or forget to take them every day, or they won't work so well."

"I won't!"

"I know you won't."

I leaned over and kissed my son's cheek.

"Now, sometimes the medicine doesn't work as well as we want it to. If that happens, I will adjust how much you are taking or even put you on a different one. We will just have to see what happens. In the meantime, I want you to tell your parents whenever you get those smells or have that funny feeling in your stomach. That will help me know if this medicine is working."

Dr. O'Rourke settled his gaze on me and Sam. "I want you to keep a journal of Conner's seizures. You will catalogue each and every one that he tells you about in a notebook. Bring it to every appointment so that we can assess any pattern. I hope that we will achieve complete control over the seizures, but if some occur, there might be a pattern to the breakthroughs. A journal should help us learn what specific changes we can make to improve the situation. It is common for pills to be skipped or forgotten, especially with all of the distractions in life. And as Conner grows we will increase the dosage to keep up with his body size."

"I don't like those big pills!" Conner protested.

"Just listen to the doctor, Conner." I instantly regretted my stern tone.

"I'm sure you'll be able to swallow these new pills with water or some juice, Conner." He took that black pen from his chest pocket, unscrewed the cap and stuck it on the end of the pen. He bent over his desk and wrote on a small pad.

"Here's the prescription with the instructions." He tore the sheet free and handed it to me as he said, "Conner, you'll take one tablet in the morning and one at night, with or without food. It doesn't matter. These Keppra tablets will not be as big as the Dilantin capsules you have been taking. Okay?"

Conner nodded. "I eat them with whipped cream," he said. His voice was filled with the innocence of childhood.

The doctor looked at Sam and me. "What?"

"That's how I've been getting him to swallow the Dilantin capsules, Dr. O'Rourke," I said with a shallow laugh. "He couldn't do it with just water. Chocolate ice cream and whipped cream does the trick." I winked at Conner and kissed the top of his head.

"Yeah, it works," Sam chuckled.

"Well, that's a new way to take medicine. It sounds delicious." Dr. O'Rourke laughed with us. "I'll have to remember that. Do you have any questions?"

"I think that you answered them all, didn't he, son? We'll just have to take each day as it comes and hope for the best. That's how it's going to be." Sam reached across the desk to shake the neurologist's hand. "I'm sorry if I got a little antsy. We're just...overwhelmed. But thank you for everything that you're doing."

Conner slid off Sam's knee as everyone stood up.

"Please speak to Hannah on your way out. She will schedule Conner's EEG with you and give you some literature and the forms about the Epilepsy Foundation and the bracelet Mrs. Golden and I discussed. The radiology department will call you in a day or two to set up the MRI."

Conner walked around the desk without any prompt. He grabbed Dr. O'Rourke's hand as he looked up at his neurologist and flashed a wide smile. He pressed the side of his head against the man and said, "I'm glad you're my doctor."

"Thank you, Conner. I'm glad, too." Dr. O'Rourke touched the top of Conner's head with his other hand. His face had become taut and he blinked rapidly a few times; it seemed that his smile was forced.

Then I saw him swallow and he looked down at the floor. I turned my head away.

We started toward the waiting room. The doctor moved into the corridor to watch us leave. Sam and I each held one of Conner's hands as he walked backward between us. I looked down and saw Conner's face had lit up with a laughing grin. Dr. O'Rourke returned the smile with a wave of his bent fingers and returned to his office, shutting the door behind him.

CHAPTER 29

On the drive home, Sam told Conner, "You were terrific, old man."
"I *love* my doctor, Daddy. He is really nice. I'm glad he's helping me. And I don't need any more blood tests. Yay! That's best, Daddy."

I twisted around in the front seat to look back at Conner. Now I, we, knew why Conner had been having learning problems. Now his schoolwork should improve. Today was a turning point in all of our lives. But I knew that we would have to live with whatever happened.

Conner waved his hands with excitement. "Dr. O'Rourke said my dings are called seizures. Will the em—em—whatever scan show them? Can we see more pictures of my brain, Mom? I wish I could show them to Michael and everybody. Do you think Dr. O'Rourke will give us some? Do you think he will, Daddy?"

"Sure, why not? We can ask him, son." Sam looked at me without smiling.

Conner's smile spread across his face. "Mom, I'm not scared anymore."

My gaze met his sparkling eyes. "That makes you special. You are very special, my darling boy. You're very, very special." My throat tightened as I bit my lip and faced forward again. Was this going to be my new world now? Medicines, appointments, tests—and maybe more seizures? Dr. O'Rourke said the new medicine should stop the seizures. Of course, he couldn't guarantee that would happen. I turned around again and grabbed Conner's hand. He looked out the window, giggling and smiling.

"Do you want to get some books about epilepsy? Should we read about seizures, Conner?"

"Sure."

How would I protect him now? There must be kids' books that explained epilepsy without going into all the terrible things, the discouraging things. They couldn't.

I stared out the window. I felt empty, drained. The sun had disappeared behind dark, heavy clouds that threatened an early-spring rain. I wanted to just dissolve into them. As I watched passing trees, I noticed for the first time new green buds of the winter-spring transition. Then there were crows—always black crows—perched on branches and on telephone wires. The closed car windows muffled their harsh, defiant caws.

We passed a little girl on the sidewalk. The older woman beside her had gray hair packed into a tight bun. They held hands, looked at each other and laughed. I smiled. I was surprised that I felt lighter inside. The sensation was therapeutic, as welcome as ice chips that melted on a burn. I became aware that the muscles in my jaw had relaxed and the fists in my lap unclenched.

I leaned my head against the cool window. Its vibrations were soothing. I closed my eyes; I had to let go of this panic. I was so tired… soon, I was half-asleep. I was eight years old again, walking with my grandmother to the corner bakery for my after-school treat—our daily doughnut. Grandma Audra always bought me the one with creamy lemon inside that I loved…doughnuts? Grandma Audra couldn't even speak English when she came to America as a little girl…Grandpa died when I was an infant, but Grandma continued to live upstairs…We were together every day—kisses and hugs—until she got sick…Grandma Audra was the first person I ever knew who passed away, as everybody says now. Why didn't people say what they *really* mean? People didn't "pass away"—they *died,* they died and they were gone forever. Just say it! I shook my head.

My thoughts returned to Conner. My temples ached again, and my stomach twisted. If a problem in his brain was causing the epilepsy, he was not normal, no matter what anybody said! Dr. O'Rourke insisted that Conner would be fine. *Fine?* I saw how torn-up the doctor was when he gave us the diagnosis. By the end of the appointment, the neurologist was on the verge of tears, himself.

I snorted and tried to stifle a fit of giggles.

Sam looked over. "What's so funny?"

"I'm thinking about the whipped cream—Conner swallows pills with it. It works, doesn't it?"

"Yeah. That was funny, all right. Dr. O'Rourke looked like he'd never heard of that one."

"Yeah, Mom. I like whipped cream. Don't we need to get more? The can is running out."

"I'll buy some more tomorrow, honey. You'll learn how to swallow the pills without the whipped cream, soon."

"Aw, I hope not, Mom."

I sat back and considered the myriad of dangers we now faced with Conner's epilepsy. I would tell the other moms what to do if Conner had a convulsion at their house. I was also worried about his friends' reactions. Would they abandon him once they knew about his epilepsy? What if their parents wouldn't let them have anything to do with Conner anymore? What if they wouldn't even let him into their homes for play-dates and sleep-overs? I turned my grimace toward the window.

I knew that lots of parents must have experience with this; they survived. We really should look into a peer group. We could do this. God, what was I thinking? This horrible thing was happening to Conner—to us.

Epilepsy. Such a horrible word. I was determined that Conner must never know how afraid I was.

I pressed the side of my head hard against the window, trying to blot out my tortured thoughts and those painful images of how society still treated people with epilepsy. What if Conner researched epilepsy when he got older? What if he got hold of articles about those archaic laws that prevented people with epilepsy from marrying? Some laws had forced them to be sterilized—and that was not so long ago. Conner was bound to come across the horrible pictures of drooling institutionalized epilepsy patients from long ago, with their repulsive skin sores from those awful bromide drugs. Doctors used them to treat epilepsy back then. Would Conner ever get like that? I shivered. What would children's books say about epilepsy?

I looked at Sam. He focused straight ahead, but his jaw muscles quivered. I wondered what was going on in his mind behind those intense eyes. Sam had been okay in the neurologist's office. No one could blame him for those panicky questions about his—our—new reality. I took one of his hands from the steering wheel and brushed it against my lips. Sam squeezed my hand and smiled—a touching, soft smile that barely moved his lips. Then his hand went back on the steering wheel.

I glanced over my shoulder. Through the seat gap my hand sought—and found—Conner's knee.

CHAPTER 30

T hat night, Conner took the Keppra with squirts of whipped cream. He didn't need the ice cream. We all laughed about this little game. Madison had to get a squirt, too, and I couldn't leave out Sam.

Conner was already in his pajamas when I went into his bedroom to tuck him in. "It was a real busy day, kiddo. Now it's bedtime."

"I know, Mom. I just want to finish this. I'm almost done." He was at his desk, his Crayola crayons were scattered around him. The crayon in his right hand squeaked as Conner moved it across the page.

I stepped closer. I thought I had seen that drawing before: a stick figure with a large, round head and a straight, unsmiling mouth. Yellow and orange squiggles radiated from the head in all directions like rays of sunshine or bolts of lightning.

"What is that? I think you've drawn that before." I brushed a wisp of hair off his forehead. "You'll be getting a haircut real soon, young man."

"Yeah. Okay, Mom." He twisted around in his chair. "I'm drawing what my dings feel like when I get them. Like this. It just feels like electricity, like when I touched that old waffle iron...like...when I was little."

Conner pointed to the jagged "bolts" that he had just drawn. "When Dr. O'Rourke explained what happens in my head—what my dings are—I just knew that this is what they...um...they looked like. This is what they feel like. I never really knew what they were. They

211

were so…uh…funny, you know? Now I know. And Dr. O'Rourke told me everything. Maybe I'll even get to see them on my em…em ahrr… and, know what?"

"What, honey?"

"Um, I don't think I want to be a videogame developer anymore. No! Um, guess what I want to be when I'm big."

"What do you want to be when you're big, Conner?"

"I want to be a doctor. A doctor…just like Dr. O'Rourke and… um…do what he does to kids." He wrinkled and scratched his nose and twisted his mouth. "I want to be able to help people with dings…like mine. Uh, he said it was epi—eplep—"

"He said you have epilepsy, honey. Do you need a tissue?"

"That's it. Yeah, I want to be just like him! Would that be okay?"

"That would be wonderful, Conner." I kissed the top of his head. Would it be possible? Could Conner get through medical school with epilepsy? Dr. O'Rourke did say there are doctors who have epilepsy. I just wasn't sure that Conner could really be *that* normal.

Sounds from the TV in the den drifted upstairs. I watched Conner finish his design. What if I had paid more attention when I saw that drawing months ago? Would that have helped him?

Conner turned his head and looked up. "What's wrong, Mom? Why are you crying?" He half-stood out of his chair and hugged my waist.

I wiped my face with my palm. "Oh, Conner. I just, well, we had such a big day today. We are all tired. But, now that we all know what's been happening to you—at school, your homework—everything should get better now." I wrapped my arms around him and squeezed tight.

"I love you, Mom. I can't wait to tell all my friends at school about Dr. O'Rourke and my com—my com—epi—what are they called again?" Conner smiled up at me.

"Complex seizures. Uh, no. Complex partial seizures. That is what he said. That's your type of epilepsy."

"Ri-i-ght. Complex partial seizures. They come…from here." He tapped the side of his head.

I cleared my throat. "You remembered! Okay, my smart young man; time to brush and floss."

"I did already, Mom!" he said with a challenging tone.

"Good. Okay. Let's put your crayons away. Daddy will be right up to tuck you in."

He scooped his crayons back into the box and climbed into his bed.

"Goodnight sweetheart. I love you," I whispered. I kissed his cheek and then the top of his head, and turned off his bedside lamp.

Sam cleared his throat and swallowed hard several times. Then he turned toward me in our bed. "I've been thinking, Sandra. We're one of those families now with a special kid, aren't we? What do they call it, a kid with 'special needs'? The neurologist said that Mark Twain's daughter had epilepsy, and she drowned in a bathtub. Can you believe that? Dr. O'Rourke said we'll just have to watch him real close. But then I think of all those other people with epilepsy. Famous people! Dr. O'Rourke mentioned some. I remember some congressional leader was living with it; there was a story about him on the news. There was that actor, Danny Glover; he talked about his epilepsy during a TV interview. Why it made an impression on me then, I'll never know. These people don't have seizures all the time. They have important jobs, too."

I nodded and put my arm around him.

"And I've been wondering: will the MRI and the EEG give Dr. O'Rourke a different diagnosis? Will the new pills stop his seizures? What if they cause those bad side effects? Will Conner grow out of the epilepsy? Will he be able to drive in another few years? Will his school grades really improve? Will he be able to go to college? Will he be able to get married, have a family? We are all going to be different, now, aren't we? It's hitting home."

"Sam, don't you think I've been worrying about all this, too? What can we even do about it? We will join that support group, okay? Many people have this condition. We have terrific doctors. We're all together. We'll get through this, okay?" I nestled against his shoulder. "But, listen to me, Sam. I am worried about something else. I'm worried about you. I'm worried about us."

"What? You think I drink too much. That's it, isn't it?" He pulled away.

"You've seen terrible things, Sam. I—I've heard about vets and PTSD. I'm worried about you. I think you've got it."

"Aw, c'mon. I'm okay."

"No. You're different since you went to Iraq. You lose your temper so quickly now, with me and with the kids, too."

"What do you mean? No…"

"I want us to go to therapy, Sam. I am really worried. I'm worried about Conner. I'm worried about you. I'm worried about our family."

"No. C'mon Sandra. It's not that bad. I mean, Conner, yeah. But—"

"I've told you how I feel. Just think about it. We're all going to need therapy to survive everything that has happened to us this year. There's just so much we have to deal with."

He opened his mouth; I put a finger over his mouth before he could protest. "Uh, uh, uh. No more. I am not going to argue with you now. Hey, you won't believe what Conner just told me. He said that he wants to do what Dr. O'Rourke does when he grows up. He wants to help people with dings, with epilepsy."

"That's wonderful, if he can do it. Yesterday, he wanted to work on videogames. The doctor did say that Conner could do anything he wants, didn't he? Even go to medical school. I'd better start saving, huh?" He laughed.

"Well. That's a lifetime away, but who knows?"

"Listen. I got through war, Sandra. I was ready to get back on my feet with Tom and really build the business. I'll need—"

I put my finger over his lips again. "You need me, Sam. You've got me." I switched off the light.

When I awoke, it was still dark. I was curled against Sam's body, my arm draped across his chest. For a few blissful seconds I didn't know where I was. Then a groggy reality sank in. The world that I had lived in this year—a troubled, disjointed world that had turned upside down for me—one that was still not right. Did this recognition come only hours ago? Doctors...Conner...Sam...the family...

What was that? My head shot off the pillow. A moan? Please, not that again...I listened. Nothing. I turned onto my other side. I heard only Sam's quiet breathing and the pounding in my ears.

My eyes rested on the photo of Mom and Dad. Their images were just visible in the sliver of moonlight on the wall. I blinked several times and sighed. Eventually, my tormented thoughts gave way and I drifted off again. My legs twitched; I startled. An image surfaced: *sparks struck stones—fire—a raven circled.* My lips moved in silent prayer. A dream ...did my eyes rove?

In my dream I was running from storefront to storefront, panicked and confused, pounding on every door in a high-rise shopping/office complex. Where was it? I was just there...where did it go? Where? The elevator had just brought me down from the Epilepsy Office. I couldn't find it. I was gasping. I was not safe.

In the morning, I had vague memories: circling ravens—elevators. Was I remembering it? Was it a nightmare?

Bright, early-spring morning sunlight streamed through the window.

I felt exhausted. I was clammy. The pillow was damp. I heard the children laughing in Conner's room. It was another day.

My eyes meandered between the shadows and brightness that played on the ceiling and on the walls. I sat up at the edge of the bed and stretched my arms. I yawned, twisted, groaned and pushed my hands down into the soft mattress. My toes danced for my tan slippers and my feet slid in.

I gazed at the collection of framed photos on the dresser. In one, my arm was wrapped around my best and oldest friend Kathy's shoulders. Next to that was a portrait of Conner; it had been taken last year at school. He was so handsome, smiling, still innocent of this thing—epilepsy. Or so I thought. God, what I didn't know then. I squinted and felt a pang of grief stab my chest.

Then Grandma Audra's voice spoke to me: "You can't control what life throws at you, Sandra dear, but it's up to you what you do with it." I smiled.

I stood and went to the window. I crossed my arms and looked at the bright world outside. All those bitter questions surfaced again. Would I ever understand what had happened to us? It would be me; I knew that. Sam seemed not to be part of it. Was Conner on Sam's mind the way he was on mine? Were these worries instinctual—that bond between a mother and a child? My stomach tightened; my morning mouth was dry.

I thought about my college Faulkner seminar. I gorged myself on Faulkner's writings then. I have never forgotten what Faulkner stood for. How his works emphasized his philosophy about the human spirit: that it was undaunted and tough. Man would outlast all degradation and strife. Man would always endure. His novels were full of those themes.

If I ever needed a philosophy, I need that one now.

But, wasn't that me? Wasn't that really me right now? I would get through this. I would prevail, too. We were all together—me and my family, together.

The sound of more high-pitched laughter burst down the hall. I tilted my head and smiled. To my surprise, despite everything that had happened, I was able to laugh a little. Dr. O'Rourke was with us. So were all those other families that lived with epilepsy. We would get through this. A peer group would be good.

Sam rubbed his eyes and looked at me. "Wh—what?"

I shook my head. "No, everything's fine, Sam." I got into bed and crawled back under the covers next to him.

EPILEPSY GLOSSARY AND INFORMATION ASSOCIATED WITH THIS NOVEL

*Terms that are italicized are defined elsewhere
in this alphabetized glossary.*

Age at Onset: childhood had been the most prevalent, but in recent decades we commonly encounter *epilepsy* developing in the elderly.

This is due to our extended longevity with its attendant increase in strokes, head trauma, brain tumors and other abnormalities that irritate brain cells and cause brain scars.

Aura: the warning the person perceives that a *seizure* is starting.

Often it is a mood change, a thought, a memory aberration or perception of smells/tastes, sensations or movements. *Auras* generally last just one or several seconds but can last many seconds to minutes prior to progressing to the full *seizure*.

Bathing/Swimming/Athletic Dangers: people suffering from *epilepsy* should avoid swimming unless someone capable of rescue is present should a *seizure* occur.

Avoid bathtubs and showers (falling face-down in the shower and blocking the drain has resulted in drowning) unless someone is home and the bathroom door is open. Mark Twain's daughter had *epilepsy*; she drowned in the bathtub. Mothers who have *epilepsy* need to use care when holding their infants, especially around bathtubs and hot surfaces. Always wear seat belts in vehicles. Wear protective helmets when biking, skateboarding and other such activities. Athletic participation is to be encouraged so long as a *seizure* wouldn't endanger life and there is proper supervision.

Blank Outs (Black Outs)/Staring/Confusion Spells: commonly represents a form of *seizure*, usually *petit mal* or *complex partial* type.

Seizures can be differentiated from normal staring/daydreaming by the difficulty of gaining the person's attention during a *seizure*. In addition, the person who has mental "blank outs" (black outs) due to *seizures* does not have conscious thoughts but the daydreamer will. During a *seizure*, the person will neither recall what was said nor be aware of his environment. In order to ascertain whether a person actually lost contact with the environment, he may need to be challenged and tested by observers (e.g., give him commands and assess if they're carried out), since he often will deny and is unaware of any loss of contact.

Chewing/Lip-Smacking/Licking/Swallowing and Other Movements: called *AUTOMATISMS* as they are stereotypical (repeated) automatic actions common in *complex partial seizures*.

During a *seizure*, people in the seizure are unaware of performing these *automatisms*. Some people move around a room, perform simple actions, cross a busy street or endanger themselves in other ways.

Clues to Suspect Epilepsy: persons presenting with their "first" witnessed *seizure* may actually have *epilepsy*, i.e. have had previous *seizures*, but be unaware of them.

This is more likely to occur in persons who live or sleep alone. Their only clue may be occasional bed-wetting as an adult and/or awakening to find a bloody pillow, lip or tongue, and/or awakening to generalized severe muscle/body aches from convulsive jerking that occurred during sleep. Frequently hallucinating (imagining) foul smells or bad tastes can be a clue of unrecognized *complex partial seizures.*

Complex Partial Seizure (limbic seizure): altered consciousness (not totally alert) with loss of awareness of surroundings. The person may still respond, but slowly and incompletely with confusion. They will have no recollection of events afterward.

They usually last a few minutes and are preceded by symptoms such as *foul smells and/or tastes* and unusual thoughts/memories. These are the *auras*—the warning of an oncoming seizure. The person may vocalize phrases for which they have no memory, such as "Oh, God! Oh, God!" or "Help me! Help me!" These seizures typically originate within the temporal lobe, which is located at the lower sides of the brain; some seizures begin in a frontal lobe. If the abnormal brain-pattern activity (epileptiform discharge) spreads to the entire cerebral cortex (outer layers of the entire brain) and results in a *convulsion,* it is diagnosed as a *complex partial seizure* with secondary generalization. *Complex partial seizures* are the most prevalent type of seizure.

Convulsion: this term commonly applies to a *grand mal seizure.*

These are the second-most prevalent type of *seizure* after *complex partial seizure.* These seizures are not preceded by an *aura* or a warning; the person suddenly blacks out. It involves the entire brain cortex and results in a loss of conscious awareness accompanied by a forceful tightness of the body (the <u>tonic phase</u>). After a few seconds, this is followed by repetitive jerking of the limbs and trunk (the <u>clonic phase</u>). Occasionally *convulsions* are so forceful that spinal vertebrae and other bones can be broken. The lips and tongue may be bitten; this is frightening to the observer, but it is not a serious injury. Do not attempt to prevent tongue-biting since the biting occurs immediately. It is also too late to pry open the jaws. If something hard is placed between the person's clamped jaws, teeth can be broken or the rescuer can be severely bitten. If the tongue is not bitten immediately, it generally will not be bitten during the rest of the seizure. Loss of bladder and/or bowel control may occur. Try to keep the person on his or her side so that saliva/vomit can drop out of the mouth and prevent choking. Protect the person from striking hard objects while falling or jerking during the event. A convulsion exhausts itself within a few minutes and then the person generally sleeps for several hours. Residual headaches are common.

CT/MRI Brain Scans: very useful in evaluating causes of *seizures*. CT (Computerized Tomography) scans require radiation exposure like X-rays. MRI (Magnetic Resonance Imaging) scans do not.

Each type of scan provides different information about the brain/skull/blood-vessel structure. These scans can show tumors and other growths, infections, strokes, bleeding, normal and abnormal blood vessels, pressure changes within and outside of the brain, loss of brain tissue from aging and diseases, brain deformities and other pathologies. Occasionally dyes and isotopes are injected intravenously (by IV) during the scan to provide more information and to evaluate brain function. Normal scans are common.

Diagnosis: primarily made from the medical history. It is common for the neurological examination and the *EEG* of persons with *epilepsy* to be normal. This is because the abnormal brain patterns (*epileptiform discharges*) and other *EEG* abnormalities are not always present during the interictal (between *seizures*) period when most *EEGs* are done.

Grand mal seizures (convulsive jerking) are readily diagnosed from the person's history. *Petit mal seizures and complex partial seizures* require astute history-taking and observation to make a clinical diagnosis of *epilepsy* and type of *seizure*. The family/observers must be taught to watch the person suspected of having these types of *epilepsy* for inappropriate confusion or blanking out. Observers need to command the person to perform certain actions in order to document loss of awareness.

Driving Vehicles: not advised. Risks include endangering themselves, passengers and the public if the *seizures* are not controlled.

Only six of the fifty states (California, Delaware, Nevada, New Jersey, Oregon and Pennsylvania) mandate that physicians, no matter the specialty, report persons with *epilepsy* to the Health Department. Other states recommend that these persons assume the responsibility to report the diagnosis themselves. The Health Departments then notify the Department of Motor Vehicles (DMV) that the person has a condition which could interfere with safe operation of a motor vehicle. The DMV sends medical forms to physicians for them to complete regarding the person's condition. The DMV, not the physician, makes the decision to allow or cancel the driving privilege. The DMV also decides how long the person must be *seizure*-free before the license is restored. This period usually lasts six to twenty-four months with medical observation. Some circumstances favorably influence these decisions, such as *seizures* that occur only during sleep (nocturnal *epilepsy*) or control of *seizures* by treatment. Legal, insurance, financial and moral considerations need to be addressed to safeguard the patient and society in general.

Electroencephalogram (EEG): painless recording of brain activity. Wires are pasted on the head and connected to the recording machine while the patient rests on a bed. Abnormal brain electrical patterns—i.e., the epileptiform abnormalities (the abnormal brain cell discharges that cause *seizures*) that are detected in the EEG between *seizures* (the interictal period)—are helpful in diagnosing *epilepsy*.

A normal test indicates that no abnormal electrical patterns or other changes were detected from the neuron cells' electrical profile in the cortex during that test period (usually lasting forty-five to ninety minutes). The abnormalities of *epilepsy* are sporadic and are not continuous in most patients with epilepsy. A normal *EEG* does not rule out *epilepsy*, and normal *EEGs* are very common in people who have *epilepsy*. Therefore, multiple testing should be considered. Occasionally, people suspected of having *epilepsy* are admitted to specialized *epilepsy*-monitoring wards where they are continuously attached to *EEG* machines and video-monitored for hours or days. This improves chances of recording an abnormality and diagnosing the condition. Ambulatory *EEGs* can also be done whereby patients perform their ordinary daily activities while wearing a portable device. Flashing strobe lights, heavy breathing (hyperventilation) and falling asleep during the *EEG* are routine components of the test as they tend to promote *seizure* abnormalities on the recording. If an *EEG* is performed on a patient for a reason other than epilepsy and an *epilepsy* pattern is found, a clinical diagnosis of *epilepsy* cannot be made if the patient and/or observers deny that any clinical *seizure* ever occurred. *EEG* abnormalities alone are insufficient to diagnose *epilepsy*.

Epilepsy: a chronic neurological disorder characterized by recurring *seizures* that are not provoked by any temporary problem in the brain (see "reactive *seizures*" in *Febrile Seizures* below). More than one *seizure* qualifies as *epilepsy* even if the incidents are separated in time by years. *Epilepsy* is a clinical diagnosis; an abnormal *EEG* is not required for the diagnosis.

The specific abnormality that causes the *seizures* often cannot be identified; this type of *epilepsy* is known as "primary" or "idiopathic." "Acquired" or "symptomatic" *epilepsy*, however, results from identifiable brain abnormalities (often found on *brain scans*) such as brain injuries and brain malformations, strokes, tumors, infections, drugs and toxins, alcohol, hormonal changes (including menstruation, called catamenial *epilepsy*) and metabolism disorders. In general, inherited *epilepsy* is not common. Approximately one percent of the population of the United States has *epilepsy*.

Febrile Convulsions: most commonly occurs in children between the ages of several months up to five years. Typically these occur in the beginning of a fever (*febrile* illness) and they are usually not associated with any serious cause.

They don't require anticonvulsant medications and they don't recur during that febrile illness. They are reactive *seizures*: i.e., they react to the fever-induced temporary problem in the brain. If the *convulsion* happens one or more days after the onset of a continuing fever, or if the *convulsion* happens during a *febrile* illness in children over age six or seven, other causes must be considered. Recurrent *febrile seizures* could represent *epilepsy* and would require on-going anticonvulsant medication.

Hallucinating Smells/Tastes: common as part of the initial *aura*, especially in *complex partial epilepsy*. Patients will perceive odors—usually foul (classically, "burning rubber")—that no one else in their environment can smell.

If physicians fail to ask about these symptoms, patients suffering their "first" observed *seizure* or episode of confusion commonly do not mention them. General medical practitioners seldom ask about these symptoms, but a patient reporting that he or she has experienced any of these perceptions should alert the physician to the strong possibility of a previously unrecognized/hidden *epilepsy* diagnosis.

Juvenile Myoclonic Epilepsy: sudden, quick jerks on both sides of the body beginning in late-childhood and early teens.

These seizures can be a single jerk or repetitive jerks, usually without loss of awareness, that occur shortly after morning arousal. A common symptom is an exaggerated startle reaction, such as the child involuntarily "throwing" something, like the breakfast-juice glass. This form of *epilepsy* often changes into generalized *convulsions*. It is highly responsive to *Depakote* (see Treatment) but lifelong treatment is usually required.

Petit Mal Epilepsy (absence): *petit mal seizures* consist of staring spells with loss of awareness, blinking and/or other slight movements. These symptoms last an average of five to fifteen

seconds. **They interrupt speech and thinking without causing the person to fall down, twenty to one hundred times per day. These** *seizures* **are notable for their lack of any warning (***aura***) and their lack of confusion afterward.**

Patients are typically unaware of having lost contact with their surroundings. They will commonly ask companions to repeat what was just said. When the *seizures* are unrecognized, observers may consider these people as "ditzy" or "odd" due to their periodic mental dullness. The specific *petit mal EEG* abnormality is a three-per-second spike-wave complex that is provoked by heavy breathing and less commonly by flashing strobe lights. Petit mal is one form of *epilepsy* that can be familial (i.e., inherited). It begins during early childhood and often ceases by the late-teen years. Why these *seizures* cease is unknown, but the process in lay terms is referred to as "growing out of it." *Petit mal seizures* occur less frequently than *complex partial seizures* and *grand mal seizures.*

Postictal Confusion: the groggy/confusion period immediately following *convulsions* **and** *complex partial seizures.*

The confusion routinely lasts minutes to hours and people commonly fall asleep afterward. People who are unfamiliar with the person's diagnosis typically call for emergency personnel/ambulances when they observe the *convulsion* and/or *postictal* confusion and sleepiness. Once hospital personnel learn that a previous *epilepsy* diagnosis had been made they will discharge the patients and send them home once they are alert.

Psychogenic Seizures/Pseudoseizures: these can resemble true *seizures* **to the observer, but they are not the same phenomenon. These events have a psychological cause that is often associated with some subconscious, secondary gain or conscious malingering.**

Anticonvulsant medications (see Treatment) fail to prevent these *seizures* but psychiatric treatment that targets the psychogenic cause of the seizure can be beneficial. The *EEGs* performed during overt "*seizures*" remain normal, so videotaping the patient's behavior is helpful for making this diagnosis. Pseudo-*seizures* can be very difficult to differentiate from actual *epileptic seizures* if an *EEG* is unavailable. An additional diagnostic challenge is that they often occur in people who also have true *epilepsy* (see above).

Psychosocial Adjustment to Epilepsy: leading full and independent lives can be a challenge in *epilepsy*, especially for those people who have incomplete *seizure* control.

School/employment opportunities, marriage, family and social life, driving and athletic participation all must be addressed. Branches of the Epilepsy Foundation and related societies help people find local *epilepsy*-support groups. They also provide a forum in which patients share common problems and ideas for living with *epilepsy*. Counseling can be very helpful in adjusting to the various situations arising from their condition.

Seizure (ictus): a sudden, temporary, uncontrolled disruption of electrical activity of brain cells (neurons) that interfere with normal brain function. *Seizures* are not a disease, but are the representative expression of the disease causing the *seizure*.

The site of this abnormal activity determines the form of the *seizure*.

- Frontal lobe (the anatomical front of the brain) *seizures* can cause jerking movements and postural changes (e.g., falling down), emotional changes and speech problems.
- Occipital lobe (the anatomical back of the brain) *seizures* can cause visual symptoms such as blind spots and flashes that can mimic migraine.
- Parietal lobe (the sides of the brain) *seizures* can cause numbness, tingling and pins-and-needles sensations.
- Temporal lobe (lower side of brain) *seizures* can cause emotional or psychological phenomena, fear and hallucinations.

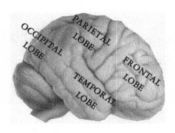

A single *seizure* occurs in an estimated eight to ten percent of the population for undetermined reasons and then never recurs during their lifetimes. Possible causes of a single *seizure* include: fevers in young children; sleep deprivation (usually more than thirty-six hours); brief loss of oxygen, excessive consumption of alcohol, prescribed medications and illicit toxic drugs; infections; and other substances and illnesses can cause a single *seizure* as a reaction to that insult to the brain. These resulting *seizures* are referred to as reactive *seizures*. *Epilepsy* is diagnosed only when the person experiences more than a single non-reactive *seizure*—even when these events are separated by years.

Simple Partial Seizure: clear consciousness is preserved during the seizure.

These patients can communicate and remain aware of their surroundings with full recollection of events despite *seizure*-induced jerking, numbness or tingling. The *seizure* can originate in any lobe of the brain. It contrasts with *complex partial seizure* in which awareness is lost.

Spinal Tap (lumbar puncture): This procedure is useful to diagnose central nervous system (CNS) infections, inflammation, cancers, bleeding, abnormal pressure within the central nervous system, multiple sclerosis, peripheral nerve disease and other conditions. The spinal tap is usually far less unpleasant than patients expect it to be when it is performed by an experienced physician. Ideally, the test is completed in less than thirty minutes and can be done as an outpatient.

Typically, the local anesthetic is the most uncomfortable part of the procedure. It is injected within the skin layers, which stretch apart; this causes a burning sensation. Next, the spinal needle is directed deeper into the space between the spinal vertebrae and into the spinal canal; this is usually painless. Pressure within the central nervous system is measured and then cerebrospinal fluid is collected as it drips from the end of the hollow needle into test tubes. The red- and white-cell count, protein level, glucose level and other components of the cerebrospinal fluid are evaluated. Testing for various types of germs can also be done. The spinal tap is occasionally performed after the patient has a seizure—especially if a fever accompanies the *seizure*—to rule out meningitis/encephalitis (inflammation/infection in the central nervous system) as having caused the *seizure*. Headache is a common side effect of the spinal tap and occurs in one-third of patients. It is caused by cerebrospinal fluid leaking into the deep tissues from the tiny hole in the coverings of the spinal canal made by the needle. It is the cerebrospinal fluid that supports the brain structures within the skull against gravity. If it leaks through the hole created by the spinal needle when the patient sits or stands up, the brain structures can sink a small amount because of gravity, causing head pain. This headache is relieved when the patient lies down and the brain structures no longer sink. One out of three patients experience this unpleasant but not serious side effect whether they remain lying down for many hours or stand up immediately after the test. This headache usually resolves within a few days by healing of the puncture hole. The body replaces the cerebrospinal fluid that is removed for testing in one-half hour.

Status Epilepticus: occurs when the *seizure* activity recurs, and lasts longer than ten minutes without the person regaining full consciousness between *seizures*.

This is a serious medical emergency that requires immediate medication, breathing and medical-support treatments to prevent brain damage and other serious complications.

Sudden Unexpected Death in *Epilepsy (SUDEP)*: very rare.

Theories about this phenomenon consider changes in the brain's regulating centers for breathing and heart rhythm. In this case the person—one in one thousand—is often found dead in bed with no identifiable cause.

Tongue Swallowing During *Seizure*: this does not happen.

Treatment: the goal is complete cessation of *seizures*.

If the most appropriate anticonvulsant, or anti-*seizure* (medications to stop *seizures*) medication is administered at the "correct" dosage, approximately fifty percent of people with *epilepsy* will gain complete control of their condition without having any more *seizures* as long as the medication is taken as prescribed. Determining the "most appropriate" medication in the correct dosage is a process of trial and error. Physicians choose an anticonvulsant based on the type of *epilepsy*, treatment trials and their medical experience.

Following is a list of commonly prescribed anticonvulsant medications by brand and generic names: *Depakote* (Divalproex), Dilantin (Phenytoin), Keppra (Levetiracetam), Klonopin (Clonazepam), Lamictal (Lamotrigine), Lyrica (Pregabalin), Mysoline (Primidone), Neurontin (Gabapentin), Phenobarbital, Tegretol (Carbamazepine), Topamax (Topiramate), Trileptal (Oxcarbazepine), Zarontin (Ethosuximide), and Zonegran (Zonisamide). Generally, if *seizures* persist while the patient is taking a specific medication the dosage is increased until *seizures* are controlled or side effects can't be tolerated. Other anticonvulsants are then added or substituted. This is the "art" in the practice of medicine. This process can take many months of trial and error.

Another twenty to thirty percent of people with *epilepsy* will gain incomplete *seizure* control and may experience an infrequent *seizure* despite trying many of the current anticonvulsants. A further twenty percent have uncontrolled *seizures* despite all anticonvulsant trials. Surgical removal of the *seizure*-causing abnormality, or focus, in the brain can be very successful with surprisingly normal brain function and *seizure* cessation or marked *seizure*-frequency reduction. The ketogenic diet can be beneficial in patients with uncontrollable *epilepsy*, but it is difficult to follow and requires a very demanding dietary change.

Treatment Cessation: *epilepsy* **that begins in the late teens and older generally requires lifelong treatment with anticonvulsant (see Treatment) medications. The medical profession cannot cure** *epilepsy.*

Epilepsy is considered to be "inactive" or "cured" under these circumstances: no *seizures* for two years, and the physical examination, *EEG, brain scan* and pertinent laboratory blood tests are all normal. It would be prudent to ascertain that the *EEG* is still normal before tapering the patient off of the anticonvulsant. Before commencing the discontinuation process, patients should strongly desire to stop their medications and must be aware that driving privileges will again be withdrawn if another *seizure* occurs. Adults whose *epilepsy* began after their teenage years will frequently experience a return of *seizures* within weeks to years after stopping their medications; this is unpredictable. If this scenario occurs they may then be convinced that medications will be required—most likely, for life.

Violent Behavior during Seizures: this is most associated with *complex partial seizures.* **People who are physically restrained while suffering a** *complex partial seizure* **often involuntarily strike out.**

Planned violent or criminal behavior during a *seizure* does not occur in the real world, despite what popular novels and movies would have us believe. The violent response to the restraint is a non-directed, unconscious defense mechanism, and patients will not recall their outburst after the event.

CPSIA information can be obtained
at www.ICGtesting.com
Printed in the USA
LVHW101442100522
718412LV00017B/346/J